THE HIGHLANDER'S HELLION

ELIZA KNIGHT

KNIGHT
MEDIA

Cover Design by Kim Killion @ The Killion Group, Inc.

Edited by Heidi Shoham

Published by:

More Books by Eliza Knight

The Sutherland Legacy

The Highlander's Gift
The Highlander's Quest — in the Ladies of the Stone anthology
The Highlander's Stolen Bride
The Highlander's Hellion
The Highlander's Secret Vow — Spring 2019

Pirates of Britannia: Devils of the Deep

Savage of the Sea
The Sea Devil
A Pirate's Bounty

The Stolen Bride Series

The Highlander's Temptation

The Highlander's Reward
The Highlander's Conquest
The Highlander's Lady
The Highlander's Warrior Bride
The Highlander's Triumph
The Highlander's Sin
Wild Highland Mistletoe (a Stolen Bride winter novella)
The Highlander's Charm (a Stolen Bride novella)
A Kilted Christmas Wish – a contemporary Holiday spin-off

The Conquered Bride Series

Conquered by the Highlander
Seduced by the Laird
Taken by the Highlander (a Conquered bride novella)
Claimed by the Warrior
Stolen by the Laird
Protected by the Laird (a Conquered bride novella)
Guarded by the Warrior

The MacDougall Legacy Series

Laird of Shadows
Laird of Twilight
Laird of Darkness

The Thistles and Roses Series

Promise of a Knight
Eternally Bound
Breath from the Sea

The Highland Bound Series (Erotic time-travel)

Behind the Plaid
Bared to the Laird
Dark Side of the Laird
Highlander's Touch
Highlander Undone
Highlander Unraveled

Wicked Women

Her Desperate Gamble
Seducing the Sheriff
Kiss Me, Cowboy

Under the name E. Knight

Tales From the Tudor Court

My Lady Viper
Prisoner of the Queen

Ancient Historical Fiction

A Day of Fire: a novel of Pompeii
A Year of Ravens: a novel of Boudica's Rebellion

About the Book

Lady Greer was a hellion from the moment she could walk. So, when the young woman is forbidden by her father, the Earl of Sutherland, to sail, she steals a boat and rows it out into the firth anyway. But her relaxing jaunt turns into so much more when a storm ravages the chill waters and the prospect of death is soon upon her.

The last thing Roderick MacCulloch, Laird of Gleann Mórinnse Castle, expects to find while out scouting his property is a soaked lass upon his shores. When she demands he take her back to her clan, he recognizes her as the mischievous lass who taunted him at a festival when they were children. Roderick realizes this might be his chance to have a bit of fun and give Lady Greer a taste of her own medicine

But Roderick's chance at revenge turns into a merry chase across the Highlands that leads them both to unexpected passion, perilous danger...and maybe even love.

Prologue

Scottish Highlands
Gleann Mórinnse Castle
1320

The laird's sister was dead.

Roderick MacCulloch cradled his sister's cold body in his arms, sobs wracking him. He'd failed her. He'd failed his parents.

All the life had drained from her broken body, leaving her skin an ashen color. The visage of her eyes closed as if in sleep tormented him.

He shouldn't have left her alone.

In one of her spells, she'd managed to sneak up to the castle ramparts, climb between the crenellations and then toss herself into the wind. It was not the first time she'd attempted to put an end to the demons that tormented her. But Roderick had always been there before to coax her down.

With her still held tightly in his arms, he leaned his head back and let out an unrelenting battle cry, until his throat hurt from the effort. But there was no one to fight, save for the Devil himself.

Jessica had been a special lass from the moment she'd screamed her way into this world, in a birth that had taken the life of their mother. When he'd first seen her, pink and wrinkled and squalling, Roderick had known it would be his sacred duty to protect his wee bairn sister, for she'd been a gift from God to his parents who'd lost so many children in the time between his brother Jon's birth and Jessica's twelve years later.

She was barely sixteen, with so much more life to live. But internal torments had haunted her for years, luring her to the brink of madness.

Pushing the hair away from her brow, he studied the peaceful face, so like his mother's in the dim light. The wounds she'd suffered upon impact had not marred her beauty.

"Why?" Roderick asked softly. "Why, Jess?" He turned his gaze to the heavens, as if expecting the clouds to part and give him the answers he sought.

But she didn't answer, and neither did God.

When their da had been killed in a raid just a few months ago, Roderick had been given the lairdship and full responsibility over everyone. Why did he have to lose so much in such a short span of time?

An intense urge to leap from the ramparts filled him—to join her in death so he might protect her in the afterlife. A firm hand pressed to his shoulder, and he glanced up to see their clan priest, Father Robert, sorrow etched in the lines of his face. "She is at peace, my son."

Roderick stared up at the man, incredulous. This was a man of God saying that his sister was at peace when one and all knew that to commit the sin of taking one's own life was to condemn oneself to the eternal flames. What could Father Robert possibly mean by mocking him this way?

"Lady Jessica," Father Robert started, then he shook his head and pressed his lips together as if caught up in emotion. "She was a troubled lass."

"Ye think I dinna know that?" Roderick shouted. "I have been there for her every day of her entire life, and the one time I was not—"

"Dinna blame yourself." Father Robert's sincere gaze never wavered.

"Who else will I blame?"

"The Devil's work has surely been accomplished today."

Roderick would have gladly called the Devil out to battle if he could. Destroy the evil that had cut his sister's life short.

"I dinna accept this." He shook his head, trying to feel any bit of warmth left in her body.

A flash of pity crossed over the priest's countenance, which only made Roderick angrier. He clutched his sister tighter, willing with everything in him to bring her back to life.

"I *willna* accept this."

This was a nightmare from which he couldn't wake. How many men had he seen fall on the field of battle? He'd lost his mother, his father, and yet, the death of his sister brought him to his knees in iron-weighted denial.

Father Robert let out a great sigh, but not one filled with irritation, rather one that said he knew how Roderick felt. "Death is hard to accept, my son. We will miss her. She was loved greatly by all. The vibrant memories ye have of her will keep her alive in spirit."

Roderick gritted his teeth. He didn't want memories. He wanted *her* in the flesh—her smile, her songs, her dancing. Those good moments when she was happy heartily outweighed the moments when she was so deep in despair that not even her most favorite things could bring her back. "She's gone too soon."

"A sentiment we feel often when we lose those we love."

"I didna *lose* her," he shouted. "She was *taken* from me."

Again, that soft, reassuring hand rested on his shoulder. "Aye. I think ye can only take comfort in the knowledge she is no longer tormented by demons."

"Ye keep saying that. But ye know verra well where she is." Roderick couldn't even say the word. He didn't want to give voice to that very fiery place where he was certain his sister must have been sent.

"Nay, my son. Nay, nay." Father Robert choked on his words. "I want ye to know that I have blessed her, for she didna... This was not entirely her doing. God knows that. He would not want her to suffer more. She will be buried in consecrated ground. She is with Him now in Heaven, and with your parents."

Roderick sat back on his heels, his hold on his sister momentarily lightening as first confusion and then gratitude overwhelmed him. Not in Hell. She was not being burned for eternity. She was where she belonged, in a place filled with peace and love. His chest swelled, and when he spoke, his voice was choked with emotion. "God, I would fight every battle for her if I could have."

"She knew that, my son." Father Robert pressed a piece of paper into Roderick's hand. "And she wanted ye to know it, too."

Roderick slowly opened the parchment to find his sister's words scrawled.

Ye are free, and so am I.

Chapter One

Sutherland Castle
Scottish Highlands
1323

Lady Greer, daughter to the Earl and Countess of Sutherland, was a hellion. If one were to jumble up all the deeds in her life and make a fair assessment, one would see it was true.

Greer preferred to think of herself as spirited. After all, to be called a hellion was not very flattering, now was it?

Spirited on the other hand was quite a compliment. It meant she wasn't an utter boor, and that she could always be counted on for a smile and an entertaining story. If one needed help with a little reprisal, Greer always seemed to know just what to do.

So why was she sitting here in the corner of the salon glowering at her mother, who sat embroidering beside her younger sister, Blair? None of them really enjoyed embroidering, but they wouldn't admit to such.

Greer was here because she'd just received the dressing down of all dressing downs from her father—and in the great hall within earshot of everyone. She wasn't willing to admit that what she'd done was wrong. Why was everything so black and white with her father? Her older sister, Bella, had been able to get away with murder! Everyone knew Bella snuck out to shoot arrows at all hours. She probably still did, even now as a married woman. So why couldn't her parents see that Greer was old enough to marry, and that her hobby wasn't nearly so dangerous as sending deadly weapons through the air?

Greer stood abruptly, enough so that her mother and Blair both startled. Matching, questioning gazes fixed on her, and suddenly Greer felt self-conscious.

"What is it?" Lady Arbella's eyes were wary, those of a mother waiting for an explosion.

The air in the solar crackled with tension, echoing the fire in the hearth as it popped and a log split in half, falling through the grate, forcing a cloud of ash to whoosh around their ankles. Was that a sign she should sit back down? Keep her thoughts to herself and swallow the words she was about to say?

Greer chewed her lip while her mother watched her expectantly.

Normally one to shout at the least cause, Greer decided to temper herself. If she was to prove she was who she believed herself to be, she needed to start somewhere, didn't she?

Greer cleared her throat, wringing her hands in front of her. When she noticed the nervous habit, she forced her fingers to unwind and swiped her sweaty palms over her thighs, but one of her rings caught on her gown. She could feel the thread stick before she even looked. There was nothing to do but to ignore the string now attached to her ring and simply say what needed saying in the calmest manner possible. "Mother, I am disappointed in Da's decision."

With a great sigh, Lady Arbella put down her embroidery and crooked a finger for Greer to come closer. She had long white fingers that used to stroke Greer's forehead when she was sick, and still now braided her hair. Despite the sigh that said she was preparing herself for conflict, Lady Arbella's eyes sparked with interest. Greer always thought her mother held a soft spot for her. That was probably because they were so alike in nature.

Her mother carefully removed Greer's ring from where it was hooked and cut the thread.

At last, her mother said softly in her English accent, "What has you so nervous?"

This was her chance. She had her mother's full attention. "I'm one and twenty. A woman." Her mother's brow raised, and Greer feared if she didn't hurry, her mother might assume she was telling her she wanted to wed, which was the furthest thing from her mind. "I'm a skilled boatwoman, and I can swim faster than any man in this clan. I think 'tis only fair with my skillset that I be allowed access to the *currachs* like any man." She didn't add that her sister had been allowed to compete in archery competitions plenty of times, which was also known as a man's sport. If she brought that up, then her mother might only mention the incident from a couple of years prior where Greer had been in a competition that didn't end as well as they'd hoped. Besides, she'd argued that point enough previously, and right now, she needed her mother's support in debating with her father.

A flicker of amusement flashed in her mother's gaze, mixed with what she thought might be relief. "I understand, sweetheart, but your father has told you he does not want you to go alone. The sea is dangerous, and the Highland weather can change with the wind. What would happen if you were alone, not close enough to land to swim, and a storm hit? We would not be able to find you. You could drown. Do you not see that what he is insisting isn't that you not be allowed to use your skill, but that you not go alone?"

I am drowning here, cooped up in this castle.

"The men dinna want to escort me, Mother, and I also dinna want to wait for when they are available." She was fully aware that some part of her petulance was showing, but she couldn't help it. What she said was true. She'd heard the men complain. They drew straws over who would have to join her. Half the time, they pretended to be seasick when they returned, swearing she wanted to kill them all. It was offensive, and it hurt her feelings, but she wasn't about to complain about it. Not if she wanted to be taken seriously. "What if I didna go as far as I usually do? What if I stay closer to shore?"

Lady Arbella pressed her lips tight, a sign she was getting close to shutting down the conversation as mothers were wont to do when their children argued for a sweet. But this was no sweet. This was Greer's life. Her passion.

"Your father has made his choice, my dear."

"And how many times have ye convinced him to change his mind?"

"That is none of your business." There was a sharpness to her mother's voice that was offset by the twinkle in her eye. What did that mean?

"But it is a fact. Ye can change his mind. Mother, please." Greer rushed forward, dropping to her knees in front of her mother. "Soon I shall wed, and then I will be doing nothing but running my husband's household and having his bairns." Her mother raised her brows at that. Greer waved away her comment. "I mean no offense, or to imply the duty of mother and wife are anything less than what a lady should aspire to. Only please, Mama, allow me this one last season of freedom."

Just then, a knock sounded at the salon door, and in walked her da —the great and mighty Magnus Sutherland, Earl of Sutherland. He took one look at Greer on her knees before her mother and raised his hands into the air.

"I'll not be changing my mind, Greer. Ye might as well give up on your campaign now." Exasperation filled his features. "Allow your mother a moment of peace."

Greer stood, hands fisted, spine straight, prepared to go into battle. "But, Da—"

"That's enough. I'll not hear another word. It's time ye acted like the grown woman ye wish us to see ye as. I've already had messengers sent out. In a fortnight's time, the great hall will be filled with lads for ye to choose from."

She refrained from making a comment about them being her escorts when she realized exactly what her father must mean. "Choose from?" Greer nearly choked on the words. Blood drained from her head, making her sway slightly.

Magnus walked to the hearth, took hold of a poker and shoved at the broken log before adding another. "Aye. Ye're to marry. And ye're lucky that instead of plucking a bachelor from a loch, I'm allowing ye to have some choice in it. 'Tis only fair, given I allowed Bella the same freedom."

Freedom to choose the shackle. As if that was a consolation prize compared to the freedom she found at sea. Greer should be happy her father was allowing her the choice. That he'd even thought to do so without her having to beg showed how much he really loved her. She knew that. There were plenty of women in Scotland, and indeed the world, who had no choice at all. They were simply shoved into the grasp of their new husband and told to honor and obey the stranger they would now be on a most intimate basis with. Greer would rather drown than do that. A fact her parents must also comprehend. Their tempering of her desire to be at sea was born out of love, and nothing more, but that didn't make it any less disappointing.

"Married," she breathed out, pressing her hand to her chest and shaking her head. Why did it feel like a horse was sitting on her torso? She struggled to draw in breath. "I'm not ready to marry."

If she were to marry now, her life would be over. No more trips out to sea. No more lying in the middle of the ocean with the sun beaming down on her, daydreaming that she would meet a selkie who would turn into a handsome warrior determined to give her the life she'd always dreamed of. Aye, childish thoughts perhaps, but ones she wasn't willing to part with just yet.

"None of us are until 'tis time." When her father said this, he glanced at her mother, who returned his gaze with a knowing look that only proved to triple Greer's frustration.

"What does that even mean?" Greer tried to hide her exasperation, but the feat proved difficult. This was her life they were talking about, not what to eat for supper.

"At the feast, ye'll find a man that will honor ye and cherish ye, one ye can honor and cherish. And then ye will be ready." Her father nodded as though she should understand this information without question, or at the very least accept it.

"I dinna think that is the way it happens, Da," Greer argued, looking to her mother for support.

But who was she kidding? Her mother had been plucked from a battlefield and forced to marry her Da. They were lucky to have fallen in love. And Bella was no different. She'd had to choose, and she'd chosen the most unlikely bachelor. She too, was lucky it had turned out to be a love match with her husband, Niall. Her eldest brother, Strath, was also married quite happily, to a woman who should have been his enemy.

Was that how it was in this family? That one sought out the most unlikely person to be their spouse? That didn't sound in the least bit appealing. Quite the opposite. And how was she supposed to get behind the idea in just two weeks? She wouldn't, and so she'd likely make a fool of herself, which would only increase her parents' frustration with her.

She peeked at Blair, who was wide-eyed and biting her lip. Her sister probably expected her to blow at any minute. Blair was much subtler. A rule follower. In fact, Greer could count on one hand the number of times Blair had got in trouble their entire lives, and even those times had been nothing important. Tiny little infractions that most people couldn't even remember.

Magnus stepped forward, placed his hands gently on her shoulders and ducked down a little to meet her gaze. "We love ye, *mo chridhe*. Give it a chance. I promise ye this, if none of the men at the feast catch your fancy, I willna force ye. Not yet. But I do ask that ye give me the same respect and actually try."

Greer's stomach churned, knotting itself like the line she used to tie down her *currach*. What choice did she have but to nod, to at least let her parents think she was accepting of this fate they were forcing upon her. A fate that Highland society itself would push for. One she knew was coming, but hadn't thought she'd so vehemently oppose in her mind.

As the third child born to the Earl and Countess of Sutherland, she was quite distant from inheriting. Now that her two older siblings both had children of their own, she was even further away. A marriage with her would be advantageous to a man because of the size of her dowry, coin her father had been very generous in offering. But that was it. There wasn't land or a great castle that she'd be adding to the bargain. Just a chest full of coin. Which meant that any man coming to the feast would be either completely penniless or had a desire to shackle himself to her, the latter of which she thought very unlikely, considering her reputation. Most men found her difficult to get along with.

"What if... What if none of them find me...worthy?" she whispered, half shocked she'd said the words aloud.

"They'd be mad not to," her father said. "Your wit alone is enough to warrant every eligible bachelor in Scotland to come calling."

"Ye're only saying that because ye're my da, and ye have to say things like that."

"'Tis true, I am biased when it comes to my children, but, lass, ye must believe in yourself on land as much as ye believe in yourself at sea."

She could do that. She hoped.

Nodding, she fell against her father, hearing his heart beat solidly in his chest. From behind, her mother approached, and she too hugged her.

Not to be left behind, Blair leapt up from her chair and joined them.

If only she never had to leave the circle of their arms, the place she felt safest when not at sea.

"No *currach* for two weeks," her father said. "We want to make certain ye're safe until then. And...no competitions when the men do arrive."

Greer crossed her fingers behind her father's back and nodded, feeling her face heat. Would she never live down the infamous spearfishing event?

It'd be a wonder if any of the men her father invited came at all, considering they'd be risking their lives if they were wed to her.

"Aye, Da."

"Promise." All three of her family members stared at her with different expressions.

Her father was stern. Her mother, pleading. And Blair, perhaps the only one to realize exactly who they were exacting a promise from, had the intelligence to appear terrified.

Chapter Two

R oderick "the Grim" MacCulloch, laird of his clan, rubbed at the sore spot on his leg that ached whenever a storm was near. While he'd like to claim the injury was one he sustained in battle beside his king, Robert the Bruce, the truth was far more humiliating. A mortification he could sometimes laugh about, depending on his mood.

Standing on the battlements of his castle, Gleann Mórinnse, he beheld the Dornoch Firth, and the white of the sky that would soon, no doubt, be swirling with dark clouds.

Just that morning, several shepherds had shown up on the doorsteps of his keep to lament about their missing sheep and cattle. Once more, the damned Ross clan had carried out a midnight raid of his lands.

Over a decade ago, the Ross clan had been subdued by the Sutherlands with the help of Roderick's father—the younger brother to the old laird MacCulloch. The MacCullochs had been heavily in debt. Enough that he'd sold his only daughter to the Ross clan.

When Roderick's da took the lairdship from his wayward brother, he'd vowed to protect the entrance to the Dornoch Firth—the same vow that Roderick had made—from English invasion. Roderick's father had burned down the original tower, Terrel Tower, and rebuilt the one Roderick now called home, giving it a new name, Gleann Mórinnse, meaning vale of big meadows, and to their clan, a bright future.

A bright future that was overshadowed by the losses they'd felt greatly.

And now, with over a decade's need for vengeance festering, it would appear that someone in the Ross clan had decided it was time to test their limits. The most plausible person was Ina Ross. Marmaduke, her *Sassenach* husband, had died a few years ago. And after the one bairn she'd ever produced passed away before reaching his fifth year, she'd not had another child. So why now? What was she trying to accomplish?

A few raids to test the waters? A few tiny infractions against the treaty to see who was paying attention? Or perhaps a simple need to destroy what she'd kept locked up for so long?

If he knew the Ross clan well, and he liked to think he did, then it was not only about a little raid. There was much more to it than that. Ina was incredibly devious and clever, and her thirst for destruction was akin to a drowning man in need of air. The fact she had waited over a decade was surprising.

Blast it all! His uncle had destroyed his clan's trust and that of their allies, but they were finally at a good place. The ache of the loss of his sister was still strong, but it had dulled with time, and he finally felt as though he could breathe. It had been three years now. Long years. But he had plans for his clan. Ideas for growth that would give them more security. Sheep and cattle had been a part of that plan.

And now Ina had decided to meddle. Not only were their livestock being taken, which was taking food and coin from his crofters' hands, but the clan was getting increasingly nervous. It was just a few animals taken in the dead of night now, but if the men, or women, responsible weren't stopped soon, next they'd be taking more. Robbing a croft of what they owned, taking other precious things that didn't belong to them. Even a life.

Roderick wouldn't allow it. His clan had suffered enough with the brutality of his uncle, the transition to Roderick's father as laird a decade ago, and then another transition when they'd lost his da. They'd lost men. He'd lost his sister.

How dare Ina Ross attempt to squash their attempts at rebuilding?

The MacCulloch shepherds were not weaklings. Nor were they fearful. If anything, they were spitting mad that a dozen sheep and cattle had been taken from beneath their noses. They'd taken to teaming up, doubling the manpower, extra weapons strapped to each of them, and doubling the hounds on watch.

Those shepherds that were still a bit wet behind the ears brought along their das and their older brothers. His people would fight for what was theirs, and Roderick wouldn't stop them. He'd not seen them this passionate about anything in a long while. It was as if his own grief had laid a blanket of sorrow over his people. He owed them. In fact, tonight he was planning on getting back what had been stolen from them. A raid of his own to show Ina he wasn't afraid of her. To show his people he was their protector.

"My laird."

Roderick didn't turn away from the view, but he nodded his acknowledgement to his younger brother, Jon, who'd joined him.

Jon leaned against the ramparts. He had the same coloring as their sister, Jessica. Golden and light, the exact opposite of the demons that had haunted her. She'd always had an angelic quality to her. And Jon, too. On the field of battle, men would often stop to stare at Jon, struck by his divine appearance. That was a mistake, which Jon took full advantage of. Thank God he'd been leading their army the last few years.

The lassies, too, were slayed by one wink from his brother, which Jon also took full advantage of. He was a bachelor to the core and had no interest in becoming anything other than that. A sentiment Roderick shared, though with less vigor.

"There are more crofters waiting in the great hall, Brother," Jon said.

Roderick had seen them. Every quarter of an hour or so, at least half a dozen of them arrived. Crofters and warriors alike. Their clan was small, and most of his men held duties as both. He suspected they were coming to speak to him about the recent raids, but he would not be surprised if the Ross bastards had indeed gone a step further from the last raid.

"Any word from the scouts?" Roderick asked.

"Aye," Jon said. "They've scouted along the perimeter of the land and didna find anything other than a few campfires that could be anyone. Nothing points to the Ross clan other than the shepherds who said the men wore Ross colors."

It had occurred to Roderick that men from another clan, or even outlaws, could have put on Ross colors to make it look like they were Ina's men. But that notion would be put to rest when he went on his own raid tonight and found their cattle and sheep.

He scowled into the distance. Nothing was ever easy. Not that he expected it to me. Being laird was a most honorable and difficult duty. He had to see to the welfare of everyone in his clan. A great responsibility he'd not known would be his own until he was nearly a man and his father had taken the position from his brother. And it wasn't one he'd fully embraced even when he was made laird, suffering from grief. He was ready now.

"I will do right by them," he said more to himself than anyone else.

"They trust ye, Grim."

Roderick grimaced at the moniker, only further proving why he had it. "Aye. And I'll see they are recompensed."

His brother followed him down the stairs, and Roderick frowned the entire way, the pain in his thigh intense. A storm was definitely coming. By the time they'd reached the base, beads of sweat lined his spine, but he pushed through. A warrior never showed weakness, especially physical weakness. A laird had to be a god among men.

All the same, Jon side-eyed him. "How's the leg?"

"Fine." Roderick's tone was clipped, but he didn't care. Jon knew better than to ask, anyway.

He stomped across the bailey and into the keep, where the great hall was filled with the men who spoke none too softly to each other about what they'd lost.

"Laird," Angus MacCulloch, a third cousin of Roderick and Jon's, spoke. "Thank ye for coming so quick."

"I'd not leave ye waiting after such torment." Roderick stepped forward and grasped the men by their arms, giving them his full attention.

"What are we to do about the Ross clan? We've not had trouble from them in many years."

"Aye, at least ten give or take a few by my count." Roderick nodded. "Not a whisper. They've been silent all this time. Not even seeking us out for trade, or even a minor trespass on our land." The Ross Clan silence was terrifying. What had Ina been up to while they all sat by, calm and carefree? "Tonight, we ride. See if we canna recover what they've stolen. Maybe question a crofter or two. And when we return, I'll send word to Sutherland that the bastards are up to their old tricks."

The men nodded, loudly voicing their agreement. "We'll ride with ye."

Roderick nodded. "Only three of ye. I want to keep the party small. Jon, ye'll stay here and protect the castle and lands."

"Aye, my laird," his brother agreed.

Three men stepped forward, Angus among them.

"Gather what ye need and meet me in the bailey in an hour," Roderick instructed.

The men left the great hall, and Roderick turned to gather the things he would need for the raid.

"Brother." Jon's voice stilled him.

"Aye?" Roderick turned back around, warily eyeing Jon.

"Be careful." Jon's face did not show any of his emotions, but Roderick would have to be a dense fool not to know the meaning behind the words.

What happened three years prior was enough to haunt him for the rest of his life. After having lost both their parents and their sister, whenever they parted, they each worried about whether or not it would be the last time they saw each other.

Death spared no one.

Death rarely gave a warning.

Roderick would never forgive himself for not being there when his sister needed him. And he knew Jon harbored guilt, too, for he'd been training with Roderick deep in the woods with their men. They'd not been gone long, a few days at most, and Jessica had been doing well. Had been happy, even.

Since losing his sister and parents, he had a better appreciation of the fragility of life. Thank goodness for his younger brother being willing to step in to lead their army. But he knew he couldn't count on Jon forever. At some point, Roderick was going to have to be the one who held a sword to his enemy's neck. Until now, the Highlands had been relatively quiet, save for a skirmish here and there.

And if it came down to choosing between an enemy or those he cared about, he knew he could be ruthless.

Never again would he lose someone close to him.

He'd sustained the thigh injury that would leave him pained for the rest of his days on the anniversary of his sister's death. It was almost a reminder of what he'd lost. In that single moment, a year's worth of healing had reverted, shoving him back into the brooding darkness.

Refusing to venture down the pained past his memory appeared to want to dredge up, Roderick grasped his brother's shoulder and gave a hard squeeze. "I'll be careful. Take care of things while I'm gone." And without a backward glance, he was marching toward the bailey.

His mount, Twilight, a massive black warhorse, was already saddled, and a leather bag of provisions was fastened to the side along with his targe. Hidden within the folds of the saddle blanket were two broadswords, and his claymore was strapped to his back. A *sgian dubh* graced each boot, and at his wrists were two smaller daggers.

With a nod at his stable master, he marched to Twilight and mounted, ignoring the stabbing ache in his thigh. He wiped at the sweat on his brow and breathed out a long sigh. The ride was going to be rough, but sheer force of will would power him through it. And when he returned, he'd have a tub filled to the brim with hot water brought in, and after a nice long soak, he'd rub the salve the healer had given him onto his leg.

"There's an extra plaid in the satchel as well, my laird. Looks like a storm's coming."

Roderick nodded his thanks.

"The skins are all filled with water, as ye requested, my laird."

The men would have liked whisky, especially with the storm coming. Tonight would be cold, and the whisky would have warmed them, but Roderick wasn't willing to risk anyone. Not for a dram.

Moments later, the men arrived and mounted up. Using only the hand signals they'd all become accustomed to over the years, he motioned for them to move out. It was imperative in any operation that they be able to communicate without their voices. Especially in an ambush situation, or when they had to hide from an enemy who outnumbered them.

Though the sky was white, and the wind blew in gusts, Mother Nature was kind to them, not allowing the skies to open until they reached the first herd. Spotting his missing livestock was easy. The branding symbol of the MacCullochs—a fist holding a dart—was plain as day in every flash of lightning. The first two of their missing cattle and one sheep. Two hours later, they'd managed to wrangle five cows and four sheep, and tie them up to leading ropes.

It would seem the men who'd gone raiding had separated out the bounty to various crofters. Easier to hide a few amongst many.

The victory of reclaiming nearly all of the livestock lost was dampened by the certainty that the Ross clan was definitely behind the missing animals. It wasn't as if Ina and her rabble were lacking for livestock. In fact, they appeared to have a plethora. This had been purely about offending the MacCulloch people.

What motive could the Ross clan have for such a move? They'd done nothing to offend Ina. They minded their own business.

Och, but why was he even asking?

MacCulloch lands bordered Ross to the east. As small as they were, the MacCullochs were situated on fertile lands and occupied a space at the firth. Perhaps the most important part, considering it was up to them to guard the mouth and make certain no one passed that didn't have permission. He recalled being a child and hearing his father's stories about Ross men trying to vanquish them, laying siege on any day that ended with Y. When the Sutherlands, Murrays and Sinclairs, along with the Bruce's support, had gone against Ross, and then his daughter and her viper of a *Sassenach* husband, they'd thought all their troubles would come to an end. They'd thought for certain Ina would never come back to bother them. What fools they'd been to trust her again.

Bloody hell.

"Ye go ahead. Take the livestock back to Gleann Mórinnse. I'm going to find someone and ask a few questions."

"I'll come with ye," Angus said.

"Nay. I can better escape alone, and if the men run into trouble on the way back, they'll need your help."

Angus looked like he wanted to argue, but he nodded instead.

"Get some rest when ye return, and first thing in the morning, come to the castle, and we'll figure out what to do next."

"Are ye certain?" Angus prodded.

"Aye. Trust me."

The men agreed and disappeared into the night. With their figures long since turned into shadows, Roderick took a moment to climb from his horse and rub at his sore thigh. Though the wound had healed on the outside years before, something on the inside had never felt quite right. Ballocks, but tonight it pained him something awful. And no amount of massaging seemed to help. Gritting his teeth, he hopped back up onto his horse and then picked his way back toward the first herd in search of the Ross shepherd. He found the lad dozing beneath a tree, safe from the rain. It was a sight that made Roderick amused and exceedingly angry all at once, then very suspicious. Was this a trap?

Roderick pulled out his two broadswords and held one in each hand as he led Twilight forward using signals with his calves and heels. When he reached the snoozing shepherd, he tapped the lad on top of his head with the tip of his sword.

The poor rascal jerked from his deep sleep with a lot of groaning and gasping, nearly poking his eye out with the tip of Roderick's sword.

"Calm yourself," Roderick commanded, brows drawing downward. The lad slept as deep as any he'd ever seen, and in a storm no less. Why in the bloody hell had he been put in charge of the livestock? "I've not come to kill ye, lad, though your laird might if he knew ye were asleep on the job."

He might not have seen the lad pale if not for the flash of lightning that showed his fear. The lad's eyes were wide and nearly black from the dark. His mouth was agape in a silent scream and tremors wracked his whole body.

The shepherd waved his hands in front of him, as though doing so would ward off Roderick, who he seemed to think was a demon in disguise. "Wh—what do ye want?"

The lad glanced wildly around, and then found and grasped his staff.

Roderick tsked. "Is that any way to greet an elder? And I'd not try anything with that staff, either."

The lad shuffled backward on his hands and feet, trying to put distance between himself and Roderick, a feat that was crushed by the tree at his back. "Take the cattle. Take them all."

Roderick clenched his jaw. "Again, I'm quite certain your laird wouldna appreciate your tactics. Ye may be the worst shepherd to grace beloved Scotland."

"What I get paid is not worth my life." The lad flashed him a defiant sneer.

Roderick shrugged. That was a fair point. "I tell ye what. I'll let ye go and not steal any of *your* cattle."

"What?" The shepherd glanced from side to side as if waiting for more demons to leap from the dark.

"On one condition."

The lad nodded vehemently. "Aye, anything."

"Tell me, lad, what is Ina Ross up to?"

"What?"

Roderick clenched his jaw. He supposed he'd have to deal in more plain terms with the lad. "Why is your laird raiding other clan holdings?"

"Oh..." The lad sounded as though he'd just discovered the earth wasn't flat. "Well, she wants only the best for her new husband."

"Husband? She's wed?" Roderick tried not to sound like that bit of news had surprised him, when the truth was, it had hit him like a boulder falling from a crag.

"Aye. A great and powerful man." The lad sounded enamored.

"And who might that be?"

He shook his head, then ran his hands over his face, swiping at the rainwater. "I canna say."

"Or what?" Roderick lifted his sword, letting the lad see that his weapon was still close enough to do damage. "Because if ye truly need a reason, I'll gladly cut out your tongue right now, lad."

The shepherd's gulp was so loud the rain did not drown it out.

Roderick made a move with his sword, knowing he wouldn't need more than a flick of his wrist to get the lad talking.

The shepherd's hands went up in front of his face as his tongue spilled the news. "Another great English lord, sir, Lord Ughtred."

Roderick had never heard of him. "What can ye tell me of this Ughtred?"

"He is young. Half her age, I should think. And he's chomping at the bit for land. More and more. He's been granted a constableship in the north of England, but he believes his true claim to glory will be conquering the Highlands."

"And how do ye know so much?"

The lad's shoulders squared, his chin jutting a little with pride. "I heard him tell it."

"When?"

"When he was ordering my da and some others to start raiding again."

Roderick pressed his lips together in thought. If Ughtred had been the one to order the raids, and the men had only done the bare minimum of stealing a few cattle and sheep, did that mean the Ross men were not completely behind their laird's new husband? Or had they only been ordered to steal a few?

"What does your da say?"

The lad shook his head vehemently. "I'd rather ye cut out my tongue."

"Dinna play games with me, Shepherd, for I'm not likely to be kind in turn." Och, but the pain in his thigh was growing with the increasing rain pelting against his forehead. He still had a long ride ahead of him, and he needed the lad to open up.

Perhaps a few breaths or more went by before the lad finally spoke. "He wasna pleased. Said he'd hoped to live out the rest of his life without warring between clans, when we were already warring with England. Please, dinna say anything. Go now. Else my da will be killed."

"I'll nae be telling anyone about your da." At least not giving his name. "And do the others think the same?"

"I dinna know. I didna ask."

"Have ye a sense of it, lad?"

"My da says I have no sense."

"Ye're still alive, are ye nae?"

"Aye."

"Then ye must have some sense." Roderick rubbed his thigh and found his patience had worn extremely thin now.

"All right." The lad sat up a little taller. "My sense is they are nae happy. Ughtred and Laird Ross married over three years ago when she made a secret trip to the border. She's lost at least two bairns since then, and threatened death to anyone who spilled their secret. Now all the sudden with her husband here, she's got a thirst for land. My ma says 'tis because she doesna have any bairns to keep her busy."

"I reckon your ma is a smart woman."

The lad smiled and then jumped at a crack of thunder and a bolt of lightning.

"Thank ye for your time, lad. And I'm certain ye know already, but in case not, dinna mention I was here."

"But—"

"If ye must say anything, say I knocked ye into sleep, else ye just may get that tongue cut out, and I'd hate for that to happen."

The lad nodded emphatically, covering his mouth with his hand.

Roderick retreated, heading back toward his own lands, a sick feeling in the pit of his stomach. Ina Ross was back—and this time, she had nothing to lose.

Chapter Three

Greer was in trouble.

Serious trouble.

And not the kind where she spilled strawberry jam on a light-colored gown, or accidentally knocked one of her father's men off the *currach* with one of her oars.

Nay, this time she was in serious danger of *dying*.

And there did not appear to be any way out. There was no one here to help her.

She should have listened to her father. Should have stayed inside and waited dutifully for the feast that would make her a bride. But nay. She'd succumbed to the strong desire to sail out to sea one last time— for that was what she'd presumed it would be, given her father had forbidden her from sailing until the feast where she would find herself shackled.

What could it hurt to go for one last sail?

Everything had been going well. She'd been on her way back to the castle, pleased that she'd decided to ignore her father's rule. What was wrong with a little rebellion if no one got hurt?

And then the skies had opened up. Her *currach* had capsized on a massive swell, dumping her headfirst into the water, her dog with her.

The skies were dark, and she'd been floating in the water forever—her gown long since shed to keep the weight of it from dragging her down to the dark depths and her death. Mother Nature's cruel jest.

Her teeth chattered in the cold, and even with her head above water, she got no reprieve. Rain pelted against her forehead. Her limbs were frozen, aching, and the idea of going to sleep seemed very...nice.

A muzzle bumped her face. Jewel, the large black hound she'd been given as a gift by her aunt and uncle, and who had a love of water as profound as her own, had not wanted to be left home. Now Jewel might die along with her.

"Go," she croaked, trying to point away from her, in hopes the hound that had more energy than she and could swim away.

The only thing that helped her stay somewhat afloat when her muscles cramped was the single oar she'd been able to grasp as she was tossed into the water, for she didn't want to lean her weight on Jewel. But even that didn't help much. When she put her weight onto it fully, she felt herself sinking into the darkness. And then Jewel would push her body back into wakefulness.

Any moment, she was likely to succumb. Whether to cold, exhaustion, or a shark. She just knew it. And there was no fantasy selkie coming to find her. No amount of praying would make that dream come true.

A warm tongue licked her face, and Greer couldn't hold back tears. Jewel had to be exhausted, and still she stayed beside her. Greer couldn't let her do it any longer.

"Oh, God, Jewel, go!" she cried, her voice breaking.

The dog panted beside her, just as exhausted, but ever faithful.

Not for the first time, Greer regretted disobeying her father immensely. They'd all been busy, and with the sky only marginally filled with clouds, she'd decided to take one last row. Just one. That was it. But one time was all it took for her mother's fears to come crashing down around her. After today, if she survived, she was going to hang up her oars and only do as her father allowed.

In the distance, she could make out lights. Whether they were from Sutherland lands or the other side of the firth, she couldn't say.

Perhaps an hour or two ago, she would have delighted in the sight of blessed lights, of civilization, but they seemed too far away now. No one could hear her shouts, and she'd not the energy to swim toward them. That bit of salvation was not remotely within reach. But maybe it was for her pet. "Go to the lights, Jewel. Go to safety."

She managed to lift her arm from the water, to snap and point toward where she thought there was land, and at last, her faithful hound swam away.

If one of them were to die, better it were she, instead of the sweet and faithful friend she'd raised from puppyhood.

And so, Greer floated, waking whenever she tried to draw breath and got a mouthful of water.

Och, but she was so thirsty. So tired. Maybe it would be all right to slip into oblivion. To let the water take her forever.

Lightning flashed around her, jolting her awake, and she almost wished for the shock of it to slam into her body, if only to warm her. Right about now, her entire clan would be in an uproar. Just before the evening meal, her maid would have informed Lady Arbella that Greer was not in her chamber. Her mother would have then rushed to find her father, and then the two of them would have searched and asked questions. They would have torn apart the castle. But her father, knowing better, would have gone straight to the docks, and that's when they would have noticed she'd taken the *currach*.

They would have felt the first drops of rain as soon as they readied a great *birlinn* to go out in search of her. But they'd go anyway. They would risk their lives for her.

But it would all be for nothing. And not for the first time, Greer wished she could be more like her sisters, and less of a resister. If only she had listened. If only she could find it in herself to follow the rules.

Too late for that now.

She closed her eyes.

***

BY THE TIME Roderick returned to his own lands, the sun was starting to rise. Soon, he'd be meeting with his men to go over the rest of their plans.

Without thinking, he rode Twilight down toward the beach, only realizing where he'd inadvertently traversed once his mount's hooves sank into the sand. Roderick dismounted, letting his steed wander over to nibble on some of the nearby vegetation. He pulled off his boots and sank his feet into the rough sand, the coolness of the damp beach a relief from his hot boots. The rain had stopped, and the sky had only a few fleeting clouds. The pain in his leg had dissipated somewhat.

He often came to the shore to think. There was something about the sounds of the waves lapping against the beach and the chill water against his feet that brought him clarity. He was planning on sending a messenger to the Sutherlands, but maybe it would be better if he took a *birlinn* across the firth to speak with Magnus Sutherland himself.

That was the last thing he wanted to do, but he couldn't see it any other way. He'd been the one who'd spoken to the lad about Ina and her new husband, so sending a messenger could mean some information would be lost in the translation.

"Ballocks," he grumbled.

Movement up the beach caught his attention. And then the sound of a dog barking had him focusing. A massive black dog barreled at him. He might have mistaken it for a bear, if they were not extinct in Scotland. The dog then turned around and retreated up the beach to where a shape was being rolled with the waves. Perhaps a seal. They sometimes were pushed onto shore. But this was too light in color to be a seal. Too flesh colored.

The hound was barking and trying to find somewhere to grasp on the form with its teeth, mouthing an arm, tugging at a piece of fabric near the shoulder.

Och, bloody hell… That looked like a body. A woman or child.

Roderick didn't hesitate. He ran down the shore, leaping over an oar…

Someone had been out in that storm last night.

But there was no boat.

The closer he got, the more he could see, and the more his stomach plummeted. A lass. *Mo chreach.* Dark tendrils of hair matted with sand and seawater. Pale white skin, blue in places. A soaked-through chemise showed every line and curve of her young and lithe body. No shoes. No gown. No jewels.

Flashes of Jessica tormented his mind, gutting him. He ran faster, ignoring the searing pain returning to his thigh. He had to get to her. To save her. Whoever she was. Was this God's way of sending him a message? Giving him a second chance?

Why else had he been drawn to the beach at this particular moment?

If he believed in mysticism, he might have thought she were a mermaid come to shore. But Roderick didn't. He believed in solid facts. This was a woman. The oar was evidence she'd been on a boat, mayhap a *currach,* that had capsized during the storm the night before. Were there others? He squinted behind him and ahead, but saw no other bodies lining the shore. There had to have been others with her. They must have died at sea, for how could a lass and her hound have gone out in a *currach* alone?

The hound growled as Roderick dropped to his knees and carefully rolled the body over. She was cold to the touch. Another flash of Jessica came into his mind, and he squeezed his eyes shut, shaking them away. The growling hound brought him back.

"'Tis all right. I'm going to help." That seemed to calm the animal somewhat.

The dog whined and nudged its owner. He licked her face as Roderick examined the body in search of signs of injury and found none.

Out of respect, he tried to avoid viewing the lass's more intimate parts. And then he found himself staring hard at her face. A face he recognized.

Greer Sutherland.

"Shite." He leaned his ear toward her mouth. She wasn't breathing. Touching his fingers to her neck, he felt a faint pulse. She was alive, but she was dying. Would be dead within minutes if he didn't breathe for her. Might still be dead even if he did. "Ye canna die on me, lass. Not now."

Mary Mother of God, help me...

There was no time for prayers. No time for thought. Only action. *Save her. Save her. Save her.* Roderick rolled her onto her back, pinched her nose, and covered her mouth with his, pushing his breath into her body. Her chest barely rose. He sucked a bigger breath, blew again, and this time watched her chest rise a little more.

"Come on," he urged her, panic in his veins.

He continued to breathe into her mouth, over and over, watching her chest rise and fall, begging her to breathe on her own, until her body convulsed and she started to cough and sputter water. He eased her onto her side as the water kept coming from her lungs, and then she spilled the contents of her stomach, which was mostly water, too. The amount of water that rushed from her body seemed unfathomable for one so tiny.

The hound wagged its tail and licked furiously at Lady Greer's face, then at Roderick's, as if in gratitude.

"Let her breathe, pup," Roderick said, patting the wet dog on the head. "She'll be fine now."

He hoped...

The lass didn't open her eyes. She took shallow, shuddering breaths, gulping in air, and then she started to tremor. Gooseflesh covered her skin. The lass was frozen. She grimaced, an expression that must have easily matched his own. Roderick didn't hesitate to unpin his plaid and wrap it around her as he lifted her up. With an iron will he'd not possessed in some time, he ignored the ache in his thigh, a stark reminder of just exactly how he knew her. He carried her back toward Twilight with the hound following diligently behind.

"Ye're safe now, lass," he said to Lady Greer, hoping to calm her even in her unconsciousness. "We'll get ye warmed up and fed, and then I'll take ye back to your da and ma."

Roderick eased her onto Twilight, belly down, and then climbed up behind her and pulled her back into the cradle of his arms. He rubbed at her limbs, trying to warm her as best he could.

Dinna die on me.

Lady Greer shuddered against him, her body shivering so violently it shook his bones, too. Knowing what she'd done to him two years ago, some crueler than he would have advised he leave her on the beach. But he wasn't evil. And no matter what had happened in the past, he wasn't going to let her die. Ironic as it was that he should be the one to find her.

And yet there was that little niggle in the back of his brain, that this was his chance to redeem himself.

Her lips were still blue, the tips of her fingers wrinkled, and she'd yet to even flutter the thick fringe of her lashes. Even without seeing her vibrant blue eyes, the color of bluebells, he was certain it was she. When her hair dried, it would be the same fiery red he remembered.

"What were ye doing out there?" He needn't have asked, for she'd bragged enough about her skill the first time he'd met her. That was what had drawn him into a competition with her to begin with.

But no amount of skill could go up against a storm at sea, especially alone.

And she would have known that.

Was this deliberate? Had she gone out to sea alone on purpose?

He couldn't fathom that she would have done such a thing with her dog on board, but then again, he'd seen the dark demons that could possess a person's mind before. Was Greer as tormented as his sister, or had this been a true accident? He'd not find out until she woke.

Roderick mumbled a curse under his breath and urged his mount into a gallop, leaving his boots on the shore, the dog in tow.

When they reached the castle, he shouted, "I need hot water, broth and a healer."

He took no offer of help in dismounting, swinging his left leg over his mount's head and dropping to his feet with Lady Greer in his arms. The ache in his leg pulsed, but he kept it at bay, snubbing the stab of pain at each step up the circular stair. What was pain when there was a life at stake? He carried her right up to his chamber, the only one he knew would have a bed made up. He yanked back the plaid blanket, slid her into the pressed sheets, and then started to pile blankets on top of her before recalling she wore a wet chemise.

Ballocks.

The wet garment had to be removed, else what was the point of trying to warm her? He glanced toward the hound who'd settled before the fire—and blast it all, were those his boots? Sitting near the snout of the hound were in fact a pair quite identical to his own. Had the dog brought them back?

His attention returned to the bed, where Lady Greer groaned between the chattering of her teeth.

"Dammit." He yanked the blankets off, and closing his eyes to keep her honor intact, peeled away the chemise. He tossed a plaid back over her before he reopened them. Better to be able to swear on his life that he'd not seen *the* Magnus Sutherland's daughter naked, else he'd find himself shackled in marriage or in a dungeon; either one had the same outcome.

The last thing he wanted was to be married—and especially not to a hellion like Greer Sutherland. Aye, he'd save her life, but that was as far as he'd go in commitment to the chit.

"What happened?" Jon came into the chamber behind him and took one horrified glimpse of Greer before backing toward the door. "What did ye do? Who is that?"

Roderick gaped. "Ye think because ye see a half-dead lass in my bed that I must have done something to her? When have I ever warranted that kind of a reaction?"

"Well, ye are standing only in your shirt..."

Roderick glanced down at himself. "Ye have a point. But I found her this way on the beach, and I wrapped her up in my plaid."

Jon crept forward, trying to get a better look at her face. "What the hell was she doing on the beach?"

What the hell indeed? "Swept in on the waves, I imagine."

"Who is she?"

"I'm certain 'tis Lady Greer Sutherland."

Jon flicked a worried gaze at his brother, and when he spoke, it was barely above a whisper. "Nay..."

"Aye. In the flesh." His brother was having a similar reaction to the one he'd had. It was one any MacCulloch would have. Indeed, every man in the Highlands who recalled what happened between the two of them a couple years before would react the same way.

"*Blue* flesh," Jon murmured.

"Very observant. Why do ye nae add more wood to the fire? Make yourself useful. We canna have her freezing to death, not when I saved her from lungfuls of water."

"Ye need to get in the bed with her." Jon nodded his chin toward the bed, his face entirely serious.

Roderick took a large step back, enough that he almost tripped on the hound. "Like hell I will." That was going a step too far. He'd already made certain not to see her without her chemise, but to hold her in his arms, naked? No way in bloody hell.

Jon jabbed his finger toward the lass. "She is shivering. She's at risk of hypothermia."

"I know that." Roderick grimaced and uttered a curse, followed by another.

"Body heat will help."

Roderick shook his head. "Not mine."

"Not mine, either, Brother. I want to live." Jon emphasized the last word as if lying with the lass was a sentence of death. Which it very well might be.

"And what makes ye think I dinna?"

"Wild guess." Jon shrugged.

"I'll get some maids to come and do it."

"That's your choice, Grim, but none of the maids will have the amount of body heat ye do. If I were ye, I'd get my arse in that bed afore she dies there and ye have to explain to her father how that happened."

Mo chreach. Roderick scowled all the more as he peeled back the covers and slipped quickly into the bed. The sheets were like ice from her body. He wasn't even near her yet and already felt the cold.

"Take off your shirt." Jon didn't turn around as he issued that instruction.

Roderick tore his shirt off and tossed it behind him. It landed on the healer's head as she rushed in with several servants behind her, carrying whisky, heated rocks, and boiling broth.

"Good," the healer said. "I would have told ye to do that."

Roderick ignored the old woman who'd aided in his birth. The lass was like ice as he curled his arms around her and brought her back flush to his body. The coolness of her thighs against his was actually a balm to the aching scar—and the other part of him that dared spark to life.

He tucked her head beneath his chin.

"Rub her," the healer commanded, as she carefully laid hot rocks beneath the blankets.

Roderick rubbed at the lass's arms vigorously. And then her legs. All the while, he forced himself to think of things like rubbing down a horse, or giving the hounds a bath, and not the fact that he had a beautiful, venomous wench in his bed whom he'd not invited, and yet who he was very intrigued by.

Chapter Four

Warmth surrounded Greer, cocooning her in a decadent cloud. She snuggled closer to the heat, smiling in her sleep.

Something niggled at the back of her brain, as though she were trying to remember something important. What was it?

And then she bolted upright in bed, recalling exactly what she was supposed to remember. She'd nearly *drowned*.

She jerked around to face the wide-eyed gaze of a man—a very handsome man—but still a *man*!

"I'm naked," she gasped, pressing her hands to her breasts to hide them from where the blanket had fallen.

"Aye." The voice was gruff, filled with sleep and grumpiness.

She felt him slip from the bed, unable to make eye contact with him. Oh dear heavens...

The chamber was completely unfamiliar to her. Not one at her own castle. Not one at any castle she'd ever been to. The wood floor was bare of rushes.

Weapons lined the wall, and there was a single wardrobe beside the chamber door. To the left of the hearth were a small table and two large chairs. Chairs fit for a giant. Or from the looks of the man she couldn't bear to view just yet—chairs fit for *him*.

The shutters over the window were closed, so she couldn't get a good look outside to perhaps judge from the landscape where she was. Which meant she had to rely on the stranger whose bed she'd been in. *Naked*.

She wouldn't have thought last night, as she floated in the darkened sea, that her situation could get any worse. But it would not be the first time she'd been wrong.

"Where am I? Who are ye?"

"Ye dinna recognize me?" He sounded surprised.

Greer squeezed her eyes shut. Had she drowned and gone to Hell?

"Are ye naked, sir?" she squeaked.

"As the day I was born." Why did he have to sound so gleeful?

Greer fell back on the bed and pulled the blanket up over her head, feeling her face heat with shame. She could die now. Right now would be fine. Somehow, she'd managed to drown herself and had either become a man's mistress or married him without her knowledge. Either way, her da was going to murder her, and her mother would be heartbroken.

"Bring me a sword," she croaked, her voice coming out muffled with the thick pile of blankets on her face.

Even still, he seemed to have heard her. "Are ye going to finish me off then, lass?"

Finish him off? "I canna comprehend what that means right now, but I do plan to finish myself."

"Oh, why's that? Is that why ye went for a boat ride in a storm? Ye've a death wish? Or was it some sort of mad challenge ye issued yourself? See if ye didna die in a storm?" He watched her with serious concern, which she supposed was completely warranted.

And then she felt a vicious pain in her chest.

Oh, heavens! "Jewel," she cried out, tears spilling down her cheeks. Her poor dog. Her vision blurred. She reached to swipe at the tears, only to lose part of the blankets that covered her, and so instead she clutched them for the sake of propriety and let her vision go.

An answering bark, and the clicking of nails on the wooden floor-boards, shocked her tears into submission. A bark that sounded so familiar. How could it be?

"Jewel?" She blinked rapidly to remove the water from her eyes. She was prepared to be disappointed but was gifted with a slobbery kiss on her cheek. She patted the bed, and Jewel leapt on. The man she'd still not gotten a good glimpse of protested.

"Dinna let her up there. No dogs in the bed."

Both Greer and Jewel ignored him. "Oh my, how did ye get here?" she cooed into Jewel's furry neck, wrapping her arms around her pet.

"She was with ye on the beach where I found ye."

Greer pulled away from Jewel a moment and almost glanced behind her, until she remembered that he was naked. So, instead, she stared at the canopy overhead. "Ye found me?"

"Rolling in the waves like driftwood."

"And ye brought me here." It was a statement of fact rather than a question.

"Aye."

"To your castle?" This she did ask, because though she was in a bedchamber, it didn't mean it was a castle.

"Aye."

All right, so it was his castle. Which meant he was a powerful man. Perhaps a clan chief or a relative of one. A steward even. Dear God, let her not have been saved and taken to bed by a steward. Her father would set the world on fire if she didn't make an advantageous match.

"And ye...took me to bed."

"In a matter of speaking." He sounded so nonchalant about it. As though he took helpless lassies to bed on a daily basis.

"An unconscious, drowned lass in your bed?" She frowned, and sensing her ire, Jewel barked. "Ye're a brute, whoever ye are."

"I didna bed ye, if that's what ye're asking. I was warming ye up. Ye were near frozen and would have died. 'Twas a long night I had afore then, so I fell asleep. Not that I need to explain to ye. Ye should be thanking me for saving ye when ye wished to perish."

"Oh." Heat suffused her face, and she still couldn't look at him.

"Thank ye." She bit her lip, sinking her fingers into Jewel's fur. "I didna wish to perish. I only wished for one last adventure..."

"Ye're young enough yet to have a lifetime of adventures."

She shrugged, not wanting to go into the details with a virtual stranger. Although there was something very familiar about him. Without peeking at him, she tried to recall the angles of his face, the harshness of his stare. He was as handsome as he was fierce, but there was also something sad about him. A sadness she felt an almost need to reverse.

"Have we met before?" Greer asked.

"Aye." But he gave her no explanation.

Well, if he wasn't willing to expound on that, she could certainly try to pry it out of him. "If ye know me, what is my name?"

"Ye dinna recall your own name?" He murmured something under his breath.

"Nay, nay, I but want to know if *ye* truly know me. A test."

She could practically feel him clenching his jaw with annoyance behind her. "Ye and your tests, Lady Greer Sutherland. We've met before, and ye changed my life. And not for the better."

Greer frowned. No one had ever said anything like that to her before. And there was a definite note of sarcasm in his tone. She heard the whisper of fabric and assumed he was dressing.

"Is that so?" she asked, curling onto her side away from him, sinking further into the warm fur of her pet.

"Aye. A couple years have passed." A *thunk* sounded behind her, as though he pulled on a boot. An echoing *thunk* made her certain of it.

She bravely turned then, almost positive he was dressed. "Well, I canna say I recall..." Her words died on her lips.

Standing opposite from where she was on the bed was a massive and striking warrior. He had dark hair the color of roasted chestnuts and mesmerizing eyes that could have been sapphires. Stubble covered his cheeks and jawline, but on his chin, he grew a short beard that connected to a well-trimmed mustache. There was a lump on the bridge of his otherwise straight nose, and his brows furrowed so deeply, she knew instantly who he was.

"Grim." She groaned and squeezed her lids closed, rubbing at her temples before staring at him again, just to make sure she was certain.

"Aye, lass." He glowered at her. "So ye do remember?"

Greer had lost the ability to speak. All she could remember was that day two years before when he'd been at Dunrobin. She'd challenged him...and he'd sustained an injury... She regretted never having found a way to apologize for it. As it was, they'd not spoken since.

Her scrutiny traveled toward his leg. *Which thigh was it?*

"No need to answer that, Lady Greer. Your gaze is enough of a confirmation."

"I'm so sorry." Her voice came out a whisper as mortification tightened her throat. "I should have said so sooner."

"I'm certain ye harbor regret." His tone was filled with ice. "But ye needna have tossed yourself into the firth over it."

Greer frowned. "I didna toss myself into the firth."

"Ye werena trying to end yourself?"

"Nay, of course not." She bit her lip, recalling vividly how his own sister had perished. Lowering her voice, she said, "I swear on the life of my mother, I didna want to...perish."

His lips tightened, the muscle in the side of his jaw clenching and unclenching.

"In any case, I can see ye havena forgiven me for what happened last we met." She gazed around the very bare and masculine chamber, noting the only feminine touch was her chemise that hung to dry before the fire.

"I saved your life. Isna that confirmation of forgiveness?"

"'Haps." She shrugged. "Or it was just human compassion."

"A warrior canna have compassion." He shook his head at her like she was a child. Given her circumstances, she was sincerely doubting she possessed any maturity.

"All warriors have compassion. 'Tis the reason they fight." The reason they save people... Greer knew in that moment that she needed to make a change. Turn a new leaf. The fact that he'd saved her was a chance to change her outlook on life, and her priorities.

If possible, his scowl deepened. "I dinna think ye understand a warrior's heart."

"Mayhap ye dinna understand yourself. Please turn around."

But he didn't move. Instead, his glittering blue gaze bore into her as though he wished to know all of her secrets. As though he could in fact see them outright. She felt exposed, more so than she truly was. Beneath the blankets, she was naked. He'd lain with her. Warmed her. He'd likely seen every single part of her flesh, and yet that stare right then and there while she was fully covered made her feel more bared than any bit of displaying her skin could have.

"Please," she said, breathless from his regard.

His mouth hardened, and he gave a curt nod.

Greer waited until he finally turned around, and then she pulled back the blanket. Her body rebelled against the chill air touching her skin, but she didn't care. Making certain his back was fully turned, she raced on tiptoe across the chamber, grabbed hold of the warm chemise, and pulled it over her head. Then she tugged a plaid off the bed and wound it around herself. She wrapped it beneath her arms like a gown and tied it with one of the bed curtain ropes. "Ye can turn back around now."

Grim grunted. Sadly, she did not recall his actual name. Everyone had called him Grim, and it had stuck in her memory. As had the losses he'd suffered. It only endeared him to her more, like an injured animal in need of coddling.

She supposed she should remember his name, as it was her spear that had pierced his thigh. If he knew she was unaware of it, he'd likely be insulted enough to toss her back into the firth.

Greer had never gone spear fishing again after that incident. She couldn't even eat fish anymore—criminal according to her clan, but since her mother also did not eat fish, or any other meat for that matter, she found herself with plenty of tasty dishes to eat at Dunrobin.

They came face-to-face, his startling blue eyes on her. Once more, she had the intense feeling of being bared. His gaze swept from the top of her head down to her toes, lingering in places that made her flush. Goodness. No one had ever stared at her like that before.

"Ye're wearing MacCulloch colors." His voice was gruff, but she was so filled with relief at learning his clan, she barely noticed.

MacCulloch. She recalled his name almost instantly then—Roderick. But Grim seemed to suit him much better, given she'd yet to see him smile. When she spoke, she tried for nonchalant, but she wasn't certain she could pull it off given her heart pounded behind her ribs. "I had little other choice if I did not want to wander around mostly undressed."

He nodded, his expression still set in stone.

Greer cleared her throat, nervously patting Jewel on the head. "I need to get home. My father is probably tearing apart the countryside searching for me. And I'd rather he not wage war thinking I've been taken."

Grim winged a brow. "Somehow, I believe that your father knows better."

"What is that supposed to mean?" She crossed her arms over her chest, all nerves instantly gone, and her hackles raised.

"That he willna think ye've been taken. From what I recall, ye were always a bit of a hellion. Some things never change, aye?" The man had the gall to wink at her.

Greer's mouth fell open, and she stared incredulously at him. "Ye're just rude."

He shrugged.

"Well, it doesna matter what he thinks happened to me, for soon he will know the truth of it. I need to get home. Will ye take me?"

"Aye."

A sudden pummel of panic hit her. The idea of crossing the firth so close after her accident left her wavering on her feet. "On horseback."

"Nay. A ship will be faster."

Greer felt the blood drain from her face. "Horseback," she croaked. "Please."

He frowned at her but finally gave a curt nod. "All right."

Relief flooded her that he'd so readily accepted. Although, it had been easier than she thought it would be. A little too easy.

Jewel stood at her side, peeping between the two of them, her massive tail thumping against the floor.

"Why did ye agree so fast?"

"Because ye belong under lock and key, and I'm certain your da will see to it. And also, because I can imagine the pain your family must be going through right now, believing the worst." His gaze flicked away from her, but not before she took in the note of pain that flashed through his eyes. "As for agreeing about horseback versus ship, I'd rather not deal with any dramatics."

"I am never dramatic."

He raised a skeptical brow.

"But I thank ye all the same," Greer said, determined to take the higher road.

He nodded. "I'll get ye something to eat."

"Just some bread is fine."

"Bread? Ye're not a prisoner, and I'll not be having ye go home to tell your da that all I gave ye was bread."

"But I love bread. Besides, ye will have given me more than that. Ye've given me back my life. I will be forever in your debt."

He glanced back at her, the tiniest grin doing away with his grimace. "I've changed my mind."

"What?" She swayed.

"I will take ye home. But on one condition."

Her heart started to pound. If he said anything about a ship... "What is that?" She braced herself for some bit of revenge to get back at her for his injury.

"Ye must pass a test of skill. Nay, make that three tests of skill."

Greer's mouth fell open. She couldn't hide her shock. He had to be mad. "Do ye nay recall what happened the last time we did a test of skill? I could have killed ye."

"Which means ye'll be even more careful this time."

Greer shook her head. "I dinna fish anymore. And I...I fear what happened has robbed me of the ability to sail... I canna get in a boat."

The only place she'd felt safe besides with her family had been at sea. Saints, but she prayed one day she'd be able to sail again. But not today. And probably not tomorrow either.

"Fair enough."

She pondered his easy acceptance. "Tell me what the tests are."

He shook his head, looking rather mischievous. "I'll fetch ye something to eat. We'll leave when ye finish. Unless ye need more time to rest?"

"I am eager to get home. And please..." She bit her lip. "Ye must know, I dinna eat meat."

"As ye wish."

He didn't even flinch or look at her as though she'd grown a second head. How odd.

"Bread and butter are fine," she continued to see if he'd heard her.

"Eggs?"

"Aye. I like eggs."

A moment later, he was gone, and she was left to stare out his window. The view of the firth from here was mesmerizing. It was a glittering blue-black, reflecting the trees, marsh grass, and dunes filled with gorse bushes, heather, violets, and wild thyme. In all that tranquility, she found her jaw clenching at the gentle lapping of the water against the shore. It reminded her how the waves had crashed into her the night before. She shuddered.

What a fool she'd been. This was exactly what her parents had worried about. Maybe that was part of the reason she'd gone out. She'd wanted to show her mother and father that she could handle it. Well, she'd just proven them right.

In a major way.

Greer swayed on her feet, feeling the sense of what she'd done, and what could have happened, quite deeply. She reached out for the stone windowsill and gripped the cool rock for balance.

She was lucky to be alive. And she owed her life to Jewel and Grim. Kneeling down, she grabbed hold of her pup's big head and kissed her between the eyes. "Thank ye, Jewel, for saving my life."

Jewel let out a faint bark of approval and licked her chin.

"Mayhap he'll bring ye a nice meal, too."

"She's already eaten more than all the hounds in Gleann Mórinnse combined."

Greer tried not to jump at the sound of Grim's voice. He'd returned quickly with a platter that made her mouth water. Fresh-baked scones, butter, blackberry jam, two eggs, and a cup of milk. And even though he said he'd fed Jewel, he dropped a bone on the floor anyway. The dog scrambled toward it, the same way Greer wished she could scramble toward the platter.

"That looks incredible." She followed him with her gaze as he set it on the table and tried hard not to pounce on it.

"Come eat. Our cook makes the best scones in the Highlands."

"Well, if your cook has the best scones, my mother makes the best pasties."

"Does she now?"

"Aye. Apple is my favorite. And I suppose if I pass your skill tests, I'll share them with ye when we get to Dunrobin."

He chuckled. "Go ahead. Sit. Eat."

Greer didn't argue, and descended on the platter of food just as the waves had descended upon her *currach*. The scones were filled with currents, and she topped them liberally with butter and jam. The boiled eggs were cooked to perfection. And the milk… It tasted like it had just come fresh from the dairy.

"I'm glad ye have a full appetite," he remarked.

"Is that one of the tests?"

He smirked. "Nay, but if it were, ye'd have passed with flying colors."

"I am honored." She shoved a bite of egg into her mouth.

"Are ye certain ye're ready to leave? 'Twould be best if we could depart soon. Ye've already slept through an entire day."

"I did?"

"Aye. I found ye on the beach yesterday morn. Took ye quite a while to warm up."

Greer's face heated. "I must thank ye for not…taking advantage of the situation."

"I wouldna have. Besides, there were people in the chamber with us." He plucked one of the eggs from her platter and ate it.

"Who?" She bit her lip, staring down at the jam, hoping he didn't notice her reddened face.

"The healer, my brother, a few servants."

Greer watched him go to the wardrobe, open it, and pull out a satchel. He tossed in two shirts and a few pairs of hose.

"And they all saw me...like that?" Was it possible for her to feel any more humiliation?

"Ye were covered. The healer did check to make certain ye had no other injuries. How are ye feeling now?"

She blew out a sigh and picked at a scone crumb on the trencher, rolling it into dust. "I feel good. Energized now that I've eaten. My body is a little sore, but I've spent much time swimming. So nothing I willna recover from soon."

"Ye're lucky ye didna sustain any further injury when your *currach* capsized."

Greer picked up another crumb and this time popped it into her mouth. "Did it ever show up on your beach?"

"Nay. Not that we've seen. Were ye alone?" He attached a bracer to one wrist and then the other, sliding daggers into the leather holsters.

She swallowed, watching him arm himself for a journey with her. "Save for Jewel, aye."

Grim shook his head. "A miracle."

"And ironic, do ye nae think?"

"Ironic how?" He paused with his weapons to face her.

"That I rolled up onto *your* shore? I nearly killed ye once. What do ye think that means?"

He grunted and shoved his hands through his hair. "Nothing other than I should expect more things to roll up on my shore from yours."

Greer laughed at how he deflected her superstitions so easily, but that didn't cease her from thinking there was more to it than that.

Chapter Five

"**A**re ye certain ye want to take her alone with the Ross clan growing more hostile? And should the lady not require a chaperone?"

Jon sounded like an old crone clucking around the lass. In fact, the wrinkle of his brow did remind Roderick of their old governess.

"Are ye volunteering?"

"Nay, not me, but a female."

"What female? The healer? She'd never make the journey on horseback. I intend for us to travel fast and hard. I want her home with her people, and I want to deliver that message to Magnus Sutherland myself. Besides, the more of us that are traveling, the more suspicious we'll appear to the Ross clan. They've got to have scouts watching."

"Aye. Scouts that will see ye leave with the lass and follow. Why can ye nae insist she take the *birlinn*? Ye'd be there in a few hours."

Roderick thrust a hand through his hair, feeling the same frustration. His brother was right, and yet he couldn't bring himself to toss her onto a ship. The way she'd looked when she insisted on horseback, pale as a ghost and trembling. It hadn't been Greer. Not the Greer he knew. "The lass just nearly drowned. When I mentioned it, she didna take it well. It will only be a few extra days on the road. I'll take a contingent of men, in case Ina Ross and her damned men attack. In the meantime, ye keep a tight rein on the castle, and keep the blasted Ross men away from our livestock."

"I'm on it, brother." Jon paused, then rushed out with, "and try to smile while ye're on the road with her."

"Smile? Have ye been tippling the whisky already, brother?"

Jon chuckled. "Nay, laird, not as yet. But I do recall how ye met the lass to begin with. Was it not when ye thought having her to wife might be favorable?"

A mistake to be sure.

"Ye've gone mad. I need ye to do me a favor. Take her dog on a *birlinn* to Sutherland shores. Let them know I'll be delivering their daughter and the news of a possible uprising. That way, they can stop fretting over her disappearance, and mayhap they'll meet us halfway."

Jon rocked on his heels. "I see what ye're doing. Ye want to be rid of her quick. Ye've been avoiding any talk of marriage since—"

"I'll stop ye there, brother." Roderick held up his hand for silence and shook his head with disappointment. "We've had this discussion over and over again. I've no interest in getting married."

"Ye might not have any interest in getting married, but..." Jon hesitated, perhaps thinking about his own survival should he continue. But then his tongue kept on wagging. "'Tis your duty to the clan. And as your tanist, 'tis my duty to remind ye I dinna want the job."

"Ye may be my heir," Roderick gritted his teeth, "but, dinna remind me of my duty. I'm well aware of what it is."

Jon held up his hands and took a step back. "I dinna mean to offend, my laird, only to remind ye. The elders have been grumbling to me about it, and I said I'd mention it to ye. Now there is a lass, a beautiful one at that, whom ye'll be traveling with, whom ye were interested in a possible union with previously. I only urge ye to keep an open—"

"Ballocks, ye sound like our governess. Grow some steel between your legs and leave off, Jon, else I'll be tempted to call ye out to the field and pound it into ye. Or worse, arrange a marriage for ye."

Jon exaggerated a shudder and then chuckled. "Duly noted. I willna say another word."

"Good." Roderick gave a firm nod.

Jon smirked. "The hound and your message will be delivered. And our lands will be in the good hands of this *bachelor* while ye're away, that I can promise."

"I trust it will."

A commotion by the front entrance of the keep sounded, and both Roderick and his brother turned to see what was happening. Everything transpired in a massive blur. A big, black furry shadow whirled through the great hall like a tornado.

It would seem that Jewel had decided at that moment to go on a tear—and she'd chosen the narrow circular staircase as a good avenue for it, knocking one of the maids on her arse on the way, and tackling a guard at the base. Greer, her red hair coming loose from her plait, was chasing after the hound. Roderick got a good view of them both. He was struck with the madness of it, and how very much Greer and her hound appeared to be perfect for each other. He found himself smiling for the first time in months.

Jewel was running in speedy circles in the great hall, dodging anyone who made an attempt to restrain her, and ducking beneath the legs of the seneschal. But being of such massive size, she only ended up giving him a lift for a few feet before he finally tumbled off. Jewel ducked under the trestle table, knocking over a bench and upending one on the opposite end. The rushes swirled like tempests as she ran, tangling in her fur.

All the while, Greer shouted for her pup to cease. "Jewel! Stop! Sit! Down! Nay!"

The hound ignored all of it, turning the once well-ordered great hall into a mockery. Chairs were upended. The table where he played chess was knocked to the ground, pieces scattered with indifference. Nearly everyone that came into contact with the dog was either taken for a ride or knocked on their arse.

Watching the slow destruction of both the great hall and his people as they stumbled over themselves in an effort to regain control of the animal, Roderick tempered the urge to laugh. There hadn't been this much comical excitement at his keep since he'd been named laird, and perhaps not even before then.

After a few more minutes of observing Greer attempt to coax her wild hound into submission, Roderick stuck his fingers between his lips and blew a piercing whistle.

Everyone stopped. Including the dog.

Everyone turned to stare at him, but the only gaze he paid attention to was shrouded by black fur, and completely awestruck by him.

"Come," he demanded of the hound.

Jewel, with her tongue flapping out of the side of her mouth, jogged over to him, all too keen to comply. She sat before him, appearing innocent and eager, as though she'd not just moments before been tearing through the great hall on some mighty jaunt.

Greer, too, hurried forward, face flushed, eyes as wild as her dog. "Jewel, that was verra naughty."

Jewel cocked her head as though being called naughty was quite interesting.

"What caused all that?" he asked Greer, though he was staring down into the droopy brown eyes of the dog that appeared to be the epitome of innocence.

"There was a cat..." Greer trailed off, her flush deepening. "Just outside my chamber, and Jewel gave chase."

Roderick narrowed his gaze. "I saw no cat. Perhaps your Jewel is simply mad."

Greer's mouth fell open in outrage, and she took a step in front of the dog as if to protect her. "I assure ye, sir, there *was* a cat."

"Where is it?" He glanced around, confirming there was definitely no feline present.

"Well, it disappeared, of course. But then Jewel saw a shadow. And from there, ye must now what happened."

"Enlighten me."

Greer wrung her hands in front of her. "Why, every moving thing became that cat, and Jewel was bent on seeing the feline destroyed."

Now her lip started to quiver, but he was pretty certain it was more the beginning of a laugh than nerves.

Still, he thought this was a good opportunity to coach the lass, as she clearly did not have a good handle on her animal. "Ye must learn to whistle. That seemed to catch your fiend's attention."

"I have tried to learn to whistle. It is simply not a skill I possess. And she's not a *fiend*," Greer rebuked, seeming to forget momentarily just what had transpired.

Roderick peered exaggeratingly around the great hall at the servants and guards who rubbed at their aching bones, at the upturned chairs, and the rushes that stood in piles when they had been neatly spread on the floor. "I beg to differ."

"Well," Greer conceded, obviously trying to hide her smile, "she's not normally so...chaotic."

Roderick chuckled. "Would ye say the same about yourself?"

Greer crossed her arms over her chest, the smile gone now. "Were we not supposed to leave?"

"Changing the subject doesna change what happened here."

She marched away from him and starting righting the chairs and benches. "Fine. I'll just tidy up, and then we can be on our way."

The servants rushed to aid her in righting furniture and smoothing rushes, and Roderick could only watch in fascination. They were all laughing now, recounting the unruly incident. Even Greer's frown had turned into a smile.

Roderick glanced down at Jewel, who stared up at him with eyes full of admiration. "Ye certainly know how to make an entrance, do ye nae?"

The hound let out a bark of agreement.

"Behave yourself on the ship."

"I'm not taking her on the ship." Jon crossed his arms over his chest and shook his head vigorously. "Not in this lifetime."

"I can quickly put ye into the afterlife then," Roderick countered with brows raised in challenge. "The dog goes on the ship. She is proof we have Greer and that the Sutherlands should trust ye when ye arrive."

Jon grumbled under his breath, shoulders slumping.

"What's this I hear that ye're sending Jewel on a ship?" Greer now stood before him, arms crossed and tapping her foot. "I thought we agreed ye'd escort me on land."

"I did. But Jewel is nae ye."

"I dinna want her on a ship, either."

"She'll be fine. Ye know she will."

Greer looked ready to argue, the blue surrounding her pupils deepening. Shoulders squared, she grew an inch taller as she straightened her spine. Roderick reached forward and pressed the tip of his finger to her lips, feeling the warmth and softness, and trying to ignore the tempting sensations.

"I'll not be argued with, lass."

She pressed her lips together and then made a snapping motion with her teeth. He was quick enough to pull away before she bit off the tip of his finger.

"Your antics might work at home, but I'm not accustomed to disorder, and I'll nae have it."

"Ye can put the brute away, I know how to follow directions."

"The brute?" Dark eyebrows slanted down.

"Yeah, the other side of ye." She had the audacity to poke him in the chest.

"What?" Heat started in his belly, rising up his chest. If the lass weren't careful, he'd lose his temper and send her home on her own. "Need I remind ye how we met?"

She just rolled her eyes and snapped her fingers at the hound, walking out of the great hall toward the bailey.

Roderick watched her go with confusion. She'd not countered him, and yet he felt like she'd won whatever argument they were having. It was damn mystifying.

"She's wearing your colors," Jon noted, somehow managing to appear at his side as if out of nowhere.

"She had no other clothes."

Jon grunted. "She's wearing your colors and just went out into the bailey."

Still Roderick didn't understand what his brother was getting at.

"That's a mighty statement she'll be unintentionally making to the clan," Jon coached. "The servants understand she had nothing to wear... but your people may not."

"Och!" Now Roderick understood. By her walking out to greet his clan wearing MacCulloch colors, she would be sending a message that she was to be their mistress. He raced after her, but it was too late. Greer was already descending the stairs, and everyone in the bailey had stopped what they were doing to stare after her.

***

ALL SIGNS of a storm had dissipated, save for the puddles in the bailey and the soaked coloring of the wooden stairs leading to the ramparts. Greer lifted the hem of her gown, having the distinct impression that everyone was watching her. The hairs on the back of her neck prickled, and all of her senses seemed suddenly heightened. She patted Jewel on the head and then glanced around to see that those in the bailey, men, women, and children, were indeed watching her.

"My lady." Roderick's sharp voice called from behind her just as she descended the last step at the base of the keep stairs.

"Aye?" she asked, turning slowly.

The furrows of his brow had grown deeper, fiercer, and the blue of his eyes were even more startling with the sun shining overhead. He stood at the top of the steps as she envisioned a great god would stand on his pedestal. Normally, a thought like that would annoy her, for she very much believed men should not hold themselves so loftily above others. But seeing him from where she stood, the height of him, the impressive musculature of his legs, her breath was taken away.

"Are ye prepared to return to your home?" He spoke very loudly in his deep brogue.

And being that she was a little irritated with him for trying to boss her around inside, she returned his overly loud tone. "Aye, I am, and I suppose we want to announce it to the world?"

How was it possible that his grimace could grow fiercer?

"Your father will be expecting ye, and I've duties to return to here."

"Why are ye shouting? I'm right here." She tossed her gaze heavenward, threw her arms up in the air, and then turned away from him and headed toward a large outbuilding she presumed was the stables.

If she was going to have to ride home over the next week or so with a man who drove her crazy, at least she could pick out her own horse.

Roderick jogged up beside her, his foot hitting a puddle and causing mud to splatter on the hem of her plaid. "I wanted to send a message."

She stared pointedly at the mud, and he grumbled an apology.

"What's stopping ye from sending your message then, Grim?"

He shifted his gaze away from her, seeming distracted now, or at least to be avoiding her question, or the truth of his answer. "Nay, not actually send a message, I meant I wanted to give my people the truth of our situation."

"Which is?" She continued walking in a straight path, not allowing him to stall her from picking out a horse.

"That I'm taking ye home."

"I'm not certain ye needed to do that by shouting. Why could ye not just tell them?" They reached the door to the stables, but before she could open the door, he touched her elbow, sending a tremor of warmth through her.

Every time he touched her, she felt that tremor. Was it because he'd been the one to put the warmth back into her body? How she wished she could remember what had happened. Right now, it was all a mystery. She'd been in the water ready to give up, and the next thing she knew, she'd been in his bed.

"Ye're wearing my plaid." He thrust a hand in his dark hair, tunneling fingers through his mane in an obvious show of frustration.

Greer glanced down at the gown she'd fashioned from his blanket and her mouth popped open. "I see." Her bare toes peeked out from beneath the gown.

"Ye've no shoes!" Roderick sounded horrified.

"I lost them at sea. Well, discarded them, truly. And yours seemed a bit too big to borrow." She tucked them back under the gown.

"I'll get ye some that fit. Or close enough. Ye canna ride barefoot."

Before she could answer, he was shouting again. "Does anyone have a pair of boots that Lady Greer could borrow? I'll bring them back to ye when I return from Sutherland."

Three women stepped forward, lifting the hems of their gowns to show off worn leather boots.

Greer could have cried at the kindness. First, their laird had saved her life and offered her a bountiful breakfast, then the servants had helped her to clean up after Jewel, and now they were offering her the shoes off their feet. Her throat tightened with emotion.

"I couldna accept," Greer said, placing her hand over her heart. "Though ye must know I am deeply grateful. I am so honored ye'd be willing to part with your boots."

"My lady, please, we want ye to take them. Pick one." All three of them grinned at her as though it were nothing to take off their shoes for a total stranger.

"Lady Greer, they will be compensated," Roderick said, and then with a light touch to her elbow, he spoke more quietly so only she could hear. "They will think ye dinna value them if ye turn them down."

Greer was mesmerized by the way he was staring at her. Pleading, almost. He really cared about his people. And he had a point. Whomever she chose would be honored she wore their shoes, as silly as it sounded. And if she refused them altogether, they would feel like she didn't think they were good enough. This would be a terrible thing to convey, since it was untrue.

"All right." She gifted Grim with a smile, taking in the relief in his gaze, and then turned to the women. "I will close my eyes, turn in a circle and point. Whoever my finger lands on, I will be grateful to borrow boots from."

Roderick raised a brow, his lip twitching in what she'd come to learn was his smile. He really was incredibly handsome...

The women delighted in her turning it into a game. Greer closed her eyes as she promised and turned herself three times, until she felt a little unsteady on her feet. Then she pointed.

"My lady," one of them said with a giggle, "ye're pointing at the steward."

"Oh," Greer laughed and shifted her finger to the left.

"That's the stairs."

Again, she shifted.

"The laird."

The laughs continued, and then she felt Roderick's hands on her shoulders twisting her just slightly.

"No cheating," Greer said.

He bent low, and whispered in her ear, "I never cheat."

Greer bit her lip, frissons of heat prickling her skin. She liked the sensation of his lips near her ear, his breath on her skin. Och, but he was a distraction! Clearing her head, Greer lifted her finger and pointed.

Hearing a squeal from one of the lasses, she opened her eyes to see she'd chosen exactly the lass in middle.

"My lady, an honor," she said as she bent to untie her boots. "And please, I've a gown for ye, too."

"Thank ye, ever so much." Greer spoke to the lass, but her gaze fell to the side where Grim stood beside her, filling her body with awareness.

Chapter Six

"So, Grim,"—he'd not instructed her yet to call him laird, and if he wasn't going to do so, she much preferred his fitting moniker—"what is my first test of skill? I'm eager to see if I can live up to whatever expectations ye set. I imagine ye'll have chosen three tests ye believe I will fail to meet, and I'd prefer to get them over with."

They'd been riding over the moors thick with green grasses and heather for the better part of an hour, and most of that stretch had been spent in silence. Every time she glanced over at him, he appeared to be deep in thought, ignoring her altogether as though he had the world's problems to solve. He didn't even speak to his men, who remained just as aloof.

Already she missed Jewel. Even if her hound couldn't actually talk back, she was an engaging conversationalist. And Grim, well, he seemed like he only wanted to scowl and brood.

She hoped her dog was fairing well on the ship. Within the next hour or two, Jewel would be back on Sutherland land, home and safe.

When he didn't answer, she kept going. "Oh, I know, my first test of skill can be to see if I can get that frown off your face?"

The muzzle of Grim's horse inched forward, and she glanced to the side to see that he was subtly urging his mount to go faster. Was he trying to escape from her? Well, she wasn't going to call him out on it, but she wasn't going to let him get away with it, either.

With each nudge he gave his horse, she did the same to the spritely mare she'd chosen to ride, and her horse was quite eager to keep in step with the massive warhorse. Nothing wrong with a friendly challenge.

Greer found it hard to hide her smile. This was a fun little game. And one she'd played many times before with her brothers.

They went faster and faster until her hair was flying behind her and she had to lean forward slightly over her horse to gain more speed. When she glanced to the side, she could see that the frown had completely left Grim's face. Indeed, the twitch of his lip had gone into a full-on smile as they raced across the moors, their horses' hooves clomping into the ground and churning up the freshly soaked earth. Flecks of grass and mud flicked up to splatter on their faces, but Greer didn't care. She didn't even stop to swipe them away. If one didn't get dirty while racing, one wasn't having enough fun.

She'd forgotten how much she enjoyed it. The rolling hills passed them by in blurs, mile after mile of road gone behind them. The men followed but stayed well enough away to give them a bit of room. As she observed the smile on his face, he slowly turned to flash it at her, and Greer's heart could have stopped right then and there.

She'd thought him striking before, but to see him with that smile... It was a sight that could knock a woman right off her horse. And maybe that was the point, because she seemed to be holding on to the mare for dear life and completely forgotten how to ride. Her body shifted from one side to the other as though she'd never ridden before.

When her horse leapt over a large rock jutting from the ground, Greer did tip backward, arms flailing, and she feared for a minute that she'd go end over end, but Grim reached for her, his strong grasp on her hand tugging her back.

He grabbed her reins and slowed them both to a stop.

"Were ye trying to kill yourself?" he asked, the scowl returned.

Greer laughed, much like she often did when presented with a challenge. "I won!"

The men stopped a dozen feet away, averting their gazes as though she and Grim weren't even there.

"Nay, ye most definitely did *not* win." His striking blue gaze locked on her.

"Aye, but I did." She pointed at him. "Ye smiled."

Grim scoffed, though she saw the telltale twitch of his lip. "That was not the test of skill."

"Was there a test of skill?"

"To see if ye could ride? Aye."

"Canna every Highland woman ride?" She tried not to be put out.

"Nay." He shook his head. "Trust me."

"Well, then, I did pass, for I can ride."

"I'm not certain I would brag about such a thing when ye nearly fell off the horse just now." He raised his brows as he observed her.

"That was because of your smile." Oh, dear heavens, had she really just admitted that? Her hands started to fly around her face as though waving around a lot might get rid of the words she'd just admitted. "I mean, I must be the first person to ever see such a thing."

There was a gleam in his eyes, and he pulled in a deep breath. "Your teasing is noted."

"Oh, come now, it is funny." She bit her lip. "Are ye always so serious?"

"In my position, one must always be serious."

"And in your position, one must also see the joy in life so ye can offer hope and joy to the people who look up to ye and trust ye."

He grunted.

She tilted her head. "'Tis your duty to spread cheer."

"I think not." He leaned back and stared her down as though he were trying to discover all of her secrets. "What fairy tales have they been feeding ye at Dunrobin?"

Greer waved away his words. "Dunrobin is one of the happiest places. Well, mostly." She frowned.

"Why the long face? Are ye not supposed to always be cheerful?" he mocked.

"That isna what I said, and ye know it." She stared out at the rolling hills that went for miles and miles until the sky touched the earth before flicking her gaze back up toward his. "Besides, no one can be cheerful all the time."

"Finally, ye speak some sense."

Greer leaned forward to stroke the mane of her mount, not realizing he still held her reins, and the back of his hand brushed her breast. He jerked away, and while sparks of pleasure coursed through her, she attempted to pretend she hadn't noticed. Through quickly drawn breaths, she murmured to her mare about being a good lassie for not completely killing her rider.

But her mind was on that simple brush. The way her nipple pebbled, and how very much she wanted him to do it again to see if the same thing would happen.

After several long moments, her heartbeat had finally calmed.

"Ye're one of a kind, Lady Greer," he said.

She glanced over at him sharply, surprised at the new tone in his voice. It wasn't jesting or mocking or angry. In fact, his expression was one quite full of admiration, and she found herself stunned once more. Thank goodness, her horse wasn't in motion, else she might have found herself fallen over for good this time.

"My family has said that often. Is it really so bad?" She bit her lip. Did he think she'd leaned over on purpose? Was he labeling her hellion and harlot?

"Bad?" He appeared puzzled. "Nay, 'tis not bad at all. When most people are busy trying to conform, to fit in, to remain the way society says they should, ye're happy and confident being yourself."

This time, when she glanced down at her hands, they were gripped tightly to the reins. They were a little red from the cold wind of their fast ride, so she held them to her lips and blew hot air on them.

"Ye make me sound verra arrogant, not in the least bit humble as a lady should be."

Grim took her hands in his, rubbed them vigorously, and then brought them to his own lips to blow on them. She could have died and gone to paradise. The sweet heat of the friction he created against her skin mingling with the warmth of his breath sent pleasure over her. And something else... A spark of something inside her that made her crave more of his touch as new, enticing sensations wound through her. What had happened when she'd nearly drowned? She should yank her hand away. Tell him not to touch her this way. Remind him she was a lady and had entrusted herself into his care.

But she didn't want to.

And wasn't that what she struggled with most on a daily basis—the things she wanted and didn't want, and the things she should?

She knew exactly what her mother would expect from her at the moment. Exactly what her father would. She also knew what her sisters, Bella and Blair, would do.

But Greer would do the opposite—which was let him blow on her hands until the sun set and rose again.

Alas, he did stop when her fingers warmed up.

"Better?" he asked.

"Aye."

"And ye were right. The ride was a test of your skill. I was curious if a lass who spent so much time on the water had been able to develop a skill for riding. Despite ye being nearly unhorsed by my smile, I think ye did a fairly good job of it."

Greer couldn't help but grin now. She'd take the compliment for what it was—and she now knew she'd passed his first test. Pride swelled inside her, and so she just had to say, "Only fairly good?"

Grim chuckled. "All right, better than most. Dinna let it go to your head."

"Too late." With that, she urged her mare into a gallop once more, and this time, she swore she was going to hang on.

***

BALLOCKS! How was he going to survive the next few days with Lady Greer?

Just over an hour into their journey, and she'd had him smiling. Then his hand had accidentally grazed her lush breast. He'd been working hard not to recall just how they'd felt when he'd held her in bed and they'd been pressed to his chest as he warmed her. Then he'd gone and grasped her hands just now to warm them... What in the bloody hell was he thinking? Did he want to prolong his own torment?

And now, his cock was hard as stone, and he had to ride like the wind to catch up with her.

Jon's urging to smile and try to get along with the lass came back to haunt him. He'd scoffed then, certain he'd have no problem keeping her safe and otherwise ignoring her.

But there was something infectious about her personality. She was so full of life and spirit. So much so, that he did in fact believe her when she said she'd not gone out to sea with the thought of ending her life. The lass was simply impulsive, as evidenced by this race—a flaw that would have to be tamed by the man she claimed for a husband.

A sudden spark of what he refused to believe was jealousy twinged his insides. Shoving it away, he focused fully on the beast beneath him.

Here he was, chasing after her, even holding back a little to let her have a bit more room to race, in order to think she was winning.

He'd not thought a fig about the three tests of skill, figuring they'd be something he could come up with easily enough as they went. But now that the first test had been something fun, a race, he wanted to the next one to be just as fun, if only to see how she might surprise him again.

"*Mo chreach*," he murmured under his breath.

Of course, it wasn't helping matters that the view he had was of her perfectly rounded bouncing arse. An arse he remembered pressed against his groin—*naked*. One he'd had to rub heat into. Och, but he was going to Hell. There was no doubt. She'd been unconscious, and he'd told himself he'd not recall every dip and curve. And yet, here he was doing just that.

He groaned and forced himself to concentrate on the road ahead.

The rising hills were the perfect place for an enemy to hide. With Ina Ross and her new *Sassenach* husband traipsing about the countryside, perhaps it wasn't such a good idea to let Greer take the lead. The lass was pushing him to distraction.

Roderick urged Twilight into a full gallop. When he caught up to her, he was unable to stop himself from winking in her direction. He took in the brilliance of her eyes and the flushed look on her face. He could watch her all day, marveling at her beautiful face. He felt his horse slowing, relaxing as Roderick let up on his grip. Bloody hell. That wouldn't do. He edged forward several feet until the muzzle of his horse jutted past her own and then shouted, "I won."

Roderick slowed his horse, and she did the same beside him, wearing a pretty blush and a wide grin.

"Good game, Sir Grim." She leaned over her horse, rubbing its neck.

He grunted but then smiled all the same. "I am but your humble servant," he said, letting the tease drip from his words.

"If only. Then again, I've a feeling ye dinna know how to plait hair properly, and I do have the most unruly hair."

Oh, she was full of wit, and speaking of her hair... He wanted to wrap a tendril of it around his finger and give it a nice tug. So he did, without hesitation. Just when he was about to pull it to his nose to breathe in her scent, he came to his senses and dropped it.

She slapped at his hand but laughed, too. "My brothers used to do that to me all the time."

"Did ye laugh at them, too?"

"Nay, I would attempt to lead them into a duel." She winked, showing him exactly the hellion she was.

Roderick laughed hard at that, feeling truly amused. "And did it work?"

"Aye, until my mother caught us."

"She didn't want your brothers to hurt her precious wee angel." He smirked.

"Ha! Nay, it was for quite the opposite reason. She was fairly certain I would harm them." Greer flashed a saucy grin. "And she was probably right. As ye yourself witnessed just a few years ago."

"Are ye saying ye injured me on purpose, my lady?" He gave a mocking assessment, full of mirth, but his words still seemed to have hit a mark.

"Oh, nay," she was quick to gush. "That was quite an accident. But accidents have a tendency to happen around me—as evidenced this morning by my dog knocking over at least a dozen of your guards and servants." As quickly as she spoke, she ceased. Her eyes widened, and she stared down toward his thigh, the exact one that ached most of the time. But for some reason, he'd had yet to experience pain today. "How is your injury?"

"'Tis been fully healed for nigh on two years now," he teased, though it was partially true.

"But does it...ache at all?"

What did she know of pain? "Nay," he answered, his pride not allowing him to admit he felt any pain ever.

Ballocks, but that day had been absolutely entertaining, until the spear had ended up through his leg. He'd been at Sutherland for two days with the purpose of seeing about an alliance. Greer had caught his attention then as much as she caught him up now. But after what had happened, he'd been dead-set on avoiding her for the rest of his life.

Several of them had been racing their *currachs* over the firth, trying to see who could catch the most fish. The Earl of Sutherland had agreed to roast the fish over the open pits outside, and whoever caught the most would win the challenge.

An overly zealous rower on Roderick's boat had bumped against Greer's the moment she was preparing to launch her spear. The jar of the colliding skiffs had caused her to throw it in the wrong direction— and it had gone right into his upper thigh, which had caused him to fall overboard.

When he'd surfaced and been pulled out, she'd been laughing with the men on her *currach*. However, as soon as she'd seen the spear through his leg and blood gushing, she'd abruptly stopped. They'd all rowed back to shore, and he'd been assisted to the castle and his injury cared for. The following day, he'd insisted on going back outside and being seen participating in the festivities. He couldn't be the invalid in bed. Not when he'd barely been able to lift his sword in anger since his sister's death. His hold on the lairdship his father had only recently just claimed was still tenuous. The men respected him, aye, but it did not go unobserved that his brother was the man who led them into battle. If he'd fallen then, nothing would have stopped the elders of their clan from putting to a vote that Jon should be their laird.

He hadn't wanted that.

Jessica wouldn't have wanted that.

Ye are free, and so am I.

Her words had not been lost on him. She'd felt she was holding him back, and had thought to set him free with her death. If he had given up the lairdship, she would have died in vain, and then life would not have been worth living at all.

So, Roderick had bucked up. But when he'd emerged from the Sutherland castle, the men had teased him, saying a lass had bested him. And when Greer had come up to apologize to him, there had been such a mischievous gleam in her eyes that he'd known from that moment that she was a termagant.

He'd still thought that until this morning.

"That is verra lucky," she said. "My brother-by-marriage lost his arm in battle, and it still pains him sometimes."

Roderick grunted. Niall Oliphant was a hero among men. If he could admit that he felt pain, then perhaps it did not hold such a stigma. For some reason, he felt compelled to share with her. "Sometimes it aches with the rain."

"Ah." She grinned, though it was small. "Well, I'm glad 'tis only some of the time. Do ye use a salve?"

"Not all the time."

"Ye prefer to suffer in silence?"

He frowned. In the span of a few hours, she was already discerning just who he was.

"Aye, ye do. I can tell," she teased.

The lass was getting under his skin, and he was starting to feel...off.

He liked talking to her. Teasing her. And yet, he knew, without a doubt, that getting close to her was out of the question. "Haps another race?"

Lady Greer's head fell back, exposing the length of her creamy neck, and she laughed in such a manner that it took his breath away.

He had such an urge to lean forward and kiss her. An urge he had to temper as much as he'd tempered the urge to ride up to Ina Ross's castle gates and lay siege, if not to lay to rest once and for all the nuisance that had been plaguing the Highlands.

Chapter Seven

Exhaustion flooded Greer's body. She probably should not have agreed to leave so early after nearly drowning. And she definitely should not have tempted Grim into racing—thrice. They'd stopped only once before reaching camp to stretch, water the horses, and relieve themselves. Now, she sat like a log on the cool evening ground watching Grim build the fire she'd helped collect wood for. She'd found a patch of moss to sit on, cushioning her sore rear. Half the men stood watch, others prepared camp, and a couple went off to see if they could find a rabbit or squirrel to cook over the fire.

Grim shifted to the other side of the fire, maneuvering the wood into whatever he deemed to be the perfect position. But as he did so, there was a noticeable limp.

"Is your leg paining ye?" she asked.

He paused, knelt back on his haunches, and steadied his gaze on her. "'Tis a little sore. How about ye? I noticed ye were limping a wee bit."

She nodded, tucking her knees up under her chin. "Does that mean I've failed the test?"

"Nay." He grinned and struck the flint to set sparks on the tinder. "A lesser woman would have asked to stop more."

"I wanted to." Saints, how she'd wanted to. The last hour had been pure misery. She'd needed to *go* so bad. But she'd been too afraid to ask to stop since Grim had returned to his old self after their third race, clamping his mouth shut and staring straight ahead. It was only now, that they were at camp, that he'd seemed to soften a little. "So now do I fail?"

He chuckled, flashing his teeth. The more time they spent together, the more the twitch of his lip turned into a true smile. "Next time ask. I dinna want ye to be uncomfortable. After all, ye did nearly die not too long ago. I've not forgotten, and I willna hold it against ye."

Greer leaned her palms behind her on the ground, arching her back and stretching out the kinks in her neck. "'Tis true. I'm glad ye'll offer me a bit of reprieve for that."

"I'd be a monster if I didna." He sat down across from her, tucking a thin stick between his teeth.

"I canna see ye being a monster. I know how ye came to be at Gleann Mórinnse." She regretted now having called him a brute. Roderick was anything but a brute—unless of course one was his enemy.

Roderick grunted. "Ye speak of Emilia." He tugged out the stick and tossed it into the fire.

Roderick's cousin Emilia had been the daughter of the old laird MacCulloch. The man had been in such great debt that he'd sold his only daughter to the highest bidder—who happened to be Ina Ross. Luckily things had worked out for Emilia in the end, and the clan had been saved by Roderick and his father.

"Aye. Your cousin is verra sweet."

"Ye've met her?" He winged a brow.

"Aye. She seems happy now—thanks to her kin, *ye*."

"I canna take any credit. She met a brave man, and she deserves it."

"So do ye."

He eyed her from over the fire, the smoke making his features seem a little hazy. "I am."

Greer cocked her head, studying him. "Then why do ye frown so? There's no mistaking why ye're called Grim."

"A name I've had since I was a child." He leaned to the side, stretched out his legs, and grasped his satchel.

The man had long, muscular legs, a testament to his strength. And she couldn't help but admire them. They were vastly different from her own. His were thick with muscle, bulging and dipping in some points. Whereas hers had only a gentle curve to show a calf. Her knees felt especially bony when she beheld his, and where she knew her thighs were soft, his would be rock hard. And the scar... She was more than curious to see how the wound had healed.

"Who would give a child the name Grim?" She forced her gaze from his legs to see he'd been watching her ogling.

He turned and began to rifle through the satchel, producing a sack he tossed her way. "My mother did."

Greer caught the sack and opened it up to find it filled with roasted nuts. She poured a handful into her palm "I'm sorry to hear of your losses." There'd been so many. Both parents, his sister... She couldn't imagine the pain she'd feel at the loss of her family.

"I dinna like to talk about it."

"I understand." She tossed a couple nuts into her mouth and chewed as she thought about what had happened to his family. She'd be devastated, heartbroken.

"My mother was the life of our clan, and when her light was extinguished, it felt that a dark cloud hovered over us. Much was the same when we lost my Da and Jessica."

Greer was quiet, offering her ear, understanding it meant something that he had chosen to open up to her just after he'd said he didn't like to talk about it.

"Well, in any case," he continued, "I offer protection. I offer my life." He stood up, the muscles in his back and arms flexing through his shirt in a way she wouldn't mind seeing again.

How odd. She'd never before been interested in the way a man's body moved, but there was just something about Grim that forced her to keep looking. To think about it. To wish he'd take that shirt off...

Greer gasped at that particular thought, and then coughed to try to cover it up.

"Are ye all right? Is the smoke too much? 'Haps ye ought to move."

She waved at the smoke, pretending that was exactly the reason behind her cough. "I'll be all right. Ye're a fine protector, Grim. I'm certain your clan is grateful for it. As am I."

He grunted and then searched through the satchel and tossed her a bannock cake. "I can only offer ye this cake and some cheese. There is jerky, but since ye dinna eat meat, that will not do. And I doubt ye want the meat the men have brought back." He nodded behind her, and she glanced back to see that a few of the warriors had returned with their catches tied to a thick stick.

"Aye." She tossed back the sack of almonds. "Cheese and bannocks are perfect."

Grim passed her a hunk of aged white cheese, and she bit into it, savoring the rich flavor as it melted on her tongue. Then she bit into the bannock and was surprised it wasn't as stale as the ones she'd had on the road before. This one appeared to be fresh baked.

He watched her eat, eying her as though he were inspecting her. "Ye're not too thin."

She nearly choked on her bite of bannock and inhaled a few crumbs. She started to cough, and Grim leapt up from his spot across from her to loom behind and pound on her back, which only made her cough harder.

At last, she could breathe again. She sipped at the waterskin he passed her, and he settled beside her, his knee brushing hers. She held her breath, afraid any gasp she made might send her into a fresh whirl of coughing.

When she could speak, she said, "That is not something I would repeat to any woman, especially if she happens to be one ye're court- ing. I'm not saying we're courting, only that I offer ye advice, as a woman. Though 'tis fashionable to have a bit of meat on one's bones, dinna ever tell her she's not too thin. Ye might as well call her a mighty cow."

Grim frowned for a minute, then tilted his head back and laughed so loud several birds who'd been sleeping in the branches above their heads took flight, and the men all jerked their gazes in his direction as though they'd never heard him laugh before now.

"Ye misunderstand me, lass," he said through fits of laughter, swiping at tears of mirth. "I but meant that abstaining from eating meat hadna left ye a bag of bones. Ye appear healthy. Ye look...good."

She looked...*good*.

Greer felt her face heat and wished the sun were already setting so he couldn't see just how embarrassed she was at the compliment. As it was now, she was certain her face flamed as red as her hair. For saying she looked *good* was indeed a compliment. As a matter of fact, no other man had ever remarked on her figure before, and she felt the urge to ask him more. Her mother would be horrified, but Greer had learned a long time ago that when she tried to conform to what was right instead of doing what she wanted, she usually ended up doing the latter anyway, and in a disastrous way.

So in this case, she tilted her face toward his, finished swallowing a fresh bite of cheese, and asked, "Good how?"

Now it was Grim's turn to nearly choke on his bannock. She passed him the waterskin this time and pounded on his strong back until he'd finished choking on whatever it was he'd eaten.

"Are ye all right?" she asked, laughing.

"Aye." He blew out a breath of relief and took another sip of water while she watched the way his throat bobbed as he swallowed.

She was pretty certain that until this point in her life, she'd never so fully studied a man before.

Grim turned her way, winging a brow. "Has anyone told ye ye're verra forward?"

That took her aback. "Forward? I assure ye I am not."

"Bold then." He leaned once more to grab his satchel and his knee brushed hers.

As if he had any right to talk about boldness. She had half a mind to point it out, but then he might stop touching her, unintentional as it was.

"Again, not a good word choice for a maiden such as myself." Saints, but she was having fun teasing him.

"Direct?" He offered her another bannock, but she shook her head.

"Direct will suit."

"All right, my lady. Has anyone ever told ye that ye're verra *direct?*"

Now, she grinned and shrugged her shoulders. "All the time."

He chuckled and bit into his bannock.

"Well, now that we've established that," she said, picking up a wee pebble that was beneath her foot, "are ye going to answer the question, or just choke some more?"

"Och, but I thought ye'd nae be making me explain."

Was she seeing things, or were his cheeks turning a little bit pink?

"I'm curious. Indulge me."

"Ye look good as in...healthy."

He eyed her now, his gaze roving from the top of her head down to where her boots were tucked up against her bottom. And she felt that gaze as it roamed the length of her, making her feel hot and yet covered in gooseflesh all at once. There was a glimpse of hunger in his eyes that she felt keenly in her gut. Good God, what was happening to her? She swallowed but that didn't help any.

"Ye have a...rounded figure."

Greer groaned and fell backward in exaggeration, flopping her arm over her face as though he'd given her a fit of vapors. "A rounded figure? Again, I'm thinking cow, sir."

"Oh dear God, are ye jesting with me?"

She peeked up at him to see he was staring down at her with genuine concern. Slowly, she shook her head, trying for her most serious face. Teasing him was entirely too much fun. "I never jest about these things."

He leapt to his feet, once more drawing the attention of his men, who just as suddenly busied themselves with other tasks.

With a hand shoved through his hair, and stuffing his face full of food, he paced in front of her for several minutes before finally turning to face her. "I shouldna be saying this to ye, but I will, because ye appear overly curious. Ye're a verra bonny lass, with hair of fire and a personality to boot. Ye've a figure that makes me take a second look. Makes them..." He nodded toward his men, and then shook his head. "Never mind. Let us just say ye have a bonny figure, lass. And if ye should tell anyone I've said these things, I will have to commit a sin and lie, denying this conversation ever took place."

Greer covered her mouth with her hand to hide her smile. With every word he'd uttered, her body had heated into little fiery tingles. He *liked* what he saw. A lot, from what it seemed. And she *liked* that he liked looking. For she felt very much the same way.

From behind the shield of her palm, she said, "Thank ye verra much, Grim. I'll not tell a soul. I swear it." Then, just as boldly as she pleased, she added, "And for what 'tis worth, I feel verra much the same way, about me liking what I see, not about your men taking a second look, that is. Although I canna speak for all."

He stood there speechless and then noted that she was teasing him. He picked up a handful of fallen leaves and tossed them at her as she fell over in a fit of giggles.

Greer dusted herself off between laughs and then pitched the rest of her bannock at him, hitting him squarely in the nose.

"I ought to thrash ye for that," he taunted, a twinkle of mirth in his eyes.

"I'd like to see ye catch me," she challenged, feeling more playful than she had in the longest time.

"Catch ye?"

Greer didn't give him a chance to figure out her meaning, she simply lifted her skirts, turned on her heel, and started to run toward the forest. The men she passed regarded her as though she'd grown two heads, but she just smiled at them and kept on running. Once she reached the cover of the trees, she dared a peek behind her, only to come face-to-chest with Roderick. The grin he wore may just have been bigger than her own. It was a grin that said, *I've got ye now*, in a way that sent a shiver of wonder up her spine.

Chapter Eight

Knocking into Roderick the Grim had to be the same as running smack into a stone wall. His broad chest was hard with muscle, and his stance unbreakable.

Greer let out a shriek as she bounced off him and started to fall backward. She grappled for anything, her fingers grazing over those same muscles. The man had the audacity to laugh at her, even as he caught her. His strong grasp wrapped around the small of her back as he tugged her forward. The heat of his touch sent tingles racing all over her. If this was what it was like for him to catch her...

"Ye thought ye were quick," he said, voice full of mischief, "but ye didna realize I have a skill at chase—no one ever hears me coming." He winked at her, arms still about her, and Greer thought her knees might buckle.

She grabbed hold of his upper arms, marveling at the rippling muscle as she gazed up at him. "Ye're quite right about that," she said. "I didna hear ye at all. Seems unfair."

"Ye were running like I might imagine a giant would thump through the woods with tree stumps for boots. Ye might have passed the horse-racing test, but ye've failed at this one."

Greer frowned. "I didna realize it was a test. How about another round? Now that I know ye've a talent for being sneaky?"

Grim chuckled, pulling her a little closer. "Och, lass, while the idea is very enticing, I must remind ye that traipsing about the wood is nae safe."

"What have I to be afraid of? Ye? Are ye dangerous, Grim?" she goaded.

His gaze slipped down toward her mouth, and she had the sudden sense that though they were talking of danger from the outside world, there was also the immediate risk of him kissing her. And if he did, she was certain she'd not pull away. That was a threat worth facing. Her own gaze slipped to his mouth as she thought it. Oh, what would it be like to feel those wide, soft lips on her own?

"There are other dangers." His voice had dipped and was now gravelly with a hint of hunger.

Was it just her, or was he getting closer? Was her grip on his arm tighter? She was closer...her body was flush to his now, and their mouths were only inches apart. Her breath hitched, and it was all she could do not to lean in the extra couple of inches to make it so their lips had nowhere to go but to each other.

Oh, kiss me!

But that would be reckless...deliciously so.

"What other dangers?" She licked her lip, barely recognizing her own voice. It was so husky and filled with...*want*.

She leaned closer. He did the same, until there was only a breath between them, and it seemed as though the world around them were disappearing.

The sound of a twig snapping had them both jerking back, but there was no one there. A warning from nature?

Grim slipped his hands from her back and took an obvious step backward. "There are things in the forest, lass. Outlaws, raiders, boars. We canna control them. Best we remain on our guard and nae go running off."

A knot formed in her belly and felt like it roped up into her throat. "I ken that well..." She thought back to Bella, who'd been attacked on the road with her husband, and again by their own castle. She glanced toward the ground. "I know better. Though only for a bit of amusement, running off was reckless."

"Ye seem good at that, being reckless."

"Ye'd nae be the first to say so." She flashed a tight smile, feeling embarrassed.

"I aim to keep ye safe."

It was not a rebuke, but an honest admission, and his voice was soft in the delivery of it. For that, she was grateful.

"I promise not to be so...hasty."

"Och, lass, but that is part of your charm," he teased, "and has given us cause to come together more than once. Alas, it is probably best on this trip if we use caution, aye?"

She had the wonderful feeling he was indulging her, which she found to be exceedingly charming. The man was a laird, and a warrior. He did not need to indulge her, especially since she was probably inconveniencing him greatly. But, he was, and that warmed her heart.

"Ye're a good man, Roderick."

"'Tis a high honor for ye to say so." He gripped her hand and brought it to his lips. The warmth of his mouth on her knuckles, of his breath fanning over the back of her hand, made the hair on her arm rise, and her knees go weak once more.

All too soon, his lips left her skin, but his grasp remained as he walked backward and tugged her toward camp.

"Your hands are cold again, my lady. Let's get ye by the fire to warm up."

Greer nodded in a daze, following him as though she were a docile lamb, when everyone knew she was more like Jewel on a tear.

The men watched their return with curiosity. As soon as they were within sight, Roderick dropped her hand and marched ahead to the campfire as though they'd not been about to kiss.

No matter. As soon as she sat down and wrapped a blanket around her shoulders to ward off the evening chill, he stretched out on the ground beside her with his back against a tree. His long legs were crossed at the ankles and his arms were folded behind his head as he stared up at the slowly darkening sky.

"I used to think the stars were the torches lighting up castles in England," she admitted with a laugh. "My brother, Liam, used to tease me and say that if I didna behave, the English would come charging from the sky and sweep me back to their dungeons."

Grim chuckled and glanced back at her. "How old were ye when ye finally realized he was teasing?"

"Older than I care to admit?"

"Last spring then?"

Now it was her turn to laugh. "Not quite. It was winter, if ye must know," she jested.

They talked late into the evening, and neither of them seemed to notice when the sky darkened. Roderick had been spending most of his time gazing at Greer, though whenever she caught him, he quickly glanced away. Aye, he'd considered a match with her before, and those same reasons were all flooding back to him. The way she'd felt in his arms when he held her in the woods had been incredible. But her impulsiveness had already got him a life-threatening injury once—who was to say that she wouldn't be the death of him next time?

All those thoughts erupted in his mind, distracting him until he finally shoved them away. What was the point of dwelling on it now? He would return her to where she belonged, and then take care of Ina Ross. Getting caught up in the whirlwind that was Greer was not feasible at the moment, nor was it smart.

And so he listened. Greer told him about her sisters and brothers. How she always felt like she was the odd one out given her penchant for mischief. He told her about his own brother, and how when they'd been wee lads, they'd love to play seek and find in the forest, which drove their mother mad.

To this, Greer claimed that no one could play seek and find like her. She admitted he might be able to win at sneaking up on her, but she could hide like no other. Roderick wasn't so sure. He could find anything. Even the smallest of grains in his porridge.

"One time, I stayed put in the same spot from the early morning hours until late into the night, only finally giving up when my father promised me a mountain of sweets if I'd only come out."

"Och, lass, I canna believe ye gave up for sweets. We once played a game of seek and find that took three days."

As they laughed, Roderick told her about how he'd made the childhood game of seek and find into a training task with his men. He grew quiet when he thought how much Jessica had loved it also.

Greer touched his arm, soft, beautiful eyes searched his, little flecks of golden fire reflected in their blue depths. She did not say a word, but understanding was there plain as day. A feeling of comfort came over him, and he patted her hand, caressing the soft delicateness of her skin, wanting to bring it to his lips as he had impulsively in the wood. It would seem that her bad habits were rubbing off on him.

The gesture was more intimate than it should have been, and for the first time, he thought maybe it would have been a good idea to bring along the old healer, if only to have someone who could slap their wrists and tell them what they were doing was not appropriate.

As it was, he'd already nearly kissed her in the woods. She was so magnetizing, he was faltering in his vow of remaining diligent and protective.

But he supposed that was one of the things that drew him to Greer. She did not do what was expected of her. She was a light in the dark. A spark when one needed to light a fire. With the way he'd been so glum for months, years even, she was the energy he seemed to need. Because around her, he felt himself coming alive.

He glanced down at their joined hands, realizing then that his touch was lasting a little too long. He jerked his hand away, ran it through his hair, and turned his gaze to the flames. It felt oddly cooler than when he looked at her.

Clearing his throat, he said, "'Tis time for my shift on watch. Why do ye nae get some rest? I'll get ye an extra plaid. The night will only get a bit more chilly."

"I am rather fatigued," she said, shifting to stand and stretch her arms over her head. "I'll need to find some privacy beforehand."

Och, why did she have to stretch like that? It made the fabric of her borrowed gown stretch across her breasts, an enticing sight to be sure."

"Aye." He offered her his elbow. "I'll lead ye there so ye dinna get lost. Or try to hide." The latter he said with a bit of humor in his tone, hoping it would do away with the heated tension building between them.

But when she touched his elbow and threaded her hand around his arm, her touch sent a flash of yearning through him. It'd been months since he'd taken a woman to bed. Not for lack of offers, of which there were many. Roderick wasn't the sentimental type, and yet when he was with a woman for only mutual pleasurable satisfaction, he found he was missing something. He was growing tired of that feeling of emptiness. But he refused to think about what that emptiness might mean.

They walked in silence into the woods, but not too far from camp given the moon was not clearly lighting the woods as much as it did on other nights.

"I'll be just over here. Call out if ye need me."

She murmured her agreement and then hid behind a tree. When they were both finished, he brought her back to camp and furnished her with the extra plaid, which she took gratefully.

"Good night, then," she said, spreading the plaid out on the ground. "And thank ye."

"Ye need not thank me, lass."

"I will be thanking ye every day for the rest of my life." And then she rolled herself up, turning away from him.

Roderick knew what she meant. That she would be grateful for a lifetime to him for saving her on the beach. But the part of him that felt that yearning, the empty part that begged to be filled, saw it another way. As in, him and her together for a lifetime.

He grimaced. What the bloody hell? How dare the inner part of himself even wish for such a thing? Marriage was not in the cards for him. Not now. If he couldn't protect his sister, how was he to protect a wife? And one like Greer would be likely to put herself in danger daily.

He would not be the first laird to never marry. Would his clan understand that? That he was their leader, their protector, but that Jon would produce any heirs. Would they accept that? Could *he*?

Jon had loudly protested he didn't want to be Roderick's heir. Was it selfish of Roderick to even think of pushing something on his brother that he didn't want? Roderick stomped to his post, relieving one of his men who reported that all was quiet. The others on duty were also released. He watched his men shifting around, those who'd been sleeping woke to take their positions, and those who'd been on watch settled on the ground to sleep until the next shift.

Guilt riddled Roderick. Neither he, nor Jon, had expected to become Laird MacCulloch. Roderick had hardly been a man when his father had had to forcefully take the position from his own brother. And his father had been in such fine health and vigor that Roderick had not expected to take up his own title for many years—possibly even when he was an old man himself.

At the sudden loss of his father, he'd barely been prepared for his new role. Aye, the men followed him because his father had allowed him to help in their training. But training men for defense was not the same as being a laird. A laird had to be diplomatic. A laird had to communicate with allies and enemies alike. A laird had to care for his clan, making certain all their basic needs were being met, in addition to protecting them from their enemies. He had to pass judgment on those who committed crimes, and do so in a way that did not alienate anyone. All through that, he was supposed to also wed, produce heirs, and protect his wife and children. He was supposed to mold his children into future warriors and caretakers, so that the MacCulloch line his father had fought to take would live on.

It was a lot for one man—and even more so to push it onto his brother, who adamantly didn't want it.

Aye, he was being selfish where his brother was concerned. Roderick glanced toward the small lump on the ground that was Greer. Curled up on her side, her hair covered her face. Was she the answer to that? He'd thought she was years before. So, what if she'd thrown a spear at him? It had been an accident.

As if to remind him, the pain in his leg was suddenly sharp, and he rubbed it away.

Would she make a good wife? He was attracted to her, no doubt, but she was a troublemaker, too. Could he trust her to be the Lady of MacCulloch, mistress to his people? Was she ready to take on the responsibility of putting others first before her impulses?

That was a question he didn't know the answer to. Greer was reckless, fearless. She'd leapt into a boat right before a storm. On one hand, he could see that being a good quality to have in a lady who would lead beside him. One had to be willing to take risks and show no fear. She'd throw her whole heart into protecting her people and make certain they were all well cared for. On the other hand, if she decided she wanted to toss herself off a cliff to see if she could fly, that would not be good for him or his people.

Reminding himself that Greer was not his sister was something he'd have to do often. She did not seem to have the tormented soul his sister had, but from what he'd learned in his thirty odd years of living was that those candles that burn the brightest often burned the fastest, leaving those who'd followed their light in the dark.

Gritting his teeth, Roderick turned away from her. His watch shift was going to be one hell of a long one if he kept his thoughts going on that course. He scanned the trees, searching for anything out of place.

Throughout the evening, the scouts had been going out one by one, returning with no news of anyone following, which was a surprise.

He felt for certain there would be an encounter with Ina Ross's men. Either they truly weren't being followed, or the Ross warriors were being very careful to remain hidden. With not having been hostile in over a decade, the Ross men had to be rusty, which made Roderick think maybe they just weren't following.

That notion, of course, worried him more, because it meant that Ina might have issued an order for her men to attack more of his crofters, or even the castle itself now that he was gone.

Whenever he left his lands, he was agitated, antsy, and eager to return. He didn't like leaving his brother, wanted to be there in case something happened. All the same, returning the lass did do away with two tasks at once, for he desperately needed to speak to the Sutherland.

Unintentionally, he glanced behind him where she slept. He was supposed to be ignoring her. She'd rolled over and was facing him now, though her eyes were closed. Moths flew over the light of the fire, one landing on the tip of Greer's nose before she batted it away. The flames had gone low, and he wasn't planning to rekindle it. The scent of smoke and the light put off by the fire were a dead giveaway to where they were, and in the dark, his enemies didn't need the extra help.

If the night got a wee bit chillier than it was now, which was very likely, he'd have to make certain his charge was warm enough. It hadn't been too long since she'd been near death, and with how exhausted she must be from their travels today, he imagined her body might rebel at having to warm itself up again so quickly.

Of course, his mind went immediately to warming her up with his body, and with that came many reminders of her silky skin, the roundness of her hips, the softness of her buttocks. So different from himself. The lass was exquisite, and he'd never even seen her naked, only felt. But he was certain if she were to stand before him right then and there in the moonlight without a stitch on, he'd know every dip and curve already.

Mo chreach! He was growing hard.

What he needed was a good fight to expend the energy that had been building since he'd lifted her up at the beach.

Roderick regarded the forest surroundings, forcing himself to discount the sounds of his men shifting about, the horses stomping or puffing their breath. In the woods, he made out the constant crackling sound of the grasshoppers, the chirping of bats, and the occasional sound of a fox pouncing on its prey. Occasionally, he could hear the smaller scurry of mice and squirrels, and the larger steps of game. Not once did he hear anything remotely human.

When his shift was up, he unpinned his plaid and rolled the extra long piece around himself to keep warm, and lay right beside Greer. He made sure not to get too close, but not be too far away, either. There was a hand's breadth between them. Good enough. His job was to protect her, and maybe just being in proximity to her would help lend her some warmth.

Some time in the night, he woke to find her rear pressed hotly to his groin, and himself raging hard. His arm was draped over her waist, and hers was on top of that. Their legs entwined. As if in sleep, they couldn't help but join together, their bodies fighting against what his mind had determined must be so.

Ballocks!

Carefully, he removed her arm from his, pulled away from her waist, and then worked to untangle their legs. She didn't make a sound at first, but then she mumbled her protest. He stilled, waiting for her to wake, but she fell right back to sleep. Holding his breath, he went to work again until he was free. He shifted away from her and put two hands' breadth between them. But to his surprise, she only came closer. Then he saw her teeth were chattering. Bloody hell, the sweet lass was freezing. He'd willingly provided her warmth in his sleep, only to shove her away when he woke.

Blast it, he was between a rock and a hard place. He wanted to warm her, felt the inane urge to do so. To protect her. And yet at the same time, doing so made him want to bury himself deep inside her.

"Roll over," he whispered to her.

At least if she were facing him, he wouldn't have her lush arse against his cock.

Greer obeyed, rolling over to face him, and he pulled her against him and wrapped the blanket around them both. To keep her away from the turgid part of himself that threatened to ruin both their reputations, he bent a knee slightly over the other and tucked her legs overtop of his. As much as it helped, she was still close enough for it to be torture.

The lass sighed and snuggled closer, burying her frozen nose in the crook of his neck. Her hands were tucked up near her throat, thank goodness, for the last thing he needed was her roving to any of his warmer spots.

Roderick rubbed her back swiftly and with purpose until her teeth stopped chattering and it seemed she'd fallen back to into a deeper sleep. Well, at least one of them was going to get sleep this night. It wasn't going to be him. Instead, he would be up all night thinking about the various ways he could make love to her.

Alas, sleep did eventually come to him, and when he woke with the dawn, he found her arse once more against his arousal.

Mo chreach...

He was a saint. He was pretty certain of it.

Before the lass woke to feel him hard against her, he climbed to his feet, glaring around the camp in hopes that no one could see just how hard he was. The entire front of his plaid was tented like he were a lad only just come into his own. He also prayed she didn't wake, else she'd see him standing over her with the bloody erection. When he went to grab the other half of his plaid, he realized she was lying on it, burrowed deep into it.

This was not going to end well, he was fairly certain of it.

"Lass," he murmured. "Let me have the plaid back. I'll find ye another."

"Nay, 'tis mine," she murmured, burrowing deeper. "Ye canna have it."

He narrowed his gaze. Had he heard correctly? Roderick gave the plaid a little tug, but she only clutched it tighter. It was on the tip of his tongue to tell her if she didn't give it back, he was going to thrash her hide.

The struggle went on for a few minutes until he bent back down and whispered in her ear. "If ye dinna give me back my plaid, I'll be forced to unbelt it, and then I'll be quite naked," he exaggerated, for he'd still have on his shirt. However, with the spear jutting out of it, she was certain to get a scare. "Is that what ye want, lass? A naked Highlander beside ye?"

As he'd hoped, she gasped, and her eyes popped open to see him smiling quite confidently beside her—and thankfully, she did not stare at his groin.

"Nay! I dinna want ye naked beside me."

"Ye'd not be the first lass who did. 'Tis nothing to be embarrassed about."

Faster than he could blink, she'd unrolled herself from his plaid, and he quite happily pinned it back in place.

"Do ye want me to fetch ye another?" he asked.

"Nay. I need to..." She bit her lip, suddenly shy. Gingerly, she stood. She kept her gaze toward the ground, the other plaid she'd used as an extra blanket tucked around her shoulders. "I need to make use of the woods."

"Come now, ye've not been shy before. I'll escort ye to a private place."

She neatly folded the extra plaid and then smoothed out her tousled hair.

He found it endearing. "Suits ye, lass, the tumbled look. Your hair knows quite well the disposition of its mistress."

"Do nae think I've not heard that afore, Grim. My ma, da, and entire clan have been talking about me being a hellion since the day I was born."

"And they must love ye for it."

She smiled up at him. "I should hope. But I dinna pretend they wouldna wish for a calmer child. My younger sister Blair is quite calm. So I suppose they got their wish after all."

"Dinna discount that some like an element of surprise."

Greer snorted.

With a wink, Roderick took her hand in his and led her toward the wood. "I think I saw some berries back here last night. Want to pick some when ye finish your business?"

"Oh, aye! I love berries."

"We'll just have to make certain they are nae the poisonous kind."

"I know which is which." She nodded confidently.

"As do I."

"Then we should be in good hands, aye?"

"Indeed."

He left her at a thick tree and went in search of his own only a few feet away.

"Thank ye for keeping me warm last night," she called from her place.

"I would not have ye freeze." No lass, not even his sisters or his previous mistresses, had ever spoken to him while in the midst of relieving themselves. He didn't know whether to laugh or be concerned. He thought it was a good sign she was comfortable with him. He had, after all, told her he didn't want her to feel shy about such things.

"I hope ye slept well."

"Aye," he lied with a smile on his face. Even though he'd hardly slept at all with desire tunneling through him, he'd do it all over again in a heartbeat.

They met between the trees, and it seemed a transformation had come over her. Gone was the shy lass from the morning, replaced with the same vixen he'd been getting to know more over the past day than he had in the near fortnight he'd spent at Dunrobin before. There was a constant twinkle in her eye.

She was truly enchanting.

"Let's find those berries. I'm starved." She rubbed her hands together in glee, which made him laugh.

Roderick led her to the brambles full of berries, both black and red.

"Ah, we can eat these." She pointed to a cluster of purple-blue berries climbing from the bushes. "Bilberries. Delicious."

"Are ye certain?" He stepped closer, wary as she plucked several berries from their limbs. They did indeed look like bilberries.

"Why do ye nae try and see what ye think?" She held out her palm filled with several berries.

Roderick eyed them. "All right, but if I fall into convulsions, 'twill mean ye never make it home."

Greer rocked on her heels, leaning toward him, taunting him. "And what if that was my plan all along, Sir Grim? To get ye out in the woods where I could poison ye with berries and finish the job I started with the spear..." She let out a haunting laugh that told him exactly how serious she was—which was not at all.

He plucked a berry from her palm, intent on playing this game out.

"I'll tell ye what, Grim, I'll eat one at the same time as ye, and then when your warriors find both our convulsing bodies, neither one of us will be blamed."

"A test. I like it." Roderick grinned and brought the berry close to his lips. "On the count of three?"

"Aye. One." She brought the berry as close as he had. "Two." She opened her perfectly shaped pink lips, making his mouth water, but not for the taste of a berry, but for her kiss, one he'd almost taken the evening before. "Three." They both popped a berry into their mouths.

Chapter Nine

Sweetness burst onto Greer's tongue, and with it, relief that she did not immediately die. She'd been pretty certain they were bilberries, but there was always the chance she was wrong and had confused deadly nightshade with an edible fruit.

"They are good," she said, plucking several more and popping them into her mouth.

Roderick did the same. "Aye," he spoke around a mouthful. "A sweet breakfast treat."

"Ye sound surprised." She stuffed another handful into her mouth.

Roderick shrugged. "I dinna normally go for berries."

"Oh?"

"I much prefer a hearty meal." He winked, sending a frisson of heat running through her. How could he make the idea of eating a meal sound so...sensual?

Greer's face heated, and she turned slightly away, picking more berries in hopes he couldn't see her cheeks growing redder. "So ye'd rather have had a stale bannock and dried leather?"

He chuckled. "Nay, I'd have rather had a fresh-baked scone, poached eggs, and bacon."

Eggs... That sounded delicious. "I'd take the first two, along with a bowl full of berries and cream."

"Berries and cream?" He, too, picked more, leaned his head back, and tossed them into his mouth.

Greer stared at him in shock. "Dinna tell me ye've never had berries and cream?"

"I'll nae tell ye then, but let ye draw your own conclusions."

"I canna believe it. We shall remedy this. Once we're at Dunrobin, ye will have my mother's fruit pasties and berries with cream."

"A dream." But then his eyes went wide and frantic as he searched her face.

"What?" she asked, her hand stilling near her mouth.

His mouth popped open, his tongue flapping out, and he gripped his neck, making a chocking sound. Within a breath, his face was turning pink, and then red.

"Grim!" Greer dropped her berries. "Are ye choking?"

He shook his head, pointed at his tongue, which was stained purple from the berries. Was it swollen? She couldn't tell. What did he want her to see? She didn't know.

"What?" Panic flooded her. Had she made a mistake? Were they indeed poisoned berries? Her hands came to her face as she racked her brain for options. Should she pound him on the back? Somehow figure out how to make him retch? "Oh, Heaven help us, I dinna know what to do!"

Then he chuckled, his hands falling from his neck. "I'm only teasing ye, lass."

"That's not funny." She crossed her arms over her chest and tapped her foot. "I thought ye were dying."

"But ye said ye brought me out here to poison me. I thought it only fair I gave ye a wee bit of a fright, dinna ye?"

"Ye really are a brute. Death is never something to joke about."

The laughter left his eyes, the muscle in the side of his jaw ticking. Was it something she'd said? Suddenly, Roderick looked as if he'd seen a ghost, or rather been reminded of one.

Greer cursed herself and bit the inside of her cheek. "I..." Panic rose in her chest.

But then his features softened, and whatever ghosts had momentarily haunted him seemed to ebb away. "Och, come now, I didna mean to upset ye."

"Perhaps I'm not the only one who acts a bit reckless at times."

"Mayhap." His gaze never left hers. "Though I didna pierce ye with my spear."

Greer's face flushed red at the double meaning in his words. Had there actually been a double meaning? How was she to know? In any case, she grew flustered. She wished she could pluck a berry and toss it at his forehead, if only to make herself feel better, or at least break whatever spell he held on her.

"I'm calling this test my win, since the berries did not actually poison ye. Though I wouldna mind right now if ye choked a wee bit for having scared me to death."

"Verra well, ye can have it."

"Two wins and one loss. That means I've won a majority of your silly tests of skill."

"Silly?"

"Aye, silly." She didn't know why she was getting so irritated. Maybe it was because she was nearing her women's courses, or maybe it was because she *did* want him to...pierce her with his spear.

She started to march away, but he grabbed her hand at the last minute, stopping her. The warmth of his fingers seeped into her bones, and all the irritation seemed to melt away.

If she wanted to yank away from him and go back to camp, she could. If she wanted to turn around and slap him for touching her, she could. But she wouldn't do either of those things.

The thing was, she wanted his hand on hers. She liked the feeling of it, and the way little tingles raced from the spot on her fingers where he grasped her, all the way up her arm, settling in her chest.

She turned slowly and gave him her best I'm-annoyed-with-ye expression, but the goofy grin on his face and the tender look in his eyes was her undoing. The frown fell away from her lips, and she shook her head.

"Ye really scared me. I...I thought I'd done something reckless once more to get ye killed, and as it is, I'll never forgive myself for what happened on the firth two years ago."

"Och, I'm sorry, lass. I truly didna mean to scare ye."

"I forgive ye. But, please, dinna ever do that again."

"Aye, ma'am."

She squeezed his fingers and then let his hand drop. "Let's get back to camp. Suddenly, I'm in the mood for bannock cakes."

"No more berries?"

"Definitely nae." She laughed.

They packed up camp, mounted their horses, and were on the road shortly thereafter. Greer's eyes kept closing, and she jerked awake. She was exhausted. She really should have stayed in bed a few days to recover. Och, wouldn't it be nice to climb into Roderick's lap the way she had when they slept? To feel the heat of his arms around her, or the solidness of his chest against her back? Aye, that would be glorious, and then she could nap all the way to Sutherland. Alas, it was but a dream, and she pinched the inside of her arm to wake herself up.

Around midday, they stopped to rest and eat a bite, and then were off again. By late afternoon, they came to the River Ness with its blue-black water reflecting the foliage around the perimeter and the mountains in the distance. The water rippled gently, disturbing the reflections, and Greer found herself staring hard, waiting to see if the river monster would raise its head from the chilly depths to greet them.

As a lass, she'd heard a thousand stories about the river monster. A particular story stuck in her head about a wee child being taken from the shore to live in the depths of the river. Of course, this was likely told to keep children away from the water—a fear tactic. But it hadn't been for Greer; nay, it had only excited her. What would it be like to live at the bottom of a river in a village filled with mysticism? There had to be all sorts of creatures there besides the river monster, like mermaids and nymphs, and selkies. It would be incredible.

Of course, she'd waited hours by the water near Dunrobin, hoping that her prayers would be answered and a river monster would come, only for her hopes to be dashed when her father found her there and admitted it was all a ruse.

How disappointed she'd been. But what relief her father felt knowing she no longer harbored a desire to dive deep.

"She appears rather tame," Grim remarked, the rumbling in his chest as he spoke startling her. "Let's find the most shallow part of her."

They were going to ford the river? A knot formed in Greer's belly. She tried to quell it, but it only grew until her stomach burned and she felt very much like retching up her breakfast.

They rode along the edge of the tranquil river—which now seemed to hold much to be desired for her—until he found the spot he deemed most perfect.

Before he urged his horse into the water, Roderick tipped her chin up, turning her slightly so he could peer into her eyes. His expression was serious. "Will ye be all right to cross?"

Greer bit down on the tip of her tongue. She couldn't show him her fear. Already, she'd cost him days by refusing to go on a ship. If she refused to cross the river, they'd travel for days on end to find a place where they didn't have to get more than toe deep.

With a great sigh, she said, "Aye. I believe so."

He let her go, and she stared hard at the water, unable to make out the bottom. She would be fine. Had to be. It wasn't storming. She wasn't swimming. And she had Grim and all his men. Plus, she'd be on horseback. What could possibly go wrong?

But even thinking that question had her stomach quickening. She'd said the same thing when everything had gone wrong before.

"Is this a test? A test of my fear?"

"Nay, lass. We've several rivers to cross. I'd not make ye take a test over and over. Besides, our three tests are over, aye? Ye won the majority. Ye're the victor."

"But it is a test all the same," she murmured, biting her lip.

"A personal test then."

"Aye."

"I'll nae let anything happen to ye," he promised.

Greer glanced at him, saw the seriousness of his expression and nodded.

"Ye can ride with me if ye like."

Her eyes widened. It was as if he'd read her mind. Had she not been fantasizing about that all day, if only to get some rest? She peered behind them at all his men. What would they think of her if she did that? They would definitely think less of her, would have to. They might already, considering she'd not been brave enough to board the *birlinn* that would have made this journey take hours rather than days. Probably some believed she'd unnecessarily put them in danger because of her fears.

Well, she needed to prove she was stronger than that, didn't she?

Squaring her shoulders, she said, "I can do it."

A flash of pride crossed his expression. "That's it, lass. Conquer it."

Grim had no idea how his words spurred her forward.

He nodded toward the water. "I'll go first, and the men will be behind ye. Ye'll be surrounded should something happen, but I've faith ye can handle it."

She nodded, staring at the rippling water.

"Have ye ever crossed a river afore now?"

"Aye," she said, her voice coming out stronger than she imagined it would, thank goodness.

"Then ye ken what ye're doing."

With that, he faced forward and clucked his tongue, giving his mount the go-ahead to step forward. Grim's horse's hooves splashed into the water. He took it slowly, feeling out the bottom of the river so as not to harm his horse should he get caught on something, or should the bottom of the river suddenly give out.

Greer let them go on about a dozen feet forward before she, too, clucked her tongue and urged her mount into the water. The mare seemed excited about the prospect of being in the water, and that made Greer smile. The horse nickered and pranced forward with eager steps and so much enthusiasm that Greer had to slow her down, fearful the mare might get stuck or spooked and toss Greer off in the process.

Ahead, Roderick had already traversed quite a ways in, and behind her, the men were coming along, too.

"Ye all right?" Grim called from ahead.

"Aye."

"Good." He flashed her a smile before turning forward.

This was good. She was doing it, and while her heart pounded as the water slowly rose up over the horse's forelegs and close to her belly, Greer forced herself to take deep breaths.

She was fine. Nothing was going to happen. When the water touched the bottom of her boots, she felt a moment of panic. A sudden need to leap off the horse and swim back to shore hit her, but the very idea of being in the water also made her want to retch. This was not good. The more she thought about it, the more her panic rose. And her mount must have felt that.

The horse let out a whinny, shook her head, and pranced uncertainly to the side. Greer held tightly to the reins, nudging the horse with her calves to go forward in the right direction, but the more she nudged and tugged at the reins, the more antsy the animal became—which only made Greer panic more. It was a vicious circle, tightening ever more like a noose around her neck.

"My lady," one of the men hurried to stand beside her. "'Tis all right. Loosen your grip and let the horse lead the way. She'll want to follow Laird MacCulloch."

Greer nodded, but it was easier to agree than to actually do. They went forward a few more feet, but soon her calves were encased in the cool water, even though she'd yanked the fabric of her borrowed plaid up above her knees. Soon, she would be in it thigh deep with the horse fully submerged and swimming.

Roderick seemed to sense her panic, for he turned his horse and started riding back toward her. When he reached her side, he smiled softly.

"Ride with me?" It wasn't an order, of that she was certain.

He was merely making a suggestion, one she was extremely grateful to hear.

Without a word, Greer nodded, but she wasn't certain how to get to him. She peeped down between them, seeing the water widen into what looked like an impossible gulf. Grim wrapped strong hands around her waist, lifted her out of the saddle, and expertly transferred her onto his lap.

He was solid beneath her. All hard thighs and strength. He was warm, too, and she found herself wanting to sink into his arms and stay there. There was something so incredibly comforting about being in his embrace, his arm snaked around her middle, her back flush to his chest, her legs slung over one of his thighs. She wrapped her arms around him and leaned her head against his chest where she could hear his heart beating steadily. The solid *bump bump bump* soothed her, and she worked to breathe in and out with the beats, matching them in rhythm.

"Thank ye," she murmured. "I tried, but the deeper we went..."

"I know, lass. Ye're safe now. And when we get across, I'll build ye a fire to warm yourself by."

She nodded, and the top of her head bumped against his chin. "Once more, ye've saved me. Seems like I should be the one saving ye."

He didn't say anything, and she peeked up at him to see if her reminder of the grave injury she'd given him had made his mood sour. But there was only a soft smile playing on his lips and no trace of annoyance.

Greer studied him as they continued through the water, shuddering when it continued to rise. Watching him was a good distraction, although she couldn't hide the fact that the cool river depths were now rising up her thighs. And like all fabrics, the wool soaked quickly.

It was only when Grim started murmuring against her ear that all would be well, that she realized he thought her shuddering was from fear. Perhaps some of it was.

She clung tighter to him, sensing he liked being her savior, but also knowing she liked the feel of him holding on to her too. What was a little trickery to get the sweet taste of being held in his arms? Oh, how she wished he would have kissed her in the woods.

When they finally made it to the other side, they all dismounted and gave their horses a chance to catch their breath and steal a few sips of water.

Greer wrung out her gown as best she could, leaving a massive puddle that trickled through the grass in long wet fingers to join Grim's puddle.

He gave the orders for his men to set up camp just beyond the river and the line of trees, and then she helped him gather wood for a fire. It was early yet for supper, but even still, he handed her a bannock, and she gratefully took it.

The heat of the fire was warm, and she hoped that by nightfall, her gown would be dry, else it was going to be a chilly sleep with the wet garment clinging to her skin. The cold and wetness of it sent her mind flashing back to those unbearable hours she'd floated in the firth, waiting, praying, believing she was about to die.

From across the fire, Grim stared at her in a peculiar way that warmed her from the cold thoughts. The hoods of his eyes were heavily lidded—just like they'd been when his mouth had been inches from her face. Was he thinking about that lost opportunity in the woods? Or perhaps they were only slitted to keep the smoke from the fire out. Whatever the reason, she had the oddest feeling that his regard was actually one filled with...*desire*.

Chapter Ten

✿❦✿

The smoke in Roderick's eyes did not do anything to hide the woman who sat before him. From where he sat across from her, the smoke made her look hazy, like a fey tempting him to cross over the flames.

He couldn't stop thinking about what it had felt like to hold her against him. To cradle her and keep her safe. Though he'd attempted to put a stop to his craving for a kiss, it was all he could think about. How he'd like to leap up from his place on the log, walk through the blasted campfire, lift her up, and kiss her until neither of them could breathe.

Greer was the last woman that Roderick should ever want to hold, and yet...he couldn't seem to get the idea out of his head.

If he'd not been certain his waterskin was in fact filled with water, he might have thought he'd imbibed in a bit too much spirits. Maybe there was something about the berries after all. Some sort of drug that made him feel...

What did he feel exactly?

An intense need to protect her. For all to *know* she was under *his* protection and no other's.

It was this latter desire, the one to proclaim to one and all she was his and his alone, that shook him to the very core of his being. How many times in the past couple of days had he tried to talk himself out of these feelings? Perhaps just as many times as he'd found himself being talked into them.

But it had felt so right holding her. And she'd trusted him to protect her. To take her to safety without judgment, and he'd fully given her that.

This was madness. The lass had thrown a spear into his leg, an injury that still pained him often. She'd laughed at him. And he still wanted to walk across the flames, scoop her up, and carry her into the woods where he could lay her down on a bed of nature's own making to show her all the ways in which he could worship her.

Bloody hell.

Roderick shook his head, breaking his gaze away from her. He was in trouble. Massive trouble. He'd been *jesting* with her. Teasing her with the berries, laughing, toying, flirting. It had been the same when he'd run after her in the woods and then held her against him. The sheer willpower alone that it had taken not to kiss her in that moment...

Mo chreach! This was not the way a warrior behaved. This was the way of stable hands with the maids. He could not recall his father ever having behaved this way. Nay, a laird had to be a leader at all times. No time for games. Playing games got men killed.

Was it the rebel in her? The hellion brought out the part of himself that had been rightly repressed as a child? For men needed to be men, and women needed to be women. When people counted on him, he could not turn into some wayward lad looking for a few laughs. He had to protect his people. To hold himself accountable. To be the man, the warrior, the leader. To notice when danger was near. If he was too busy playing games with the lass, how was he to notice something such as a bloody Ross coming up behind him?

He ground his teeth. If his father could see him now, would he be disappointed? Probably.

Guilt soured his belly. He had to be better. Had to put her out of his mind. At least until he'd got her back to her father. Once there, he could run away as quickly as he could find a ship.

Deciding to go on this adventure with her had been the first wrong move among many. He'd played into her love of adventure and games. Stoked her reckless side and in turn, his own.

They had about three days left of travel by his guess, and in all that time, he was going to have to figure out how to break whatever hold she had on him. Because all the things he wanted to do went against all of the things he *should* be doing. Kisses, games, all of it.

Clearing his throat, he pushed to stand, and without looking at her, he marched away toward his men to get an update from the scouts.

He'd taken barely three steps when the pull to turn around and make certain she was all right with him leaving her side was enough to make him want to toss himself from the nearest cliff. What kind of a man was he turning into? One with no backbone? She had to be all right with him leaving. This was his duty, and hers was to stay put. He nodded to himself and continued his march toward the edge of camp.

"Imbecile," he murmured to himself.

Angus eyed him warily. "My laird."

"What is it?" Roderick snapped, feeling instantly contrite.

"Ye seem out of sorts."

Roderick grimaced. "I worry about the Ross clan, 'tis all. We've seen naught of them."

Angus nodded. "They'll be dealt with soon enough. We've faith in ye."

Roderick glared as far as he could see down the river and across. They were sitting ducks to any enemy, but they could not ride wet—there was no way in hell he was going to risk Greer getting sick. "Any word from our scouts?"

"Not yet."

"Go and get a bite to eat. Dry yourself by the fire. I'll stand watch for now."

Angus moved off toward the fire, leaving Roderick alone. He leaned back against a tree, took out his *sgian dubh*, and sharpened it against the stone in his sporran, then he used it to clean his nails.

A moment later, he watched Greer head to the edge of the river. She stared down at the depths, then knelt and tentatively reached out a finger to touch the water. Ripples circled out from the place she touched, and even from where he stood, he thought he could see her smile.

She dipped her hands into the water, washing them. When she stood, she approached Angus. They chatted for several moments, and Roderick had never been keener to be privy to a conversation, especially when she laughed.

Then Angus stood and led Greer in the opposite direction and out of sight. Logic told him the man was only taking his charge to a place of privacy in order for her to relieve herself, but the envious side couldn't help but come up with all sorts of other scenarios. Most of which ended with Roderick's sword at the flesh of Angus's throat. For ballock's sakes, Angus wasn't even that type of man. For him to even think such a thing was the worst sort of offense to his friend.

Och, but where was all of this jealousy coming from?

She wasn't his. Had never been. Never would be.

A few jests and games did not a romance make.

Even going down that road went against everything he'd promised himself. And yet, there was that notion again that perhaps he should rethink his previous convictions. He knew for certain Jon would appreciate that. Hell, his brother had very blatantly told him just that before he left.

Roderick had taken six steps from his post, intent on going to find Greer, when she and Angus reemerged from the trees. When they spotted him, he knelt down, fiddling with the dirt, pretending he'd seen something.

Wouldn't do for his men to know how very close he'd been to doing something he'd warned them never to do—leave their post.

Thank goodness they'd emerged when they did, because just then, one of the scouts returned, and if Grim had not been at his post, he'd never hear the end of it. It would have been another notch in the imaginary post he presumed his clan was keeping with all his faults carved in neat little nicks.

"My laird." Clayton, the scout, leapt from his horse and handed the reins off to one of the men, who took the animal away to be brushed down, fed, and watered.

Roderick nodded for Clayton to follow him to the tree where they could speak quietly and he could still remain at his post.

"Glad I am that ye've returned." Roderick clapped Clayton on the shoulder. His words were not spoken lightly. He was glad his man had returned. There were plenty of warriors that went out and did not return. But a scout's job was even more perilous. They were often alone and searching for the enemy. Many gave their lives for their missions, so with every one that returned, gratitude was owed.

Clayton nodded, but his face was grim. "As am I, my laird. Men are on the move."

Roderick stiffened. "How many? Ross men?"

"From atop the rise, I could see movement in the west. At least a score, 'haps two score. I couldna tell if they were Ross men or not, but since we will eventually reach them in the west, it was my assumption, aye."

"We are close to Fraser lands, too. Might it have been them?"

"Possibly. They were moving fast, though, and 'tis unlikely the Frasers would be moving at those speeds and in that number. I'd not heard any whispers of them having trouble at the moment, but that doesna mean they are not. If they dinna make camp tonight, they could be upon us before dawn."

"Damn." Roderick pinched his brow. This was not good news. "We have to move. Now."

"Aye."

He didn't want to break down their camp at night with Greer in tow. Blast it all. This was not ideal. The horses needed rest, and so did she. There was naught he could do about it though. Safety came first, and the horses had had some time to rest already. Perhaps they could find a safer place to make camp, something hidden close by.

Roderick glanced toward where the lass once more sat before the fire. She'd have to ride with him. Not that he didn't trust her to ride well on her own. Hell, she'd more than proved she could already. But he couldn't risk something happening to her on her own mount. If the horse spooked or tripped, she'd be in danger. Danger he could have prevented by having her ride with him or one of his men. But the thought of her riding with anyone else was unacceptable. He told himself it was only because he wanted to be certain she was safe, and he couldn't risk her not being safe with anyone else. Although he knew well enough a lie when he heard one, even when he told it to himself.

"Put out the fires," he commanded his men. "We need to move."

The horses were loaded back up, and Greer stared at the men as they moved quickly to do Roderick's bidding. Her face was pale, and when he approached, her worried gaze locked on his.

"Ye're going to ride with me," he said.

She straightened. "I'm fine to ride on my own. I am grateful for what ye did before—"

"Ye'll ride with me." Roderick cut her off before she could continue. There was no time to argue. He turned his back on her to oversee putting out the fires. The men dumped lake water onto the pits to cool them so whoever came upon their makeshift camp would not be able to tell exactly when they'd left.

However, Greer did not seem to care that he'd dismissed her. And he should have known better.

She marched right up to him, tugged on his arm, and did not wait for him to acknowledge her before she started talking. "I dinna appreciate your tone, Grim, or the way ye're ordering me about. I'm not one of your men. I'm a lady, and I expect to be treated as such."

When he ignored her, she continued. "I can ride well, and I think I've proven that, save for the whole river fiasco, but if we're just riding on land, I prefer to have my own mount."

Roderick stopped what he was doing, turned toward her, and narrowed his gaze. "Ye'll ride with me, and that's final."

Greer stomped her foot, and her face transformed into the fiercest glower he'd seen from one so pretty and small. In fact, it was so ferocious, he was a little taken aback. But perhaps he shouldn't have been.

"I am not accustomed to taking orders." Her hands flew to her hips, and her chin jutted forward.

Roderick's brows drew together, wondering if he'd missed something. She appeared to have taken great offense to his attempts to keep her safe, and yet she'd not balked before.

He faced her fully, taking in the hands on her rounded hips, the angry flush to her cheeks, and the way her chest puffed out. The overwhelming urge to kiss her struck him. He wanted to smooth away the anger and show her that all that bluster, all that energy, could be put toward something more useful, like kissing and pleasure.

Then again, knowing her, she'd probably bite off his tongue and toss it in the fire. Arguing right now would get them nowhere, and she didn't seem to understand the urgency.

"Dinna fash yourself, lass. I dinna think less of ye for needing my help afore. Now go on and do as I've instructed. I've the camp to oversee, and quite frankly, keeping the men, and *ye*, safe outweighs your need to make yourself known."

She narrowed her eyes even more, if possible. "What?"

"Go and get on my horse. We'll talk more when we're away from here."

"Did ye nae listen to a word I've said?"

"Hush now, sweetheart, and go do as ye're told." That only seemed to make her more angry, which he was kind of enjoying, though he really didn't have time to relish it fully. "Dinna make me toss ye over my shoulder, for I will. And I'm entirely positive that your da would agree with me. Ye've got yourself in enough trouble lately. Go."

Her mouth fell open at that, but she must have sensed from the way he was staring at her that he was not jesting. She glanced around the camp, following the men as they dismantled everything to make it appear as though no one had been there in some time.

Roderick counted in his head, wondering just how long it would take for her to turn around, and if he was going to have to make good on his promise to toss her over his shoulder. Thankfully, Greer turned away from him and marched toward his horse with renewed purpose. Smart lass.

With no assistance needed, she grabbed hold of the pommel, lifted her foot to the stirrup, and tossed herself up onto the horse that was easily two or three hands higher than her. He'd seen grown men struggle more with mounting his mighty beast than the wee lass had. Tiny and fierce.

He couldn't help but grin in her direction, but she only glowered back.

He returned to his tasks, and once he was satisfied, he ordered his men back on their horses. He mounted Twilight and tugged her onto his lap. This time, he didn't have to worry about ignoring the feel of her against him, because their second scout, Joseph, returned, his face fierce with worry. Instantly, Roderick knew it was bad news.

Joseph reined in his mount. "Another group of men, this one approaching from the south."

Roderick's stomach tightened. "Did ye get a look at them?"

"Aye. I believe they are Ross men, my laird."

Roderick muttered an oath under his breath. He'd been hoping the first party spotted would be the only one, and that by racing away now, they'd have enough time to make camp later somewhere safe. Now it seemed like that was an impossibility. In fact, it was looking very much like a battle may be coming their way.

"Joseph and Clayton, linger behind us, double back and then bring news."

"Aye, my laird," they said in unison, and then they were rotating their mounts. They would both keep an eye on the two approaching parties, and Roderick prayed that before the night was through, he and his men would manage to escape both.

A battle wasn't what he feared; he loved a good fight. But it would be hard to protect Greer if he was in the midst of a fray. Worse still was knowing she'd probably grab up a sword and jump right in.

Chapter Eleven

Why did she have to be so obstinate?

Greer held tightly to the front of the saddle, though Roderick's grip around her waist was firm enough she knew she'd not fall off. Even still, she squeezed the leather, hoping it would stop the trembling in her fingers.

What was happening? Why could he not have just told her they were in danger?

Of course, she'd had an idea that the scout had told him something that had made him want to move their camp, but she'd not realized the peril was so great. But she supposed she should have. She shouldn't have second-guessed him. He was laird, a warrior, and a fine one.

At first, she'd just assumed he thought her weak, that after the fiasco on the river, he didn't want to deal with her when they were on the run. She'd only been trying to let him know she was fine on her own, but then she'd grown embarrassed.

And what did she always do when she was embarrassed? She grew obstinate and confrontational. Every time.

Add that to her list of flaws. They seemed to be growing exponentially, and bringing all of their ugliness out in front of the one man she wanted to kiss her.

Goodness, what must his warriors think of her now? No doubt, they supposed her to be a silly woman. Which she supposed she had been, displaying quite a bit of silliness arguing with him. In fact, she was surprised he'd not thrashed her for being so ridiculous. Or at the very least, tossed her over his shoulder and gagged her. She might have...

All these flaws, the need to argue, were so ingrained within her, that she couldn't curb them even when it was necessary. Grim had to be growing impatient, she was certain, had to think that this was all she was.

How many times had her father and mother lamented of her obstinacy? Aye, she was a troublemaker. A rule breaker. A debater. A mischief maker.

But that wasn't how she wanted to be recognized. And she wanted him to know her for the other good parts. There were other things she was skillful at, too. Sailing, swimming, and a skill she'd taken note of that Roderick also possessed—finding things that were lost.

Aye, she could find anything. Children who'd gone off to hide, a chicken who'd escaped the yard, a pin that fell through the cracks in the floor, or a match to a pair of hose that had been lost in the wash. One time, she'd even found her mother's missing earbob in the loch.

Despite being so good at finding things for others, she seemed to be struggling with finding herself.

"Who am I?" she murmured.

"What was that, lass?" Roderick called in the wind at her back.

And she was thankful that the wind created by their quick gait had muffled her words, because she did not want him to know the question of her heart. Yet she kind of *did* want him to know. To talk to him about it. Roderick seemed a man with a good head on his shoulders, and he'd had to change fairly quickly over the last few years, to find who he was supposed to be.

All that didn't matter now. He had other things to pay attention to besides her. So, Greer shook her head and tried to tuck the hair loosening from its plait back in place so that they wouldn't whip in his face and obstruct his view.

This was a step in the right direction. Thinking before acting. Not putting her desire for knowledge first. Of course, with her mind no longer wondering, she now worried about the threat that followed them. The MacCulloch men were fierce, to be sure. Thick with muscle, deadly gazes, and loaded with weapons. But the truth was, there wasn't that many of them. And if there were two hordes headed their way from opposite directions, she could only pray her father had gotten the message to meet them halfway.

As the sun began to set, they continued over the moors, riding until their horses were slick with sweat and they were forced to dismount. Though their pace slowed, and they now walked on foot, they still didn't stop. Roderick led his horse and held her hand tightly as they tread through thick grass, over rocky terrain, and up and down hills.

"Up there," he called to his men, pointing at a rise over their heads. "Find a way for the horses."

Two men separated from their group.

"How do ye know what is the perfect spot?" she asked, hoping he wouldn't take offense to her curiosity,

"If possible, I try to be on higher ground in order to see my enemies as they approach. That rise is verra steep though. And I'm nae certain we'll all fit on the peak."

The men returned a moment later and confirmed this, so they continued until the wooded area turned into moors once more, and then into more crag and cliff than grass. At last, they came across a cave. By the time they did, Greer could no longer feel her feet. They had to be blistered in her boots, and possibly bloody. The boots had not dried all the way, and the water had quickly soaked into her hose. She was a mess. An utter mess. And she had no one to blame but herself. She should have simply gotten on the *birlinn*, curled up in a ball, and closed her eyes until she was home.

"I'm sorry." Though her voice was soft, Roderick heard her.

"For what?"

"For not riding the *birlinn*. This is all my fault."

"Nay, lass. Ye've nothing to worry over. The Ross men have been raiding my lands for months. At least we've drawn them away from the castle."

Greer bit the inside of her cheek. There was so much confidence in his words, as if they were simply luring the enemy away, and the idea they were about to be attacked was a mere fancy.

"I trust ye to protect me," she said, but the words were meant more for herself. For she did trust him, but she wasn't entirely certain why. "I dinna think ye would have saved me on the beach only to toss me into your enemy's sword."

"I'd never do such."

They crept closer to the mouth of the cave, but when Greer started to head inside, Roderick held her back.

"Wait." He nodded to Angus. "Could be wildcats inside."

Her heart leapt at that. She'd been willing to walk right inside without even thinking about the fact that wildcats liked to make their dens in caves. Roderick disappeared inside with his claymore drawn. Her stomach twisted up into knots.

As the seconds ticked by without him returning, her skin started to prickle with nerves and sweat slicked her palms. Just when she was about to order Angus to go inside and find his laird, Roderick reappeared.

"All clear. 'Tis not as deep as I'd hoped. The horses will have to stay outside with the men on watch. Those not on watch will sleep inside after settling their mounts."

This was not ideal. If the horses were spotted, their enemies would know they were within, but she supposed there was nothing they could do about it now. Their mounts were exhausted, and if they continued to ride them, they'd run the risk of injury, and then there would be no escaping.

"Come, lass. Get some sleep." He held out his hand, and Greer accepted it as he led her into the cave.

It was pitch black inside. She stilled her feet, resisting the tug of his hand. No amount of blinking helped her vision to adjust.

"How did ye know there were no wildcats? I canna see my hand in front of my face." She waved it there just for emphasis, though she was certain he, too, could not see it.

"A sixth sense I suppose."

"Perhaps ye're madder than most think me."

"I dinna think ye're mad."

"Nay? What would ye call sailing out into a storm?"

"A passion for sailing?" The jest in his tone was loud and clear, but she wasn't in a jesting mood.

"Ye'd be the only one, for not even I would call it that. If anything, I'd call it foolish," she grumbled.

Grim stopped walking and let go of her hand.

A sudden rush of fear filled her, and she gasped, hands flailing out for him in the dark. She came into contact with his back and gripped the linen of his shirt. He moved quickly back to standing and pulled her against his chest, the steady beat of his heart calming her.

"Sorry, lass, I should have warned ye I was letting go. I but wanted to set out a plaid for ye to sleep on."

Greer shook her head, wide eyes frantically searching in the dark. "I dinna want to sleep." She supposed being scared of the dark was a new flaw she was supposed to deal with, for it wasn't one she'd had prior to this journey.

"Ye must."

She bit her lip, certain she was going to have nightmares. Probably of getting her throat ripped out by a wildcat. He didn't say anything as he worked, and she kept her hands on him the entire time without him protesting. And when he rose, she still did not release him, her fingers falling to the muscles of his chest. They stood close. Close enough she could feel his breath fanning her forehead and the heat of his body. He smelled of warm wool, leather, and something unique to him, an enticing spice. Greer breathed him in, memorizing that scent and desiring all over again to kiss him.

Still, he didn't move.

Should she?

Aye, she should, and very far away, too. From there went a whole litany of *should she, should she not* that warred constantly within her.

Well, if she was going to try to turn a new leaf, then she supposed this was as good a place to start as any. Greer let her hands start to slip away, only to have Roderick press his larger, warm and calloused hand over hers, stilling her, flattening her palms against his chest. Her breath hitched, and she could have sworn his did, too. Beneath her fingertips, his heart thumped. Her thumb brushed over that beating organ, and she found it hard to keep herself from stroking over his muscles, wanting to hold tightly and never let go.

She let out a breath she wasn't aware she was holding, only to suck it back in when his thumbs caressed her knuckles and he tugged her slightly closer so that the tips of her toes touched his. This was the forest all over again. The teasing whisper of a kiss.

She'd never been as intimate with a man as she'd been with Roderick. Never felt the length of her body on another until him. And she was certain after the moments they'd shared, she would never be able to think of being close to any other man than her Grim.

Her Grim.

Och, I am in trouble.

They were so close she could almost imagine his strong thighs braced against hers. The flat of his muscled belly flush to hers, enough so she could feel him breathing with her, as though they were one. Only a few inches separated them. All she had to do was take a step forward, and then she would experience all of the things she imagined.

Greer licked her lips. She should say something, but what? Was he going to kiss her? Oh, how she wanted him to kiss her, and how she feared blurting out those very words.

"Lass," he murmured, his husky voice barely above a whisper. Another little tug, and her belly was flat to his, her thighs lining up to his strong stance, and his breath was closer now, fanning her cheek.

She couldn't find her voice, didn't know what to say even if she could. All she wanted to do was get up on her tiptoes and press her lips to his. To do what she'd wanted to do for days.

He hovered closer, and then just as abruptly, she felt the coolness of his retreat. She didn't reach out for him, knowing it would do no good, also knowing it was for the best. She tried not to be disappointed. But she was. No matter what, she was pretty certain she'd not be able to get rid of that feeling. She wanted that kiss. Wanted it badly. Enough that her heart still pounded and it was on the tip of her tongue to tell him not to leave just yet so she could grab the front of his shirt and tug him close. To fumble in the dark until her lips were pleasantly pressed to his so she could taste what a true kiss should be, and satisfy the craving she'd had ever since she'd turned to see him lying in bed with her.

But she wasn't brave enough for that. Not by half. For all the risks she was willing to take, the idea of kissing Roderick when he might reject her seemed one she couldn't quite take the leap on.

"Get some rest." His voice was even more gravelly than it had been before, as though he were straining to get the vowels out. It made her think that just maybe he wanted to kiss her as badly as she wanted to kiss him. "I'll be back with something for ye to eat."

Greer didn't argue, though the idea of staying in the cave alone, even if only for a few minutes, was terrifying. Balling her hands into fists, she resisted the urge to reach out and grab hold of him.

She nodded.

"Lass?"

"Aye," she croaked, realizing he'd not been able to see her. Her sense left her more with every breath.

She clamped her lips closed when she nearly begged him to hurry back. Instead, she sat down heavily on the floor, tucked her legs up under her chin, and wrapped her arms around her legs. She curled her fingers into the plaid, which had thankfully dried before the fire, even if the same could not be said about her boots. Sitting down now, she let out a great sigh. The weight was off her feet, and she could allow them some time to dispel the ache.

Who were they running from? Who were Roderick's enemies? She didn't realize until just then that she'd never taken the time to find out. Aye, he'd mentioned the Ross clan had been raiding, but there were two armies headed their way. She knew for certain he was an ally of her father. It was one of the reasons she'd trusted him so readily. He had to be well respected if he were an ally of her father's. That meant he might have fought alongside Robert the Bruce like her father, uncles, and brothers.

Then a terrifying thought occurred to her. What if Grim's enemies were her father's allies?

Greer kept her gaze toward the front of the cave where the dark-ness faded from pitch black to dark gray. Her vision played tricks on her, showing shadows that were there and then weren't. The men moving in and out she was certain of. Then a figure loomed in the mouth of the cave, and she slammed her hand against her mouth to keep in her gasp. In the darkness and shadows, she could only make out the breadth of him. The hilt of his claymore over his right shoulder.

Roderick's scent reached her, calming her to his presence, and she thanked the heavens it was he and not the enemies that chased them down.

"Who's there?" she whispered, needing the confirmation of his voice beyond his mesmerizing scent.

"'Tis only Grim, lass." His soft tone was comforting, and she breathed out the breath she wasn't even aware she'd been holding.

"I never thought I'd hear someone say they were Grim and I would be so pleased to see them."

He chuckled, shuffled forward, and sat down before her. His fingers brushed her folded legs, and she reached out and took the bannock he passed her.

"Sorry, this is all I have for now, lass. We've gone through the nuts, and 'tis too dark to forage for anything else ye might be able to eat."

"And too dangerous. This is more than enough. I'm not all that hungry, besides." She spoke the truth. Her stomach had been twisted up in knots for hours now, and there was no point in forcing food into a belly that would only rebel.

"Water?"

"Aye."

He passed her the waterskin, and their fingers brushed again. Every time he touched her, a jolt of awareness ran through her limbs, and her skin hoped for another gift of his touch, however small.

"I'm going to take first watch. Ye'll be safe here. Sleep."

As he said it, men started to shuffle inside to roll out their plaids and sleep. At least she wouldn't be alone. That made her feel more comfortable about sleeping with him outside the cave, rather than him holding her like the scared bairn she felt like.

"Thank ye," she murmured, handing him back his waterskin.

"No thanks required, my lady. I aim to protect ye and return ye to your father."

Roderick cleared his throat, stood, and retreated without another word. What had she expected him to say? Sorry that he'd not kissed her? Sorry that he'd made her think he might?

It wasn't as if he were going to admit to anything in front of his men, nor did she truly expect him to acknowledge such things to her anyway.

Greer finished her bannock cake and then lay back on her makeshift bed, listening to the sound of the men snore and the odd way it echoed in the cave. She put an arm over her face and concentrated on her own breathing, but despite how exhausted she was, she couldn't get the idea of kissing Roderick out of her head. Och, but she was a naughty lass, that was certain.

She rolled onto her side, feeling the hardness of the cave floor straight through to her bones. Tucking herself up in the blanket, she found herself missing the warmth of Roderick's body as he slept beside her. Only a couple of nights together, and she'd already grown used to having him near. That was going to be a problem when she arrived back at Dunrobin and he subsequently returned to Gleann Mórinnse.

A little while later, the feeling of Roderick lying down beside her roused her from a sleep she couldn't recall falling into. She smiled when he wrapped his arm around her middle and pulled her into his warmth.

Chapter Twelve

Roderick jerked awake from a shake to his shoulder. His jolt woke Greer, who butted her head into the bottom of his chin, causing him to bite the tip of his tongue. He groaned, rolling back and tasting blood.

Angus loomed beside him in the dusky gloom.

"My laird, the sun will rise soon," Angus said. "Ye slept hard."

In more ways than one.

Disentangling himself from Greer's limbs, he stood and stretched out the kinks the night of sleeping with Greer had given him. He was grateful the jolt awake had at least tamed the part of him that was constantly rising to attention where Greer was concerned. "Let's pack up."

Without a word, the men all rose and packed up their horses. All the while, he tried to remain completely oblivious of Greer, which only made him all the more aware of each of her movements. From the corner of his eye, he could see her brushing her fingers through her hair and re-plaiting it. She swished some water around her mouth from a wineskin one of the men offered her. Then she rolled up her extra plaid, carried it out to Grim's horse, and slipped the roll into the satchel attached to the saddle.

Last night, when he'd held her close in the cave, he'd been so close to kissing her that if he'd flicked his tongue out, he would have touched her skin. The only thing that had stopped him had been the hitch in her breath. It wasn't that he worried she didn't want him to kiss her. Nay, the lass had given him every indication that kissing was exactly what she wanted, needed.

But kissing would lead him down a path he wasn't certain he was yet prepared to take. Pleasure didn't matter, for if it did, he would have kissed her soundly and then made love to her. God, how he would have worshipped her.

Blast it all, but just thinking about making love to her had blood pooling in his groin. Aye, he wanted her. Body, mind, spirit. To want a woman was not unusual for any man. Even to decide one was good as a wife.

But him? Him and Greer?

Together, they would be a disaster waiting to happen. So why couldn't he stop thinking about her?

Roderick marched toward Twilight, his boot heels digging a little more forcefully into the ground than they had before Greer had swept up onto his beach.

"Grim."

The soft feminine voice stilled Roderick as he was about to mount, and he turned to face Greer, sliding his hands off the pommel of the saddle.

Her face was still flushed with sleep, and dark half-moons lined the undersides of her eyes. "Am I to ride with ye?"

He'd not realized he needed to tell her. He'd assumed she would understand that was to be the way of it until they reached her father's lands. With the danger that followed them, he couldn't let her go.

"Aye, lass."

She stumbled forward, exhaustion etched on her features and in the uncoordinated way she moved. She took another step and then pitched forward, and he caught her in his arms. Her head hit his chest as he wrapped his hands around her ribs. The tips of his thumbs brushed her breasts, and Roderick gritted his teeth, quickly shifting his grip lower.

"I'm sorry," she mumbled. "I'm just so tired. And my feet hurt."

"There is no need to apologize." Roderick wrapped his hands around her waist, lifted her up onto the horse, and mounted behind her. "Do ye want something to eat?"

The crown of her head brushed his chin when she shook her head, a few strands of her locks getting caught in his beard and making him twitch as they tickled. He smoothed them out, marveling at the softness of her. Greer settled against him, her head leaning back against his shoulder and her arms over his that draped at her waist. Within a few minutes of riding, she was asleep. So deeply, in fact, that she kept slumping forward, and he had to gently nudge her back in place else she fall off the horse.

The lass had been through so much over the past few days that he was not at all surprised. They should have remained at Gleann Mórinnse. He should have sent a messenger to bring Magnus back his way instead. But she'd insisted she was well enough to travel. When they stopped to rest the horses, he eased off his mount with her in his arms and carried her toward a tree to keep her out of the sun. She woke before he got there, shifting slightly in his arms to glance up at him.

"Ye can put me down." Her voice was groggy, but when he peered into her eyes, they were bright with curiosity.

"Glad to have ye back with us," he teased and settled her feet on the ground.

"How long did I sleep?" Greer stretched her arms over her head, rolling out the kinks in her body as he watched—oh Lord, did he watch...

The gown strained against her breasts, and when she undulated her behind and hips, he thought he was going to lose his mind. He'd seen any number of women stretch after a long ride or a day working hard in a field. Yet the sight of Greer doing something so commonplace left his mouth dry and his blood rushing from his extremities toward his core. It boggled his mind.

Clearing his throat, he said, "All morning. 'Tis noon I'm guessing. The scouts have not spotted our enemies close as yet. 'Tis a good sign."

"Ah, that is a relief. I feel much better."

"I'm glad."

"I think I'll walk a bit to stretch." She glanced around as if to catch her bearings and then headed away from him.

Of course, his gaze was drawn to the sway of her hips, and then he noticed she was limping a little. He didn't want her to fall again like she had that morning. Maybe he could convince her to remove her boots and let him see her feet, wrap them at least to protect them. "Wait, I'll walk with ye."

She glanced up at him, looking surprised. "Are ye certain?"

"Aye." He glanced at her skeptically. "Why?"

"The last time we were alone..." She trailed off, and he grinned.

"I promise not to abuse your company."

Greer's mouth gaped open, and her eyes grew wide as bannocks. "I would never think such a thing about ye."

"All the same, I promise not to take liberties that are not mine to take."

White teeth scraped over her bottom lip, and she glanced away, avoiding his gaze. What did that mean?

"How are your feet?"

Greer still did not look at him. "They are better now."

"But ye limp."

"Only from lack of use."

They walked in silence, and then she asked for a moment of privacy, which he took himself as well. He waited to hear her call out to him in friendly conversation, but she was silent.

When she was finished, she rejoined him in the space between their private spots.

"Would ye care to forage?" he asked.

Her stomach let out a loud grumble, and her cheeks flushed red.

Roderick chuckled. "Ye must be starved. Ye've not eaten since last night."

A wide grin curled her lips. "I could definitely eat now, in case my stomach's reply was not clear enough."

They found the remains of a berry bush, which appeared to have been thoroughly picked over by deer and other forest creatures, although she did find three the animals had missed. She offered them to him, and then popped them into her mouth after he declined.

"I'm sorry there's not more, lass."

She grinned up at him and shook her head. "There's no need to apologize. I'll be fine. If ye've got more bannock cakes, I'd be happy to survive on those until we reach Sutherland."

"Your da will think I've starved ye."

"Nay, he'll not. He knows me well, and having been with my mother, he knows the way it goes." She ran her fingers over the bush, plucking a thin, dried stem and breaking it into a few pieces. "I want to give ye my apology for what happened."

Which part? He wanted to laugh, because since she'd come into his life, it had been nothing but one event after another—which he was coming to find quite endearing. "Lass..."

"Please, allow me to finish. I am used to arguing. To getting my way if I push for it. And if I dinna, then often I go about doing what I want anyway." A sad smile crossed her face. "'Tis the reason we have come to know each other once more."

Roderick didn't know exactly what to think about what she was saying. This didn't sound like it was about the almost kiss. Rather about a disagreement.

"In any case, I shouldna have argued with ye in front of your men about riding the horse on my own. And I'm grateful that ye were patient with me, and that ye didna toss me over your shoulder, or worse, leave me tied to a tree as ye ran off. 'Twas inexcusable for me to have acted in such a way. My father would have had my hide." She shook her head and plucked another dried stem. "I admit to being a little impulsive sometimes, but lately...I feel a little lost."

"Och, lass, I ken the feeling of being lost. 'Tis something I've struggled with myself. Ye have to trust in yourself. Become quiet and listen to your heart. Do the things ye love." He watched her dump the remnants of a torn up twig to the ground. "Know that from me, *all* is forgiven." He meant that sincerely, even the piercing of her spear. With a wink, he added, "And your hide will remain intact."

Greer laughed at that, tossing a tiny remnant of stick at him. "I'm glad for that. And thank ye. I dinna often sit and listen to my heart, or anything else. I'm a whirlwind." She held such an endearing expression at that moment, the protector in him felt an intense need to wrap her up in his arms and fight all of her battles for her.

Alas, he knew that wasn't the way. Just as it hadn't been for his sister. Aye, he could be her armor, but that wouldn't help what was crumbling on the inside.

"Ye're an amazing woman. Dinna ever doubt the power of your heart, for it is strong." Roderick tucked an errant lock behind her ear and then jerked his hand away, but she caught it, much like he'd caught her in the cave.

"Dinna pull away this time, please," she whispered, pressing his palm back against her face.

Suddenly, his throat felt very tight. Too tight. He tried to swallow, but he couldn't. And then he was nodding, accepting what she said, and smoothing his thumb over the arch of her cheek.

The feel of her skin against his palm was a decadent pleasure. Never before had he been so moved by touching a woman's face. Roderick was a man of many pleasures and had more than a few lovers. None of them had caused such a reaction from a simple, unassuming touch. Just like everything else with Greer. What would be normal for some was incredible with her.

But it was more than desire racing through him. Something caught in his chest, tightening it. He wanted to embrace her and never let go.

"We should go back," he found himself saying, trying to stop whatever it was that was happening between them. But his words didn't even sound convincing to his own ears.

"Aye. That is probably best." But her gaze was on his, and her hand now cupped the outside of his own. She turned her face, her eyelids dipping closed. Then she pressed her lips to his palm, and a jolt of pleasure rocked him. "Thank ye for taking care of me."

Good God, his entire body tensed at the feel of her lips, the faint wash of her breath on his skin. His head bobbed, and a few ridiculous comments came to mind, such as, *Thank ye for washing up on my shore.*

There was no way he could walk away from her now without kissing her. He had to. Was compelled to. Wouldn't be able to live with himself if he didn't.

Roderick stepped closer, feeling the soft wool of her plaid gown against his bare knees. She peered up at him, wide bluebells unwavering.

"When we were in the woods, when we were in the cave—" He swallowed hard. "Hell, ever since the first time I saw ye, I've wanted to kiss ye."

Her lips parted, eyes dewy with desire, and she sucked in a breath before saying, "And I wanted ye to, so verra much."

But was that permission enough?

He touched her waist, fiddling with her gown and tugging slightly as he slipped his free arm around to the small of her back. "I want to kiss ye right now."

He watched her eyebrows rise up in surprise, and she flicked a delicate pink tongue over her lower lip. "I...I still want ye to."

Mo chreach. There was absolutely no stopping him now.

Threading his hand into her hair and pressing gently against her spine, he brought her completely flush against him, feeling every line and curve of her body against his. He massaged the arc of her cheek with his thumb and searched her face, but he found only eagerness and anticipation there. Blast it all. He was done for.

Roderick lowered his face to hers, watching as her eyelids dipped closed, and then he too was letting his lids dip closed as the softness of her lips touched his.

A sigh escaped her as soon as they touched, and she caressed his arms until she clutched to his shoulders, singeing him. Roderick wrapped both arms around her, lifting her slightly into the air as his mouth slanted over hers, claiming her. He slipped a tongue over the seam of her lips and teased until she opened for him, and then he swept inside, swallowing her gasp. She tasted sweet and wild, like the berries she'd just eaten, and just like *her*.

A deep yearning to consume all of her filled him. How was he ever going to go back to a normal life having tasted her? No other woman would ever be able to compare. No other life could be lived if it were not lived beside her.

Her tongue pushed against his in gentle exploration, and he grew weak with desire. If he did not end this kiss soon, it was going to be harder and harder to pull away. As it was, he was planning his life around this kiss, which seemed imprudent. This was just a kiss. A blood-pumping, delicious kiss from an incredible woman. A kiss he'd been waiting for what felt like a lifetime to have.

Was being so moved by a kiss possible? Or had he just been worked up after waiting days—hell, years—before he could claim her?

Or mayhap, it was only that he hadn't taken a woman to his bed in a long while, and she was the first one for him to have touched since then. Aye, there had to be some logical explanation behind it.

For one simply did not plan their entire life around a simple kiss.

Chapter Thirteen

Greer was floating, and not merely because her feet were no longer on the ground. She was swept up in a maelstrom of delight, and it was all Roderick's doing.

His kiss dominated her senses. All she could do was return his touch and feel. Really *feel*. The sensations ricocheting through her body were intoxicating. Tendrils of warmth and pleasure stroked over her limbs and curled through her insides.

She'd never been kissed before, and she was certain she'd never want to be kissed by anyone else again. How could they ever compare?

With her arms wrapped around Roderick's neck, her lips fastened to his, her tongue mirroring the velvet strokes of his own, and her body crushed against him as he held her, Greer was certain she never wanted to be let down. If the world were to implode right then and there, she was content to know she'd leave this realm with the last thing she'd ever done being kiss this handsome warrior.

His beard tickled her face, but not in a way that made her want to bat him away or laugh, but in a more seductive way that had her wanting to sigh and gasp and rub her skin all over him.

Slowly, she felt herself being lowered, her feet once more planted on the ground, though not firmly. She was completely off-balance, and so she clung to him, curling her fingers into his shirt, massaging the thick muscles beneath her fingertips. Their mouths still hungrily sought out each other, pleasure for pleasure, stroke for stroke. Goodness...she could barely breathe. Her heart pounded, and all she could think about was the rapture of this moment.

But what did she know of pleasure? She'd only ever kissed this one man, right now. Sure, she'd seen plenty of men and women sneaking into alcoves, heard the rustling under blankets in the great hall on cold winter nights when they'd all camped out for warmth. Even watched a stallion mate with a mare once, though when her mother found her hiding behind a stack of hay, she'd warned Greer it wasn't ladylike to spy on animals doing their business.

At the time, she'd not known what that meant, but as she'd grown older, she'd been plenty aware that doing one's business could mean rutting. This was why she'd thought for quite some time, her father and his men were engaging in such behaviors when they retired to his study for what they called "business." Of course, she'd been mortified when she'd confessed this to her older brother Liam, and he'd laughed so hard she was certain he was going to bust open his guts.

Oh, why did words and deeds have to be so complicated?

Between their lips, she felt the slide of Roderick's thumb, as though he couldn't break himself away from her without the help of his finger. Their lips peeled apart, and she gazed up at him with eyes that were heavy and blurred. He watched her much the same way, lips red and slick, and cheeks as flushed as hers felt.

As soon as their gazes met, she felt a rush of heat to her face and was embarrassed, though she wasn't certain why. Maybe it wasn't embarrassment; maybe it was shyness and an inability to figure out what to do with her hands.

Greer unwound her arms from around Roderick's neck where her hands had become entangled with his hair without her even realizing it. She slid her palms over his shoulders and paused on his chest where she could still feel his heart thumping.

"That was..." Her voice caught in her throat. What did one say after having received a kiss?

A life-altering kiss?

"Incredible." He stole the sentiment right from her mouth.

"Aye. Incredible."

"I..." This time it was him who was at a loss for words as he ran his hand through his thick hair. "I should get ye back to camp."

Those were not the words she wanted to hear. She wanted him to hold her hand, kiss her knuckles, and declare her the most beautiful lass in all of Scotland. To proclaim that he must kiss her again, right then and there, and that he'd die if he could not taste her lips just once more.

He slid his fingers down her arm and squeezed her hand, but he did not hold on to it. Her arm fell limp at her side, and the warmth in her limbs seemed to slip away as quickly as water going over a waterfall.

She was certain she was making a bigger deal out of it than she should. While this was her first kiss, Roderick had to have kissed a dozen lassies at least. Why would he think she was anything special? She wasn't experienced with kissing, and maybe she wasn't even that good. Though he had said she was incredible; that had to mean something, didn't it?

Alas, the longer she stood there speechless, the more foolish she felt. "A good idea," she agreed. "They will wonder where we went."

"Nay, they willna." His brows furrowed, and the telltale grimace she'd come to associate with him when they first met returned.

"What is it?"

"They will know I was kissing ye. Take one glimpse of ye and see."

Greer reached up to touch her face, feeling the heat of her cheeks and the ruffled hair that had fallen out of the plait when he threaded his fingers against her scalp. Her lips felt swollen and tingly.

"Then we could stay here a while longer, until I am presentable again." She raked a hand over her skirt, then stilled, her gaze cutting back to his. "Will I be presentable again?"

Roderick grinned, a slow wink dipping his eye closed and open. "Only if I dinna kiss ye again. And if we stay behind any longer, I canna promise that will nae."

"Oh." She breathed out, touched her lips, and felt their heat against her fingertips. That was what she'd wanted. It was near enough a decla-ration for her. Enough that the foolishness she'd felt slipped away, allowing the elation of what they'd shared to return. Even if he didn't kiss her again, just knowing he wanted to was more than satisfactory. "Let me at least fix my hair."

His grin widened. "Allow me?"

"What?" She was so shocked at his suggestion that her hands stilled in mid-air toward the back of her head.

Roderick shrugged. "I can give it a go."

Greer raised her brows but pulled out the ribbon holding what was left her plait. She turned around, presenting him her back. Her eyelids fluttered when he gently threaded his fingers through the remains of her braid until her hair lay flat on her back. Her scalp tingled. This act seemed strangely intimate. No one had ever touched her hair, save for her maid, her mother, and her sisters. And now Roderick, in the middle of the forest, after kissing her breathless. Goodness...

"'Tis a lot like braiding leather," he murmured as she felt him line up the pieces and begin weaving them around each other. "Save softer."

Greer smiled. "Grateful I am that 'tis softer than leather."

Roderick chuckled and then reached over her shoulder, fumbling for the ribbon in her hand.

He tied her braid, and she slid her hands over the woven locks. They were straight and even. "Nicely done, warrior. Seems ye're good at more things than warring and kissing."

He waggled his brows. "So ye think I'm good at kissing?"

Greer gave a sheepish grin. "Aye. And me? Was I nae too terrible?"

"Was it your first kiss?" He offered his elbow, and she took it as they made their way back to camp.

"That bad?"

"I didna say that."

"I'm nae sure ye had to."

He chuckled. "I could tell at first ye'd nae done much kissing, but by the end, ye were verra, verra good." He gave an exaggerated sigh. "Verra, verra good."

Luckily, no one stared at her strangely, either, though there were a few knowing smiles tossed their way when they returned.

Was it really so obvious?

She'd never thought before that one could look kissed, but that was before she'd done the deed herself and seen the result on Roderick. His skin was darker from the sun, and his jawline was covered in stubble, his chin covered in a beard. A flush to his skin was not as easily noticeable as one on her paler, softer visage.

While Greer snacked with great joy on bannocks and a few almonds Angus found in his bag, Roderick talked in hushed tones with his men. The way he stood, shoulders slightly stiff, hands on his hips, and the set of his jaw, she could tell that whatever news he'd received was not good. The excitement of what they'd shared was now buried beneath a flood of worry. Was the enemy close?

They did not stay put long. They remounted before Greer had finished her second bannock and rode for several hours in silence. Roderick was stiff behind her, and the men mirrored their leader. Any attempt she tried to make at small talk failed, so she became quiet, watching the moors and crags pass them by.

When they stopped once more, Roderick waved her away with Angus to make use of a bush, and then they were swiftly on their way again until they came to the River Beauly. She was disappointed not to have him for company, but he was still deep in discussions with his men, and the scouts who circled back every so often.

They slowed near the bank of a river, the men letting the reins slacken enough for the horses to dip their heads and take a sip.

"I'm afraid we're going to have to ford River Beauly, lass."

"I trust ye." But even as she said it, she watched the water rushing past and scanned the sky above that was darkening well before the sunset. Gray, ominous clouds swarmed closer, clashing overhead. They were in for a storm, a brutal one. Across the river, a large stone fortress loomed, the only thing giving it away as a house of God was the stone cross at its peak. Was it too much to hope that when they crossed, Roderick would suggest they stop for a respite?

She glanced behind her at Roderick. "Should we not wait out the storm?"

He grimaced and shifted uncomfortably in the saddle. "We dinna have time."

Greer gave a curt nod. Was the fluttering in her chest simply nerves from having nearly drowned herself less than a week ago, or a warning about what could happen if they walked into the water?

Angus appeared at Roderick's side. "Wind is picking up."

"Aye." Roderick stared down river, possibly studying the swells. "If we go, we need to go now. Before the storm starts."

Greer closed her eyes as they took their first shaky steps into the water. The horses snorted as if they, too, knew the danger, which they likely did. Animals acted on instinct. But other than the snorts and the slight prancing, they did not buck their riders, so it seemed that perhaps the river was not yet as bad as it could be.

Besides, they were well-trained warhorses. They must have been in worse situations.

Unable to keep her eyes closed any longer, her imagination making up all sorts of scenarios, Greer studied each and every horse, twisting in her saddle to make certain all was well.

They went forward about five feet and the water inched slowly up the legs of their horses. By the time they had gone ten feet, the water was about halfway up the horses' legs. From this position, Beauly seemed wider than the earth itself, but in reality, she knew it couldn't be wider than the river they'd forded previously.

Despite that, the farther they went into the water, the farther the shore seemed to be. River water rushed past them at speeds she was certain would have swept her away had there not been a horse beneath her and a warrior holding her tightly.

And then their horses were swimming, and the cold water was rushing up over her legs. Greer shivered. It was freezing. Bone-chilling water seemed to sink deep inside her instantly. She'd barely warmed from the last trek through the river, and after her adventure in the firth, getting warm seemed a near impossibility. The only saving grace was Roderick's heated chest at her back and his thighs beneath her rear.

Unlike their first river crossing, where he'd talked her through it, he was silent this time. Judging from his death grip on the reins, he was worried. The horses were slowing, their snorts and whinnies growing louder as the river swirled against their bodies, trying to pull them in a different direction than what their masters commanded. Even she could feel the drag of the current.

"Steady," Roderick directed, as did the other men to their mounts.

Greer worked to breathe in through her nose and out of her mouth, slowing her trembling as best she could, so as not to make the horse more nervous.

On the left end, Clayton let out a shout as his horse broke formation and started swimming back the way they'd come. Clayton's soothing and tugging at the reins did not stop his horse's hurried strokes in the opposite direction. Panic-fueled survival instincts overtook the animal's training.

Roderick cursed under his breath and shouted out an order for Clayton to get his mount under control. The man to Clayton's right took hold of the horse's bridle, trying to encourage the horse to return to the formation, but that only seemed to make the horse more desperate to be away. The other horses seemed to sense his panic and were also becoming jittery.

Another expletive left Roderick's mouth. Greer felt completely helpless, but what could she do?

Clayton could let his horse go and try to make it to her riderless mount being led by another warrior, but there was the real risk he could be swept away by the current.

Greer bit her lip and watched helplessly as Clayton tried to rouse his horse to go the other way, and the men worked to tame their horses so they didn't end up in the same situation.

She sent up one prayer after another to the heavens. But all the prayers in the world couldn't help when a bolt of lightning flashed, followed by a thunderous crack, obliterating all hopes of an easy passage.

Chapter Fourteen

Roderick gritted his teeth, holding Greer tightly with one hand and his horse with the other.

"Talk to him," he said, against her ear. "Touch him."

Greer leaned over the neck of his mount, stroked Twilight's straining muscles, and spoke in soothing tones. "'Tis all right. Ye can swim. We're almost there."

"Dinna panic," Roderick commanded his men, letting his voice be heard over the thunder and rushing water. "Soothe them."

His own mount's body rippled with anxiety, yet his ears were perked back, listening to Greer as she stroked and soothed. Roderick himself felt calmed by her voice. As much of a hellion as she was, she was also a comfort, and when it came down to it she did exactly what needed to be done.

Though he'd respected her before for her fiery spirit, his esteem grew tenfold when he watched her take command of the horse's comfort. The men followed her lead. They watched her and repeated exactly what she did. Even Clayton was making the same attempts to soothe his horse.

"Tell him to cover the horse's eyes," Greer offered. "We've done that at sea when the swells have made the mounts nervous."

Roderick issued the order, irritated with himself for not having thought of it before. When the barn had caught fire the previous year, they'd had to cover the eyes of the horses in order to lead them out.

Clayton ripped off his shirt, and pulled it over his horse's face. Within moments, the mount had calmed, and Clayton was able to ease him around and back into formation. Sensing the panic was over, the other horses, too, fell back in line and continued to swim—despite the thunder and lightning above.

Greer continued talking to the horse, and Roderick had the distinct impression she was soothing herself as she mollified the steed.

"Ye've strength enough for this and more," she said. "Close your eyes if ye must, and push through. We are counting on ye. We need ye."

Roderick smiled, holding her tightly as she leaned forward, not wanting her to pitch completely over the horse's neck.

At last, they made it safely to shore, where they wrung out their clothes as best they could with the rain still coming down. Greer walked from horse to horse and stroked their muzzles. The sun had started to set, not that it was overly noticeable with the clouds covering most of the sky. Even still, through the gloomy haze, they could make out the lights in the priory. With it being so close to the shore, there was no need to remount. Instead, they would simply walk, lead the horses, and beg shelter.

"Beauly Priory," Roderick said. "We'll see if they will accept a few wary travelers for the night, give the horses a nice place to rest."

The walk to the priory took less than five minutes, but it felt a lot longer with the wetted wool of their garments and the wind and rain of the storm pushing against them. By the time they reached the great wooden doors, they'd been opened and a line of monks were ushering them inside. Water dripped from the worried faces of the religious order. They must be wondering what had caused their visitors to rush headlong into a river during a storm.

One particular monk stepped forward. "I'm Father Wesley, Abbot of Beauly. We saw ye in the river and prayed for a miracle to help ye cross."

"Thank ye, Father," Roderick said. "I am Roderick MacCulloch, Laird of MacCulloch. This is Lady Greer Sutherland, and these are my men."

The priest considered him, gaze roving up and down, his scrutiny stilling particularly on the puddles forming beneath all of their wet clothes. "What's the rush? Why not wait until the storm passed?"

Roderick grimaced, shifting his weight onto his other leg as pains shot through his thigh. He'd barely noticed his injury the entire journey, too distracted by Greer he supposed, but once the storm had rumbled in, so too had the pain.

"We're being pursued by two caravans. We're not certain who, but I have an idea one of them is a Ross army. We're on our way to Sutherland to return Lady Greer, who had an accident on the firth and ended up on our shores. 'Twas only by an act of God that she survived," Roderick said, hoping to appeal to their faith, for it was truly a miracle she'd survived at all.

Father Wesley blanched, and the monks behind him whispered prayers, crossing themselves.

"We were verra sorry to hear about the death of your sister, and so soon after your father succumbed."

A jolt of emotion struck inside Roderick's chest. He'd not been expecting them to know who he was, let alone that his sister had passed. Their non-judgment of her death took his breath, for he feared most that though his own priest had viewed it as an accident, the rest of the world would not.

"My thanks." His voice came out a near croak.

"Blessed are ye, my son."

Roderick nodded, feeling his throat tighten again.

"Well, let us get your horses into the stable and the rest of ye something warm to wear, a place to sleep and some food." Father Wesley surveyed them all with intelligent eyes. "Are ye hungry?"

"We are much obliged." Roderick reached into his sporran and produced a gold coin, which he passed to the abbot. "For your troubles."

Father Wesley bit the coin. "'Tis no trouble at all."

The men were led out toward the stables to tend their horses and shown quarters nearby where laymen not of the cloth were housed when in residence.

"My laird, for ye, there is a chamber in the monk's dormitory in the upper floor of the east range. The lady will be housed in a chamber near the west range, where our visiting abbess stays. Once ye've settled, ye can meet us in the refectory for a silent meal. We were just about to serve."

"While I am full of gratitude, such arrangements are not necessary for myself. I will sleep with my men."

"If ye change your mind, the offer is open."

Father Wesley showed Greer to her room with Roderick following, despite the stares from the man of the cloth. When they reached the room, he produced a key, unlocked her door, and ushered her inside the stark room, furnished with only a bed and a small side table with a half-melted tallow candle.

"My lady, ye'll find an extra robe and tunic in the wardrobe that belongs to Mother Anne. I'm certain she will not mind ye borrowing it for the time being."

Once she was through the door, Father Wesley shut it firmly and gave Roderick a hard stare. "I'd best not be seeing ye lurk about her door."

Roderick bowed his head in subservience. "I would never dare, Father."

"Good. Come now. There is also an extra robe in the men's quarters ye can wear to dinner. And we'll expect ye to join us for all prayer times."

"I wouldna dream of doing otherwise."

Roderick could have sworn he heard the abbot snort. After changing, Roderick made his way into the cloister, walking beneath a wooden awning. Despite the covering of the awning, the wetness of the rain continued to cause his leg to ache. It was a pulsing that grew from deep in his bones and spread outward until he was gritting his teeth and sweat lined his spine.

Ballocks, but it hurt something fierce. They'd been going hard for days now, and not once had he stopped to rub the salve into his muscles like he normally did after a long day of working himself to the bone. The muscles around the scar tissue tensed, and he had to shift his weight to his other leg.

By the time Lady Greer appeared, he was leaning against a post, uncertain how he was going to make it through supper without retching.

"Are ye all right?" The space between her brows scrunched together as she examined him from head to toe.

Roderick managed a nod, certain if he spoke, the strain in his voice would give away the pain he was in. Sheer willpower alone allowed him to shove away from the post and offer his elbow. He concentrated on the heat of her hand wrapping around his upper arm and limped toward the refectory.

"Are ye certain ye're all right? Ye're limping."

Roderick grimaced. "'Tis fine." His tone was clipped, and so in a softer air, he said, "Dinna fash over it, lass."

From the side of his eye, he watched her nod, though she continued to study him. The heat of her intense gaze lingered on him even when they sat down.

Inside, his men had already joined the monks, each of them wearing a worn brown woolen robe, their faces somber as they peered down toward their empty bowls, waiting for them to be filled. He felt their moods straight to his gut. The weather, the incident in the river, the blasted Ross clan, and whoever else was coming after them... They were all exhausted, water-logged, and on edge.

Greer nudged him in the ribs, panic crossing her face. Roderick couldn't understand what was happening and glanced around the room, trying to figure it out. He realized at the last minute that she was likely worried about what exactly supper would be, given as she didn't eat meat or fish. He admired her fortitude and was truly surprised at how she could survive on the meager bits of food he'd seen her consume.

Even though it was meant to be a silent meal, he murmured under his breath, "If 'tis meat, I shall give the abbot another coin to see ye're given some bread and cheese, lass."

The expression of gratitude she gave him warmed him enough that he almost forgot about the pain in his leg.

They found their seats and sat quietly waiting. It appeared to be a vegetable and barley soup from what Roderick could see. He was pleased when it was poured into their bowls and he saw he was right. Greer sighed beside him, relieved.

Father Wesley gave a blessing for the food, and the men ate their soup in silence.

Roderick glanced at Greer to see how she was enjoying the soup only to catch the attention of the abbot, who glared at him quite fiercely until he returned his gaze to his own supper. The soup was flavored with spices and was quite good. It had soft carrots, bits of onion, turnips, and wilted greens. He could have had another helping, though seconds were not offered.

When the meal was complete, everyone carried their dishes into the kitchen and dipped them one by one into a rinsing bowl before drying them and stacking them on a wooden shelf.

Outside once more, whispers started as the men hurried into the church for their evening prayer.

"We must join them," Greer said. "Will ye be all right?"

"Aye." Roderick gritted his teeth as the pain in his thigh reminded him he needed to rest. He limped his way down the covered corridor in the cloister toward the arched opening into the chapel where music from the church's organ and harp were being played. His men knew better than to comment, but Greer was giving him a stern expression. He'd seen exactly the same expression on his governess's face as a lad.

"Your limp has grown worse."

He nodded grimly.

"Ye should rest. I'm certain the abbot will excuse ye if ye're not well."

Roderick flashed her an incredulous look. "Not well? I assure ye I am verra well. I'll rest tonight when we sleep."

"Have ye a salve at least?" She slowed her pace, presumably to continue their conversation longer, because he hated to think she did so in order to cater to his limp. Hell, if he needed to, he could run miles. Had done so before.

Monks funneled past them, but his own men also lingered behind, awaiting their laird's entry into the nave.

"I do. And if ye stop asking questions, I'll promise ye I'll apply it after the service."

She pursed her lips. "If ye warm it over the fire, the warmth will help to ease the pain."

"I will consider it."

She stopped moving altogether now, and when he stopped, exasperated, he caught her staring down at his leg and chewing her lower lip.

"Let me help, Grim."

Roderick blanched. Did she not realize what she'd just suggested? The wound was on his upper thigh. The very idea of having her hands on him sent his mind reeling in a direction it shouldn't, especially not in a house of God.

"I'm certain that is nae a good idea, my lady." He hoped his use of her title would help her understand the topic was not open for discussion.

Apparently, she did not. "Why not? I'm the one who injured ye. Should I not be the one to care for ye?"

Roderick shook his head firmly and quickened his pace away from her, ignoring the shooting pains in his thigh as he went. During the prayers, he worked hard not to rub at his thigh, hoping she'd think he was better. But he could tell by the looks she gave him from her bench in the section designated for noble women that she could see right through his lies.

When they left, she hurried toward him, even though he tried to speed ahead.

"My laird." She caught his elbow. "Let me at least warm the salve."

"Ye're not to come to the stables where I'm sleeping with the men, and I am not to come to your chamber. The abbot would send us all out into the night lamenting of our morals."

She squared her shoulders, and he waited for whatever argument she was about to give. If there was one thing he knew well about her, it was that she did not give up. "The kitchen then. Where anyone can walk in. Surely ye dinna think anything untoward will happen there?"

And somehow, he found himself nodding in agreement, because the idea of standing here and arguing more only made him sweat, and the pain in his leg was only growing worse.

Greer marched toward the kitchen with an air of importance and authority that she'd learned from her mother. Inside, she found one of the brothers, presumably the cook, hunched over a barrel. He jerked up and started to flail his arms in protest of her entry, but she set him with a glower she'd seen the Countess of Sutherland give when she was having a disagreement.

"Laird Roderick needs his salve warmed. He has a grave injury on his leg that needs tending. I ask ye kindly, Brother, to allow me to stoke the fire to warm a salve for my guardian."

The monk eyed her warily, and just when she thought he was going to deny her, he nodded without speaking.

Greer went to work stoking the fire, all while the cook stood off to the side watching her.

"I hope I am not interrupting your duties, Brother. Please dinna mind me."

He nodded again, and returned to the barrel he'd been sifting through before, pulling out one cupful of flour after another, presumably to make bread. While he did that, she found a pot, filled it with water to boil, and managed to find a spare rag she could soak with boiled water to soothe his leg prior to the salve. Preparing the injury with the heat always seemed to aid salves in doing their work, or at least that was her experience at Dunrobin.

Moments later, Roderick arrived, a small pot in hand, which Greer took from him. One whiff, and she could make out the strong contents of comfrey, calendula and ginger.

"'Tis strong stuff," he murmured.

"Aye, I hope it helps."

Leaving the cork off, she placed it on a stone within the hearth, inches from the flames. While they waited for the salve to warm, she dipped the rag in the boiling water with a spoon and then pulled it out and allowed it to cool only for a second or two before she wrung it out. Roderick remained standing, arms over his chest. He leaned against a wall and propped one foot over his ankle, as though he were simply waiting or relaxing.

"Why do ye nay sit?" Greer suggested. "Let your muscles relax. We'll put this rag on your leg to soothe ye afore the salve is ready."

"I've been sitting for days. And I dinna need soothing." The expression on his face was so full of obstinance, she could almost glimpse what he must have been like as a lad.

Greer refrained from tapping her foot or putting her hands to her hips. Instead, she decided she needed to approach him with softness. "Riding and sitting are not the same thing, my laird. Riding takes a lot of work with the legs. And your leg is angry with ye. Let's calm it down."

With the rag in one hand, Greer took Roderick by the elbow and felt him flinch beneath her touch. The cook eyed them from the corner where he was kneading dough for tomorrow's meal.

"Come sit down." She led him to the stool and gently shoved, surprised when he didn't balk and sat heavily.

With her hand out, she offered him the rag, which he took with a grumble and shoved beneath the borrowed monk's robe.

"Lay it out so it gets the most coverage."

He raised his brows, about to argue, but she pinned him with another of her sternest looks. He grumbled some more but did as she asked. Greer watched to make certain it was done right, but her face heated as the hem of his garment lifted up over his calf, then his knee, revealing the corded muscles of his lower thigh. Then his hands disappeared, keeping the wound hidden.

She whirled around, not wanting him to see her heated face—and also because she could feel the judgment of the monk behind her.

Peering into the jar, she saw the salve was slightly melted around the edges. "'Tis probably warm enough now."

"Aye."

She tapped her finger on the side of the jar and tested its warmth. It was too hot to pick up, so she fetched another small spoon on the shelf of supper dishes, promising the cook she'd wash it. She scooped out some of the contents of the jar and carefully carried the spoon heaped with salve back toward her patient. She nodded at his leg. "Dinna be shy. Show me."

Roderick raised his brow, crossed his arms over his chest, and didn't move. Greer groaned on the inside. Why did he have to be so difficult?

Smiling sweet as honey, she coaxed him as she would Jewel when the hound didn't want to obey. "Come on then, dinna be shy. Right now, I'm a healer. Would ye be shy with a healer?"

"Nay," he drawled out, and then glanced toward the cook.

"Would ye prefer he do it?" she whispered with a nod in the brother's direction.

"Nay." This response came quicker than the last.

"Then show me."

Muttering something under his breath, Roderick gripped the hem of his faded brown robe. She held her breath, forcing herself not to stare too hard as he slowly drew the fabric up over his thigh, exposing pure strength beneath bronzed skin and the slightest sprinkling of inky dark hair. He removed the wet rag.

And then she saw it—a mangled scar as wide as her palm.

She'd not realized how deep her spear had pierced his flesh. The skin was silvery in parts and an angry pink in others. With the scar so wide, it had to have pierced bone, and permanently damaged muscle. Her stomach plummeted. She'd done this to him. It was one thing for injuries to be caused in the field of battle or when protecting someone from harm, but an accident—and a silly one at that... She'd been so determined to win the fishing tournament, she'd not paid attention to what was happening around her until too late.

Throat tight, she managed to swallow around the lump and find her voice. "I am so sorry, Grim."

"Ye need not apologize again. I'm alive, and that is all that matters." There was a strength in his voice that reached across the space between them to stroke her conscience, but it did little to soothe her heart.

"Ye're lucky to be alive, and I am ashamed to have not been more careful." She dipped her finger, scooping up a glop of salve. "Did it pierce bone?"

"Aye."

Just as she'd guessed. The spear had gone deep into the bone and the wooden shaft had made the wound larger than if it had just been the actual iron spear tip.

"Ye've a powerful throw, my lady. Ye should be proud of that."

Greer gaped. "How can ye compliment me at a time like this?" She shook her head and spread a thin line of salve around the edges of the wound, the puckered skin softer than she imagined it would have been.

Roderick hissed a breath at the touch of her finger, and she felt him tense beneath her touch.

Greer winced. "Does it hurt?"

With lips clamped closed, he shook his head. Greer scooped out more salve and massaged it into the wound with Brother Cook watching from a distance, no longer rolling dough into loaves but perhaps feeling as though he could not leave them alone, either.

She retrieved more salve and spread it over the wound until she determined there was enough, and then she discarded the spoon. As she massaged, Roderick closed his eyes, and the firm press of his lips eased.

"Are ye still doing all right?"

He nodded. "It feels good."

She managed a small smile. "I'm glad."

The salve was warm and slick, and as she rubbed it into his wound, she gently rubbed at the tension in his thigh muscle. Within a few moments, he was visibly starting to unwind. The tightness in his jaw relaxed, his shoulders fell a little, and the furrow between his brows smoothed out.

Greer considered him, sitting there fully trusting her. There were not many moments like this where she'd been able to study him before. He was always awake when she rose in the mornings, and she was usually so caught up in the spark in his eyes that she could look nowhere else.

But now, with them both quiet, and his distracting orbs closed, she took her time to run her gaze over his finely arched brows, finding a thin, silvery scar that ran vertically between his brows and down over the bridge of his nose. His bone structure was exquisite. There really was no other way to describe it. Though his beard covered a good portion of his jaw, the angles were sharp, and so were those of his cheeks. His lips were full and wide, with a subtle dip at the center top, and she imagined what it would feel like to touch the place her own lips had been.

She had to stop herself from doing just that. So instead, she perused the thickness of his neck, the angles of his collarbones that faded into broad shoulders. Even in this monk's robe, he cut a fine figure.

"Tell me what ye see," he murmured.

She glanced back up, noting the lines of brown lashes still firmly on his cheeks. "Who says I'm looking at anything?"

"I can feel ye."

"That is because my hand is on your wound."

"I can feel your eyes on me."

"Ye're full of yourself."

He grinned, showing off a slight dimple in his right cheek beneath several days of growth. Fingers grazed over her knuckles, and then his grip stilled her movements.

"I feel much better now, lass. Thank ye." He flicked his gaze toward the monk and back, lowering his tone. "If we dinna leave soon, I fear the brother will raise the alarm."

Greer tried not to grin at that image. "It is no less than what ye deserve, Grim. To be sure, I feel obligated to do just this verra thing for the rest of our days. I had no idea how bad it was..."

His face darkened, growing serious. "That will be quite difficult given the distance between our lands."

Greer turned away, wiping her slick palm on a wet rag, and then making a pretense of searching out the cork for his salve jar, but only because she didn't want him to see her disappointment. Why did he have to point out how verra far they were from each other, as if she wasn't already aware?

Or was he making another point? That he wanted her to know he would not be bringing her back with him. That anything that happened between them would be folly. That the one kiss they'd shared would be the last.

With a nonchalant shrug, she handed him the corked salve. "Verra true. I suppose ye'll have to find someone else."

The furrow in his brow deepened, but she couldn't even try to imagine what it was he might be thinking at that moment. She needed to escape him. Escape the thoughts he put into her head. The cook stared them down as though he'd been watching two lovers.

One kiss did not make them so.

And she'd better start realizing that before she lost her head over it. Kissing Roderick had been incredible, even in his own words, but that didn't mean anything. *They* were not anything. In fact, there was no *they*.

The sooner she realized that, the better.

She tossed the rag into a pile of laundry by the back door of the kitchen and left him without a backward glance, making her way through the cloister and toward the spare chamber, ignoring the soft call of his voice behind her.

Chapter Fifteen

The bells woke Greer for the dawn service. Her eyes felt heavy, but no heavier than her mind. They were still at risk from the Ross clan, and closer than ever to the enemy's stronghold. She'd been restless all night, dreaming about Roderick. She relived that moment when her spear went through his flesh over and over and over again. Saw him thrashing in the water. The men jumping overboard to get him. How his pale face had stared hard at her in disbelief. The man was a powerhouse of strength. A lesser warrior would have lost consciousness with the wound and blood loss, but he hadn't. Mayhap it was because he'd been so busy staring her down, or maybe it was the cajoling the men had been doing at his having been pierced by her.

She'd made a jest, trying to make light of it, but he'd not found humor in it. In fact, after that, he'd not spoken to her until she'd woken up in his bed two years later. After barely two days in bed at Dunrobin, he'd risen like the dead and used a thick wooden staff to walk all the way from the castle to the MacCulloch *birlinn* and disappear from her life.

Sutherland warriors still talked about him, saying it was inhuman, godlike even, for him to have risen so quickly—and *walked*.

How could anyone not admire him after that, even if it had been a matter of pride that forced him from bed.

Still, no matter of accolades from the Sutherlands, which he probably to this day didn't know about, could lessen her guilt. There had been rumors he'd come to Dunrobin to ask for her hand, and despite a few quick flirtations, of which she'd shared with several visiting warriors, there'd been no other signs.

Oh, why did her heart ache so much to think about never seeing him again? It wasn't as if she was going to hop into her *currach* again and sail across the firth to end up on his beach.

The sound of the bell for morning services tolled again, and through the cracks in the shutter, she could just make out the hazy morning sun trying to push through gray clouds.

With a heavy heart, she climbed from bed and washed up, dressing in the same borrowed gown as the evening before as her MacCulloch wool was still slightly damp. Leaving the sparse room exactly as she'd found it, she followed the murmuring of the monks as they sang a hymn on the way to the chapel and took her seat in the empty row across from the men.

During the morning service, she tried to make eye contact with Roderick, but he avoided her gaze. When the service was over and they headed to the refectory, they did not speak other than formal greetings. He seemed distracted, but at least his limp had improved.

After breaking their fast in silence, Greer went back to her chamber, unsure of what else to do since the men had dispersed so quickly, Roderick with them. Was he avoiding her?

She changed into her now dry chemise and MacCulloch plaid and neatly laid the other one back on the bed for the next lady in need. She supposed it was probably too much to hope that her father would bring her one of her own gowns should they meet upon the road.

The rain had stopped at least. She looked out the tiny window in her chamber and could see a slight bit of blue marking the sky. Perhaps their ride today would be without rain. A knock sounded at her door, startling her. She leapt back from the window and opened the door.

To her surprise, her father, dressed in Sutherland colors, his golden-silvery hair pulled back in a queue, filled the entrance to her chamber.

"Daughter." His voice was gruff, brow furrowed. "What have ye gotten yourself into this time?"

Despite his rebuke and gruffness, she tossed herself into his arms, never so glad to see him in all her life, except for perhaps when he'd come home from battle. "Da! When did ye get here? I didna see ye from the window."

"Only just now." His voice was softer now, and he pressed a kiss to her forehead. "Glad I am that ye're alive. We thought ye dead. Your poor mother searched for ye to the point of collapsing."

"Nay! Is she all right?"

"Aye, she's fine. As soon as we got MacCulloch's message, she packed up a satchel and sent me on my way." Her father wrapped his arms around her, and she breathed in his familiar scent.

"I'm so sorry. For the rest of my life, I will repent."

"Ye scared us half to death. Look at my hair, 'tis nearly all silver now. And your mama..." He shook his head. "At least three new lines etched around her eyes. But I dinna think a lifetime of penance is necessarily."

Greer shook her head. "I will never board a boat again, on that I swear."

Magnus Sutherland held her at arm's length. "Laird MacCulloch's brother, Jon, said as much. But, Greer, ye canna give up on the thing ye love so much."

"But it almost killed me, Da, and I have broken your trust by following my heart before. And I've put the MacCullochs in danger. Oh, Mama is probably so angry with me, do ye think she'll ever forgive me? Will ye?"

"Ye're already forgiven, sweet lass. And ye canna let a little thing like death scare ye. To have faced death and survived is to have really lived."

Greer bit her lip. "Da, ordinarily, I would have agreed with ye, but in this, I canna."

"Walk with me outside. I think the fresh air will help."

"Fresh air willna change my mind."

"If there's one thing I know about ye, daughter, it is that ye rarely change your mind. But there is something else I know about ye, too, and that is that ye never give up and ye love adventure."

Greer paused on the threshold, searching her father's face. "I'm afraid, Da. I dinna know what I want, or who I want to be."

A smile softened his features. "On the contrary child, out of all my offspring, ye know the most. Ye just have to search inside to find the answer."

Those words, said to her not too long ago by Roderick, rocked her to the core. Even when Roderick had told her before, she'd known it, but she'd not yet had the time to really sit and listen to what her heart told her. As soon as they returned to Sutherland, she was going to make good on a vow to herself to search within.

Greer slipped her hand through her father's arm and walked with him to the cloister where she could now see several Sutherland men, including her brother Liam, who was a younger version of her own father with sharp green eyes and golden hair.

"Brat," he murmured against her ear as he pulled her into a tight hug. "Glad I am that ye're still breathing." Then he tugged her hair.

Greer pulled away, stuck out her tongue, and pinched him on the back of his muscled arm. Liam gave an exaggerated shout, and she rolled her eyes. Her gaze fell on Roderick, and the laughter left her.

Roderick gave her a curt nod, devoid of any attachment, as though he truly had been only her escort these past few days and nothing more. Disappointment flooded her, and she glanced toward the ground, not wanting to show anyone how she felt, or even give the slightest hint to her father of what might have transpired.

"I didna expect to meet ye so soon upon the road," Roderick said as he took a firm grip of her father's arm in greeting.

"Aye, well, when Jon arrived and told us what happened, I already had a *birlinn* prepared and was ready to search the seas again. As soon as I saw Jon, the first thing he said was Greer is alive." He glanced at Greer. "Your little skiff surfaced on shore only an hour or so before Jon arrived. We took our leave immediately, in hopes of catching ye upon the road. We've been following for days."

"And Jewel?"

"She is with Blair, and I'm certain both they and your mother are eager for your return." Her father nodded toward Roderick. "I can take her home from here. My gratitude for saving her life. A reward will be waiting for ye upon your arrival back at Gleann Mórinnse."

Greer's heart fell. She'd barely been prepared to leave Roderick in a few days' time. But now? Her mouth went dry. Liam elbowed her lightly in the ribs, and she glanced up at him to see he had a questioning expression on his face.

She just shook her head and tried to work the emotions from her face. But saints, it was hard to do such a thing. Not when she felt so strongly.

"With all due respect, my laird," Roderick was saying, "there was something I was coming to Sutherland to discuss with ye. And I think once ye hear it, ye may wish us to continue on with ye."

Magnus glanced down at her, concern etched in his brow. Greer hoped he would indeed escort them, but then as soon as she recalled just what Roderick would want to speak to her father about, her countenance fell once more. The Sutherlands might have arrived, but that didn't mean the Ross warriors weren't still in pursuit.

In fact, they could show up at any minutes.

A shiver of fear went up her spine. They needed to go. She knew that. "I can help ready the horses," she said.

"I'll help ye." The expression on Liam's face brooked no argument, and judging from his stubborn streak, he was going to try to get out of her whatever it was he thought she was hiding.

Which of course, was a lot.

The two men agreed and walked away. If the circumstances had been different, she might have been watching Roderick walk away to ask for her hand in marriage. But as it was, she was certain now more than ever that any dream of being with him had been just that—a fantasy.

SEEKING a private spot in the nave of the church, Roderick wasted no time in telling Magnus Sutherland about what had transpired with the Ross clan and the information he'd gleaned from the shepherd.

"We thought ye were Ross men when ye were following us. If we'd had any idea it was ye, we would have waited. As it was, we were being pursued on both sides, unsure if both caravans were enemies. Glad I am to be aligned with ye."

"Aye, our alliance is strong, ye need not worry on that account. Hell, among my men, ye're a legend."

Roderick snorted. "Ye jest."

Magnus chuckled and shook his head. "I strive to be talked of as ye have. They still talk about how ye got up and walked all the bloody way to the pier after getting your leg nearly torn off by a spear."

Roderick kept his face void of any expression, but his chest did swell with pride. All this time, he'd though the men judged him weak. They thought him a legend? Impossible.

"A leader must remain a pillar of strength, aye?"

"Ye are that. An honor it is to be aligned with ye." Magnus clapped him on the back. "And an honor it will be to go into battle with ye against the Ross men."

"Sooner than ye may have thought. Ye were coming from the east, and the other party is coming from the west—Ross country."

"Bloody hell. I thought we'd put that beast to rest."

"As did we all."

Magnus let out a low growl. "We need to get my daughter back to Sutherland. From there, we can form a plan of how to deal with the Rosses, gather our allies, and once and for all put them down."

"I fear we'll have more trouble this time now that she's wed a powerful English lord."

"'Tis nothing we havena dealt with afore now. She was married to an English lord a decade ago, as flaccid as he was."

Roderick chuckled. "Aye, he was that. But he followed her lead. Now she seems to be following her new man."

Magnus scowled and crossed his arms. "That is a terrifying thought, someone more scheming and evil than Ina Ross?"

"Exactly my fears, sir."

Magnus dropped his head and let out a disappointed sigh. "The task before us will not be easy, but with all of our allies, we will defeat them."

"Aye. Ye have the full support of the MacCullochs."

"We'll beat them this time once and for all."

"With relish."

Magnus regarded him with an expression Roderick couldn't quite decipher. "I canna thank ye enough for what ye did for Greer. How did ye find her?"

Roderick grew somber. "In an odd way, we have Ina to thank for that. I retrieved some livestock the Rosses stole in a raid, and after, I went down to the beach to think, as I do after every battle. A massive dog barreled toward me and then ran back toward something rolling in the surf. It was Lady Greer." He could still see her lying there. So still. So blue. "She wasna breathing, so I helped her get the water out of her lungs. Then I carried her back to Gleann Mórinnse to get her warmed and fed."

He waited for the Sutherland to ask just how he'd gotten her warm, but the man said nothing, nodding and rubbing at his chin instead.

"I could have lost her," the older warrior murmured. "Lost her because I pushed her into a tight corner where she doesna belong."

Roderick didn't know what to say, and he was fairly certain the laird's words weren't meant for him anyway.

"Daughters are both the hardest work and the most pleasurable," Magnus said with a subtle shake of his head. "I hope someday ye're blessed enough to know this."

An uncomfortable tightness filled Roderick's chest. How was he supposed to protect a daughter, a treasured child, when he hadn't been able to protect his own family?

"I ken what ye're thinking." Magnus stared at Roderick with an intensity that left him unnerved.

It was on the tip of his tongue to challenge the older warrior, how could he possibly know what Roderick was thinking? But he kept his mouth shut, waiting. Listening.

"I lost my parents at a young age," he said. "Had to raise my brothers and sister on my own. There is a guilt that comes with loss, is there nae? And I can see ye harbor guilt like I did."

Roderick swallowed against the tightness in his throat. He was a grown man for goodness sake. Why did he feel like he had the control of an adolescent over his emotions? But it didn't matter. Whenever anyone spoke of Jessica, the same thing happened. A cloud of guilt. The pain of loss.

Magnus pressed his hand to Roderick's shoulder. "I ken ye've the support of your clan, and a brother that'd give his life for ye, but know this, son, we are allies, and if ye're in need of something, ye need only ask." He gave a mirthful grin. "And I'm nae only saying this because my daughter nearly killed ye." The smile lines flattened into a serious countenance. "But I am saying it because ye saved her life." The man glanced over his shoulder in the direction of the cloister, though they couldn't see Greer from where they stood. "She is my heart. Of all our children, I think she takes the most after me. I'd be lost without her."

Lost without her. Wasn't that exactly how Roderick felt at the idea of leaving her behind?

"Despite the past," Roderick said pointedly, "I'd not have walked away from her on the beach."

"Ye're a good man. The Highlands are a tough place, and there are plenty of others who would have done so."

"And suffered the wrath of God, country, and the Sutherlands for it."

"God, aye, for who would have known besides Him?" Magnus's eyes drooped for a moment before the fleeting mien of sadness left him.

Greer's father spoke the truth. Roderick could have walked away from the beach, let her drift back out to sea to sink below its depths, but he'd not done that. He couldn't. Even knowing who she was, letting her die had never been an option. For despite their history, the lass had somehow managed to dig a hole in his cold chest and camp out there for years. There wasn't a day that had gone by where he hadn't thought of her.

Magnus squeezed his shoulder again, his grip firm and reassuring. "I suppose I'll be parting with her soon enough though, albeit through marriage and not death. At least I can hope."

Marriage?

Of course Greer was going to get married. In fact, she might already be betrothed. It wasn't as if Roderick had asked. Hell, there could be another man out there who might come to call Roderick out when he found out about their kiss and attempt to run him through with a sword. He wouldn't be surprised, for he'd do the very same thing. He'd hate to take that man's life.

Through a tightening in his jaw, he managed to say, "He's a lucky man."

Magnus raised a brow and studied Roderick's face intently again, not giving away his own thoughts and leaving Roderick to guess a hundred different things.

The older warrior grunted. "Aye, he is."

Bloody hell! Magnus Sutherland had all but confirmed that Greer was betrothed. Lost to him forever. The tightness in his throat returned with a vengeance, and an ache filled his chest as though a boulder had fallen from a cliff and flattened him at the bottom.

It wasn't until that moment, when he realized that Greer belonged to somebody else, that he realized just how much he'd wanted her to belong with him. Beside him for life. Kissing her every night, and waking up to that spirited smile every morning. A life with Greer would never be dull, and yet when times were tough, he knew he could count on her.

The struggles he'd been dealing with these past few days suddenly seemed so menial. He realized he didn't actually care about all the things he'd worried about as long as Greer was by his side. They could conquer the world together.

But, nay, he would not be doing the conquering with her. There was someone *else* who would. Ballocks. He was gutted. What was this? Why was he so torn up?

Because he cared for her. More than he wanted to admit.

Magnus didn't seem to notice the crushing blow he'd just dealt. "As for Ina Ross and her band of bullies, dinna fash, Roderick. Together, we'll take care of it."

Roderick mustered through his discontent. "Aye, I'm with ye. All the MacCullochs are. The Highlands have been a place of peace these last few years, even longer from the likes of Ina Ross."

"'Twas her that caused your cousin to suffer, too, aye?" Magnus asked.

Roderick nodded. "Aye, but Emilia is verra happily wed now."

"A bairn now, too, aye?"

"More than one, I believe. We went to the lad's christening last year."

Magnus grinned. "Daughters are your heart, but sons carry on your legacy."

"I should think daughters carry a legacy, too, no? Did ye nae just say that Greer favors your spirit most?"

Magnus glanced at him, a nostalgic smile on his lips. "Aye, ye're right."

Pounding Roderick on the back, he steered him out of the nave and back toward their party. It was time they got back on the road, before their enemies caught up—if it wasn't too late already.

Chapter Sixteen

S omething had changed, and Greer wasn't sure what it was, but it was very evident in the way Roderick was treating her. He spoke only in clipped tones, and while they'd ridden together the last few days, today when they were readying the horses, he brought her mare out and handed the reins over to her father with only a nod in greeting.

Of course, she'd not expected to continue riding with him now that her father was present. For some reason it felt...wicked. And perhaps that was because every time she'd been so close to him, there had been an intimacy there that she wanted to savor. Every time he'd put his arm around her waist, she'd imagined the way he'd held her when he kissed her senseless.

Aye, perhaps it was a good thing she was riding her own mount. But at least he could have pulled her aside to tell her why. Or at the very least, he could have managed more than a nod. For heaven's sake, they'd been sleeping curled up in each other's arms for days, he'd saved her life, and now he was acting as though they were virtual strangers.

She mounted on her own and rode beside her father, and when they stopped to rest the horses, she sat with her brother Liam. It was not of her own choosing. She would have happily tried to have a conversation with Roderick, but any time she drew near, even if only to ask how his leg was, he abruptly turned away from her. It was damn vexing.

By the time they stopped to sup and make camp near the Conon River, it was so incredibly evident he was avoiding her that even her brother noticed, which only managed to increase her mortification. Had Grim only been using her? Was she simply another conquest? If she'd continued to pursue their kisses, would he have dumped her off at Sutherland sans her maidenhood?

"Still mad at ye for the spear, I see." Liam shouldered her, which caused her to tip over from where she sat on a log. He caught her at the last minute. "Jumpy, lass."

Greer frowned and popped a foraged berry into her mouth. She chewed thoughtfully, watching Roderick across the camp. He leaned against a tree, his arms crossed over his broad chest as he spoke with deep concentration to her father. Even in her irritation, she admired his striking features, his height, the muscles of his calves, the way the light caught the red in his chestnut hair.

Chewing a berry into pulp, she swallowed hard, trying to sound like she didn't care when she spoke. She shrugged disinterestedly. "I had not thought it before, but I suppose he is."

"Did he ignore ye the whole of your journey? I bet that drove ye mad." Liam wiggled his brows.

Och, how she would like to pluck every hair from her teasing brother's wagging eyebrows in that moment.

Greer lifted her chin and said quite seriously, "In fact, quite the opposite."

Liam straightened, his eyebrows still raised but no longer moving. "Has he taken liberties?"

Greer almost choked on a berry. This was not something she wanted to discuss with her brother. And she supposed the two of them would have differing opinions on the definition of *taken liberties*, for she'd freely given the liberties he'd accepted. And was a kiss really taking liberties? To her it had always seemed as though taking liberties was much more than that. A greater sin. An assault. Most maiden lassies would have thought themselves wanton for even allowing a man to cup their cheek and gaze into their eyes, whereas Greer had readily accepted it and practically begged for more.

Liam's shoulder bumped against hers. "Greer?"

The note of exasperation in his tone did not go unnoticed by her, and given her brother would feel the need to protect her and her reputation if she told him the truth, she snorted. "Nay, of course not. He's a warrior, not a rogue."

To this, her brother simply raised a skeptical brow—and how he got them any higher, she had no idea. She'd never seen anyone with eyes and brows as expressive, and irritating, as his. "Not a rogue? All men our age are rogues."

Greer groaned on the inside, trying her best not to stomp her foot. "Well, I shall have ye know that while I was at his castle, I didna see any of his maids or servants or clanswomen tossing themselves at his feet begging for another night in his bed, nor did I ever feel as though I'd wake to find him fumbling beneath my skirts." *Though I did wake to find myself naked beside him the first morning, and our limbs tangled every morning thereafter.* That, she kept to herself.

A low rumble left her brother's throat that was half-laugh, half-growl. "Greer!"

"Dinna act the modest lad now, Liam, ye're the one who brought it up, and while I may be your wee sister, I am not so naïve as all that. Virgin I may be, but stupid, I am nae."

Laughter danced in her brother's eyes. "Being stupid and being ladylike are two different things. I know I've heard our *lady* mother say the same thing to ye."

"Ye think a lady canna talk about fumbling beneath skirts? Ha! Do ye wish your bride to be flat as a skewered fish on your wedding night and for the rest of your life thereafter?"

Liam covered his face with his hand in disbelief. "I canna believe ye just said that."

Greer shrugged. Why hold back now? "Ye've known me all your life. When have I been known to not speak what was on my mind?"

"Never," he groaned. "And now I can see exactly why Grim wouldna have attempted to take liberties with ye."

Greer's mouth fell open in offense. "And why is that? Ye think because I speak my mind, and plainly so, that he wouldna wish to tangle with me?"

"Good God, if mother heard us speaking right now..." Liam fell with exaggerated motion backward.

Greer took the opportunity to punch him softly in his belly. "Mother is not here. 'Tis ye and I, and ye're my big brother. I should feel safe to speak my mind with ye."

Liam rolled his head toward her. "Ye're safe, trust me. But I'm nae so sure about any man ye may align yourself to." He braced himself for another playful blow, but she refused to give him the satisfaction.

"Men..." She popped another berry into her mouth and chewed. "Did ye hear about the great feast Da is planning?"

"Aye." Liam sat up and stole a berry from her pile.

"I'm to be auctioned off to the highest bidder. Like a sheep."

"Ye're no sheep."

"Fine, like cattle then."

"Not as docile as that, either, Sister. Besides, I dinna think 'twill ye being auctioned off; rather the other way around."

"Exactly."

"Why not choose Grim, then?" He nudged his chin in the direction of the man in question. "Ye've spent more time with him than any other, plus, ye know he'll not kill ye."

Greer tossed her head back and laughed.

"Ye laugh, but I'm serious." Indeed, her brother's face was quite grave. "I worry about that."

That only made Greer laugh all the more. "Why? Ye think Da would allow me to wed a man who might kill me?"

"Nay, but I think ye've enough...spirit, that it may warrant such an outcome."

Greer pushed her brother's shoulder and tossed a berry at his face, which he caught in his mouth with a wink. "Ye're a maggot."

Liam chuckled. "Well, this maggot says 'tis a good match, wee sister."

She glanced over toward Roderick again, feeling an achy pang of longing in her chest. At that moment, he glanced her way, and her stomach dropped somewhere on the ground beneath her when his blue eyes locked on hers. How did he have the power with one gaze to make her tingle all over? The corner of her mouth lifted in a smile, but then he turned away without so much as a twitch of his lips.

A dejected sigh escaped her. "He doesna want me. He canna even look at me or sit near me."

"'Haps he doesna know that he wants ye. Men are idiots. Trust me, I'm one of them."

Greer wanted to say that she knew her statement to be fact, because Roderick had basically told her such. He'd kissed her only once and then told her that such could not happen again. And as soon as her father had arrived, he'd thrust her off and ignored her. If the man wanted her, wouldn't he at least make an effort to show it? She might be naïve in the ways of courtship, but she wasn't naïve when it came to people's emotions toward each other.

"I'm quite certain he knows exactly what he wants, and that isna me."

"Then he's a fool," Liam said. "Oh, and I brought ye something." He leapt up from his spot, marched over toward his horse, and riffled through his saddlebag. When he returned, he had something wrapped in a cloth package. "From Mama."

Greer took the extended package and carefully unwrapped it to find a hunk of her favorite cheese and *four* mushroom pasties. The crust was crumbly at the edges and soft in the center, just the way Greer liked it.

"Oh, my... This is bliss." She closed her eyes as she bit into the buttery crust, the delicious, savory sauce a reprieve from her diet of bannock and berries.

"I thought ye'd be happy about that, even if 'tis a few days old."

"A few days, a week, the flavor is still incredible. How will I survive without Mama's cooking?"

"Ye'll have to learn."

Greer stuck out her tongue. "Ye recall what happened the last time I tried to cook, do ye nae?"

Liam started to laugh again so hard that Greer was tempted to throw something at him to get him to stop, but the only thing in her hands was her food, and she wasn't wasting that.

"What are the two of ye laughing about?"

Greer glanced up to see that her father and Roderick were standing before them, and she'd not even seen them approach.

"This donkey," she said, hooking her thumb over her shoulder toward her brother, "is having a grand old time at my expense."

"Da, do ye remember when Greer thought it a good idea to try and make Mama a birthday supper?" Liam could barely get the words out he was laughing so hard.

Magnus chuckled. "Och, aye, but that was not a pretty sight."

Greer's face started to heat, and she flicked an embarrassed glance toward Roderick. "It wasna as bad as the two of ye make it out to be."

Magnus sat down and indicated for Roderick to join them. He was again staring at her, but there was an iciness in his glittering blue gaze. What could he possibly be upset with her about?

"Tell the story," Magnus goaded his son. "I'm certain MacCulloch would be happy to know he's not the only one of Greer's victims."

"Da, nay!" Greer sent her brother a frosty glare. "Dinna say a word."

Now Magnus was chuckling, and when she glanced once more at Roderick, the glitter in his eyes had hardened. "Do tell, Lady Greer."

No one else seemed to notice the coolness in his tone, but she did. After having spent so many days with him, and having spoken to him on an intimate level, she could now tell the difference in his moods easily. Besides, there was a big difference between the heated tension she'd been wading through for days versus this aloof and stony man who'd taken over her Grim.

Och, *her* Grim? In no uncertain terms, he'd made it very clear he was not hers.

Greer shoved a large bite of pasty into her mouth and chewed. She started to talk around the large mouthful of food, so the words were purposefully muffled, but Liam and her father both protested.

"Come now, tell the story right."

Greer pretended she didn't hear and took a long swallow of water, and then with great dramatics, agreed. "I wanted to make my mother's mushroom pasties, but as a surprise for her birthday. So I foraged for the mushrooms myself."

"First mistake," Liam piped in.

Greer pinned him with a glower. "Hush, brother. I was only ten or twelve at the time, so 'tis not like I had a vast amount of experience. Not like Strath's wife." She glanced at Roderick and explained about her eldest brother's wife and her uncanny ability to find edible things in the forest and make a delicious meal out of them. "I am not her, and never will be. In any case, I found some mushrooms, got some eggs from our chickens, and went into the kitchen, where I rummaged to find flour and butter. The flour was a bit off, chafed my skin even, but I didn't think anything of it until I lit the fire and started to bake my pasties."

"'Twas lye powder she found! On top of that, the mushrooms were poisonous! She quite literally baked my mother a poison pie. But that's not the worst of it." Liam was cackling again.

Greer considered shoving her brother off the log he was perched on.

"When Cook found me, the kitchen was filled with smoke, to which I'd already succumbed. He found the source of the fire, but the strength of the poison from the smoking lye burned his eyes. And he stumbled around blind, screaming for help until several other servants roused from where they slept in the great hall and came to our rescue."

By now, her father and brother were in fits of laughter, but Roderick had barely cracked a smile. Even though no one else noticed his stony expression, she did, and it made her mortification all the more complete. She avoided eye contact with him as she finished the last bite of her pasty and then held out the cloth to him.

"These are my mother's pasties, and I assure ye they're nae poisonous. Would ye care to try one?"

Roderick started to protest, but her father cut in. "Aye, ye must try some, even just a bite. Though once ye have a bite, I dinna think ye'll be able to stop. Even after a few days, my Arbella's cooking satisfies."

He muttered an agreement.

With Roderick's gaze on hers, he brought the pasty to his mouth and took a bite. As his teeth cut through it, and his lips clamped on the crust, Greer had the distinct impression it was his way of biting into her. She suppressed a shudder, wracking her brain to figure out what she'd done to offend him, and coming up empty. Unless he was still mad that she'd walked away from him in the priory kitchen.

That could be it, although she'd assume he would move on from that fairly quickly. It wasn't as if walking away from him had been worse than arguing with him in front of his men, and he'd forgiven her easily for that. It seemed like something deeper troubled him, and she desperately wished she could pull him aside to ask him. But doing so would only garner the attention of her brother and father, who were both watching her like a mother hawk guarding her nest.

The rest of the night was quiet. Some men took shifts, while the rest of them lay down to sleep. But Greer had a hard time falling asleep. The ground was harder than it had been the previous nights. She was cold despite the two extra plaids she'd been given. She missed the warmth of Roderick behind her. When he was not at his watch station, he perched himself against a tree on the opposite end of camp —as far away from her as he could possibly get.

Chapter Seventeen

Roderick woke with a jolt.

He jerked forward, hand instantly on the sword at his hip, expecting to see a hoard of Ross men either descending upon them, or to feel the steely edge of a dagger at his neck. But there was nothing save for the sweat trickling down his back and the hairs on his arms raised on end.

The camp was mostly quiet, with warriors sleeping huddled around the banked fire, and Greer curled up in a ball. Soft snores reached him, and the occasional snort or scuffing hoof from a horse. The few Sutherland and MacCulloch warriors on watch were standing at attention, their gazes focused on something beyond their sight. They were camped in the woods with no discernable clearing, but it was enough of a good spot that they could hide from their enemies.

Dawn was just awakening. The sky was hazy and pink, the sun a ball of fire on the horizon, and a mist curled around their feet. An ordinary sight in the Highlands, but somehow, this morning, it felt like a warning.

A drop of water fell from a leaf above him, splashing on his nose, but it was only the remnants of rain from the day before mixed with morning dew. The rain and clouds had gone, thank the saints, because his leg had ached something fierce by the time he'd gone to bed last night. The massage Greer had given him had helped him sleep through the night they slept at the priory, but as soon as dawn had broken, a dull ache had started up again. After a full day's ride, he'd been ready to tear into anyone who spoke to him.

Lord, he'd even been a bear when she'd told the charming story of the poison pie. He'd not even been able to quip that he'd be sure to run in the other direction if she ever offered him a homemade meal. The ache in his leg and the knowledge she was already taken by someone else left him in a murderous rage that was barely banked beneath his skin.

With his free hand, Roderick rubbed the drip of water from where it dangled on his nose. He wasn't certain what had woken him other than a warrior's instinct, for there was nothing that seemed to have alerted him or his men, and yet his skin prickled, and clearly the men were also aware of something.

Roderick came swiftly to his feet and pulled out his claymore at the same time the men on watch did the same. A glance at Greer assured him that she was safe, eyes wide with fear. Even from this distance, he could see her throat bobbed as she swallowed. Och, he wanted to go forward and comfort her himself, but he had to be satisfied with her father and brother providing that.

He raised his finger to his lips, indicating she should be quiet, and she silently nodded, coming to stand on her own.

With his gaze outside their camp, he sidestepped slowly to the first warrior around the campfire and nudged him awake with his foot. The man was instantly alert and rousing the rest of those still asleep.

He bobbed his head toward Greer to Angus, indicating without words that the warrior was to protect her at all costs, even though she had the protection of her family and clan. Even if he was angry she'd not told him she was betrothed to another, he couldn't begrudge her safety. Besides, she'd not promised him anything, nor indicated to him any sort of attachment other than kissing and needing him for a protector. But now was not the time to be thinking of such things.

Knowing that Angus would take care of Greer, Roderick headed to where Magnus stood, claymore drawn and gripped in his two massive hands. The morning air was chilled, and the warriors' breaths came out in clouds to match the mist around their ankles.

Then he heard it. Swift footfalls. They were quiet, but the sheer number of them combined grew loud and distinctive to a warrior's ear. They were coming from one direction, or at least that was what it seemed like. Even still, the MacCulloch and Sutherland men formed a circle, swords drawn, and in the center were Liam and Angus with Greer. They'd covered her head with a plaid, but it was still obvious she was a woman.

There was no time for her to be whisked away, and he wouldn't have wanted her to be anyway since they were about to be ambushed, and there was no telling where the enemy was.

No one spoke. Everyone stood still and listened as the whistles in the wind picked up the hurried steps and the faint whisper of armed bodies cutting through air.

They were coming, any second. Tension crackled the air. The hair on the back of his neck prickled. Gooseflesh rose on his skin, and from every angle he could sense the eyes of the enemy on him. The men held themselves motionless, waiting. This was not the first time he'd fought beside a Sutherland, and though he was a laird in his own right, Magnus Sutherland was an earl who had fought beside Robert the Bruce for longer than Roderick had been alive, so he would follow the great man's lead.

It seemed the world was still and quiet, and then a sudden piercing whistle came from the left, and with it, men were leaping from what seemed like thin air, their swords raised, eager and angry faces painted with black pitch. The Ross colors of their plaid were unmistakable. Though they'd yet to cross onto Ross lands, they were close enough.

"Hold the circle," Magnus bellowed.

And the men complied, keeping the fighting sphere tight, unbreakable, even as they fought off the attack. The air sang with the sounds of iron clashing against iron, and moaned with the sounds of men falling.

"Where is your laird?" Roderick bellowed. "At home with her *Sasse-*

nach lover?" He crushed a man with a hacking blow. "Does she not command her men? Ye're all traitors to your country. Ye might as well flee to England where ye belong." Another warrior rushed him, and their swords clashed hard enough to jar the length of his arm.

His words were meant to goad, to insult, and did the trick, drawing more warriors from the woods like ants on thick, golden honey.

While fighting, Roderick tried to keep an ear perked for sounds coming from Greer. Despite her having already been claimed by another man, he couldn't help feeling concern for her. He cared about her more than he wanted to admit. More than he should. And damn it all, he was going to make sure she made it out alive, even if it was only to fall into the arms of another.

Three Rosses rushed him, their swords raised, but Grim hadn't earned his name simply because of his frown. He may not have fought for many years, but he was known as the bringer of death, and he did it with a face masked to match. Roderick let out a war cry that thundered against the trees. He swung his claymore with all his power, cutting through one, slicing into another, before he yanked it back to hit the third in the center of his forehead with the butt of his sword. He kicked the bodies away, making room for the next onslaught.

The men continued to come at them, but the line held until the enemy stopped coming as swiftly as they'd arrived. The eerie silence was deafening. And the prickles on Roderick's skin remained.

They might have ceased their attack, but they were still out there.

"Dinna run!" Magnus shouted to the forest. "For we will find ye."

The MacCulloch and Sutherland men stood in formation for a quarter of an hour, but there was nothing but the silence of the forest to answer. It would seem the Ross men had retreated, but Roderick didn't trust it. Nothing where the Ross clan was concerned could be trusted. Even a truce or a signed treaty.

"They'll be back," he murmured. "That was only the beginning." He swiped the bloody blade of his claymore against lichen on a tree to clean it.

"Aye. I've a feeling ye're right. Let's get across the River Conon. We'll be on Ross lands then, and we need to make haste to leave their lands. The farther we can get today, the better. For the longer we remain where they can claim we trespass, the more danger we're in." Magnus nodded toward the west. "Their castle, Dingwall, is not far from here, and they've got enough reinforcements to supply the English king with his own traitorous guard."

"If not more," Roderick mused.

"Aye," Magnus agreed. "Bloody bastards."

The men gathered quickly, mounting their horses. Magnus asked that Angus continue his protection of Greer by taking her onto his horse, and Roderick found it hard not to argue—even if it made him jealous.

They picked their way slowly, weapons drawn, so as to hear any approach from an enemy. The scouts rode ahead, circling back to keep them informed of any sightings. Just as swiftly as they'd attacked, the men had disappeared. But Roderick was certain they followed. They had to be following. There was no way the Ross men would have recognized the MacCulloch and Sutherland colors, and not attempt a second attack. Perhaps they'd gone back for more reinforcements, though they could have kept on fighting with the numbers they'd had. An increase in enemy cavalry, however, would likely crush the small MacCulloch and Sutherland contingent, no matter that Roderick could state with confidence they were the most skilled warriors in the Highlands. Even a great wolf could be taken if enough foxes bit into its flesh.

Throughout their quick escape, he snuck glances at Greer. Her expression never changed, nor did her stance. She kept her eyes straight ahead, and her back rigid. And he was thankful to see that her stance was not as relaxed in Angus's lap as it had been on his own.

When they arrived at the River Conon, the water was much smoother than their passage at Beauly, and they were able to find a spot that was not as deep as their previous crossings. They made it across swiftly. Instead of stopping to dry before well-built fires, they continued, soaked through to the bone. It would be a damned miracle if none of them fell ill from it. But being ill and being dead were two very different situations. He'd take the former over the latter any day.

The sun shone down on them. Though it wasn't particularly warm, it helped to dry their clothes as they rode.

They trekked for hours, until the late afternoon when the horses needed to stop. Luckily, they'd reached the edges of Sutherland lands, and the threat of the Rosses crossing paths with them had grown smaller, though the risk was not completely gone.

They stopped in a small village. Magnus wanted his daughter to sleep under a roof and for all of them to have a hot meal. Roderick completely agreed. The men needed to dry out their water-logged clothes and get a real meal in their bellies. They'd been going full force for days and then had to flee after a battle. The rush of battle had powered their flight, but it wouldn't last.

The local tavern offered Lady Greer one room, and her father another, though he declined, preferring to sleep with his men. When that same room was offered to Roderick, he also declined.

They took up all the benches in the tavern, squeezing around the tables. Those who couldn't fit stood. The proprietors worked as hard as they could to gather supplies in the town to give the men ale, a stew, and fresh-baked brown bread.

"Highland hospitality at its finest," he said to Magnus.

"Sutherland hospitality."

"The measure of a leader is his people's respect, aye?"

"Aye."

"I am honored." Roderick bowed.

"Och, stand up."

Roderick grinned, trying to lighten the mood. "They may call me a legend for walking with my leg wide open, but I dinna do the moniker justice when compared to ye."

Magnus clapped him on the back in a manly show of appreciation. "I like ye, lad. I really do."

Roderick chuckled. "Glad I am to hear it."

They clinked their mugs of ale, and dug into their stew, but the meal felt oddly empty without the smiling face of Greer and her jovial chatter nearby.

The lass had remained in her room to sup. Roderick had overheard a bath had been ordered for her along with her meal. If anyone deserved it, 'twas she. He was surprised she'd not completely collapsed in a heap yet. And indeed, as she'd climbed the steps in the tavern an hour before, he'd watched the way her knuckles had whitened as she gripped the rail. She was exhausted. If he could, he'd suggest they stay a few days until she had time to recuperate. But there was no time. Likely, she'd sleep for a fortnight when they finally reached Dunrobin.

There was a pang in his chest at not being able to join her. To talk to her. To ask why she'd not mentioned her betrothed to him. Did she think he'd judge her? Or had she avoided the topic on purpose in hopes he'd never find out? Was it too much to hope that she'd kept it hidden because she wasn't happy with the arrangement?

Was marrying someone else the reason she'd escaped her house to begin with? He wanted to pose all of these questions to her father as well. Did Magnus Sutherland know why his daughter had risked her life for one last thrill?

But with his daughter out of earshot, the man was laughing and jesting boisterously with his men and the MacCullochs, and he deserved it. The poor laird had thought his daughter was dead, had found out his old enemy had resurrected herself, and then had been attacked on the road. The last thing he needed was to be interrogated by a man who had no claim, nor place to do so.

He listened while the men joked and a few strummed on a lyre they passed around and chanted a bawdy ballad. Others pulled out their sets of knucklebones or cards. He stared into the flames, trying to under-stand why he found the ambush by the Rosses so familiar. The sense of foreboding made his head feel hazy.

"Laird." Angus sat down heavily across from Roderick on a stool he'd dragged over. "What troubles ye?"

Roderick glanced up at his clansman, seeing the concern on his face. Angus had known him since he was born, and he trusted him with his life. But he wasn't certain he wanted to entrust him with his worries now. Not that he thought Angus would betray him, but only that he wasn't certain exactly how to put his troubles into words. On the other hand, there was something that bothered him about the ambush. The style the men had taken, descending on them in hoard, disappearing, and not returning... There was a tiny niggle of an idea that had started to form in his mind and needed fleshing out. Might Angus be able to help him do just that?

"There was something familiar about the ambush. The way the men stalked us and then swept in and out, as if taunting us."

Angus set down his ale and crossed his arms over his chest, his brows furrowing in thought.

"When my da was attacked upon the road, the one warrior who survived long enough to talk about it said the men had come from nowhere. He was certain they were nae outlaws. There had been no time to escape. The men were there and then gone, and they didna make certain to not leave anyone to tell the tale. What's more, nothing was stolen. 'Twas as if the attack was made simply to inflict pain or create fear, not to accomplish anything else. Much like today."

"Aye." Angus sat forward, an elbow on his knee. "Ye think the Rosses were behind the death of your da?"

Roderick pressed his lips together. "I'm nae ruling it out."

Magnus perked up, catching Roderick's eye from where he'd been playing a game of knuckles. Roderick gave him a nod. He approached then, dragging up another stool and sitting beside them. "I heard ye say Ina Ross might be responsible for your da's death. I dinna like that we've yet to see them again."

Roderick shifted on his seat, relieved that the ache in his leg had subsided. "I worry they've gone back to attack Gleann Mórinnse."

"Aye," Magnus agreed. "Or they will attack us outside Dunrobin."

"What could the motivation be?" Roderick ran a hand through his hair. "They had both ye and I in once place, and they had to have known it. Hell, your daughter was with us. Why did they nae attack again?"

Magnus shook his head. "'Tis why I'm concerned. Something isna right."

"They were wearing Ross colors. Do ye think there is a possibility it wasna the Ross men? I didna recognize any of them, though that's nae saying much."

Magnus pulled out his dirk and spun the tip on the pad of his index finger. "I didna recognize any of them, either."

"They didna say a word. Even when I taunted them."

The grooves in Sutherland's brow grew deeper. "I've a feeling that's because they were English."

"*Sassenachs?*"

"Aye."

That was a terrifying thought. "I'd nae put it past Ina Ross to pull a stunt like that. Especially now that she's realigned herself with the English."

Magnus stood. "I'll take first watch." He glanced around the tavern. "On second thought, I'm going with the scouts. We need to find the bastards."

"I'm going, too."

He nodded. "Let's go now."

THE BATH HAD BEEN LOVELY, and the vegetable pottage the tavern keeper's wife made Greer had been delicious. But all of that goodness and even the relief of having escaped the Ross attack was dampened by what she saw now from the window of her borrowed chamber.

In front of the tavern, two distinct figures were mounting equally distinct horses. There was no mistaking it was Roderick and her father. But why? Where were they going?

She didn't like the answer that particular question led her to, for it brought nothing but danger. Not to mention it completely soured the elation of them all having escaped. Why were the two fools just going to rush headlong back into danger just after they'd managed to escape?

They met with a few of their men out front and then took off down the road and disappeared into thin air.

Greer's stomach plummeted. What if she never saw either of them again? She'd not even had the chance to say goodbye...

As their shadows disappeared into the darkness, something else caught her eye. A silhouette darting between the village buildings, drawing closer to the tavern. A flutter in her gut warned her of danger as the cloaked figure stole across the road and behind the tavern. Someone was hiding.

Dear God...what if the ambush had been a trap, and the men racing off had no idea the true evil lay right here?

Or was it just a vagabond in search of a few bites of food? Perhaps she was allowing her worries and fears over the attack to get the best of her. It wouldn't do to accuse a poor beggar of treachery when all he sought was food.

Then again, if it were someone come to do them harm, she couldn't sit here and keep quiet.

INA ROSS HAD to do everything herself. This was nothing new. Even marrying a powerful English lord—twice—hadn't seemed to give her anything other than more annoyances.

When the raid in the woods had not ended as she'd wanted, she'd decided it was time for her to strike out on her own. And what a perfectly brilliant scheme she had planned. The men were so intent on finding her army, they hadn't thought twice about dashing off to danger while she lurked right here under their noses.

She'd instructed her imbecile army to take the lass. What was so hard about that? *Just go in and take her, for heaven's sake.* Ina scoffed in the dark and stared up at the tavern. Considering she'd not shown her face in Sutherland country in nearly a decade, she doubted she'd be recognized, especially since time had not been kind to her. Whenever she observed her reflection, she barely recognized the hag who stared back.

In fact, she wasn't quite certain how she'd convinced her new young husband to marry her, though she supposed a hunger for power was a very enticing thing for a young lord. Especially one who was English and wanted to impress his king by taking land and power in Scotland.

But he wasn't doing what she wanted, which was to take control of all the surrounding lands so she could be mistress of Scotland. The Bruce was growing old, but unfortunately for her, he'd married once more. He'd not been willing to marry her; she'd already tried that. So, what was the next best thing? Ina wanted to kill them all. That would make her feel better. But her silly wee husband had decided these small raids would be best, that instilling fear in the people before swooping in to save them would somehow work. He knew nothing.

Absolutely nothing.

He was nothing but a flea-bitten mandrake mymmerkin.

She was growing tired of trying to instruct him. So she'd followed the men on their last raid and watched how they'd given up against the MacCulloch and Sutherland band, but that was not what had intrigued her the most. Nay, what had gotten her very excited was what she'd seen they were protecting—a lass. One who looked so much like her mother it could be none other than a daughter of Magnus and Arbella Sutherland.

Och, but it gave her chills just thinking about it.

What was the chit doing out in the woods with the men? Was it possible she'd been wed to the MacCulloch? That seemed likely, though she would have thought Magnus would want to align his daughter to a more powerful laird, not a usurper like MacCulloch. How was the cheater even able to maintain loyalty among his men?

He was a swindler, for bloody's sake! By principle alone, it meant he had no loyalty, the fetid churl. She would show him what happened to men without loyalty. If they could be called men at all.

Ina stole across the road, edging toward the rear of the tavern where the servants entered. With a plain wool cape pulled up over her head, she knocked on the back door. A harried-looking woman answered and eyed her up and down as though she were the rubbish that needed to be tossed out into the loch with the rest of the chamber pot contents.

"No beggars. Be on your way." The maggot-licking wench had the audacity to wave her hand at Ina, shooing her.

Shooing her! Oh, but she was going to pay for that.

Ina narrowed her eyes and flashed her best ye're-an-idiot-and-lucky-I-dinna-kill-ye smile. "Please, madam, I have a message for the lady."

The woman eyed her suspiciously. "What lady?" She crossed her arms over her chest as though she'd best Ina in a test.

Bloody foolish, woman.

"Lady Sutherland. I've only just seen his lairdship, and he asked me to come right away."

The woman thought about this for a moment, clearly trying to decide if she should trust Ina.

Ina pulled back her cape, letting the jewels she wore at her neck show, as if proving her right to be there by demonstrating her wealth. As sad as it was, that seemed to do the trick.

"She's up in her chamber."

"Will ye show me to her, please?"

The woman nodded, and as soon as she turned around, Ina grabbed up the nearest pot and hit her on the side of the head with it, relishing the sickening cracking sound her skull made on impact. The bitch dropped like a sack of wheat, her head hitting the floor once more. A trickle of blood spilled from a gash on her scalp.

That was going to hurt like hell if the wench ever woke up. Ina searched the meager area, not finding a suitable place to hide the body. Och, she supposed it was all well and good to take her out back anyway. Less chance of discovery then. Ina lifted the wench's feet and dragged her outside with a power that often surprised others. She might be thin, but she'd always been strong. Alas, dragging the woman did cause her to break a sweat, and it had her panting a bit more than it would have when she was young. Blast it all. Ina abandoned the woman behind the woodpile. When she came back inside, she locked the door in case the wench woke up and tried to regain entry.

A wide grin crossed over Ina's features as she slipped up the stairs.

This is much too easy.

Chapter Eighteen

G reer opened her chamber door slowly, the hair on the back of her neck standing on end. Just as she was about to step out, a blur of movement barreled toward her. But she was faster.

Greer stepped aside at the last minute, and her assailant fell forward into the borrowed chamber in a heap of limbs and woolen cloak. Her mother and father probably would have advised her to close the door tightly then, locking the person inside while she shouted for help. That would have been the least risky thing to do. Alas, Greer was not one to always listen to advice, so she leapt on her assailant and yanked back the hood.

A woman most assuredly older than Greer's mother, with hair that had likely once been nearly black, snarled beneath her. Deep grooves were etched into the corners of her eyes and the sides of her mouth, giving her what seemed a permanent frown—probably because she'd spent most of her time like that. Beady eyes narrowed on Greer, and the woman spat out obscenities Greer had not even heard from her father's men.

"That'll be quite enough," Greer snapped. "Who are ye, and what do ye want?"

The snarl faded and was replaced by a terrifying smile. In that one gesture, her features seemed to transform. Beneath the ugliness, Greer could see she had at one time been a rather handsome woman. But the vileness in her heart and the lawless way she lived her life had soured everything about her. Greer supposed the smile was supposed to be disarming, but it only made the hair on the back of her neck stand more on end.

"I've come with a message, dear child, now will ye not let me up? Is that any way to treat a guest?"

"Ye're no guest, and messengers dinna sneak and try to attack people. Ye must think me verra naïve."

The woman clucked her tongue. "Nay, I would never think a clever lass like ye could be naïve. Look at me now, I'm on the ground with ye atop me." The nauseating smile only grew. But the honey in her tone had an underlying hint of malice. "Clearly, ye are far from unintelligent. Now let me up so we might discuss why I've come."

Despite the woman's saccharine air, Greer could tell that something wasn't right. She didn't know who this woman was, but the sick feeling in her gut told her to remain on her guard.

"I think I'll be the one deciding when ye can get up, hag."

A flash of anger screwed up the woman's face, showing the side of her she'd noticeably been trying to keep hidden before.

"Let me up, *bitch*."

Greer grinned. "I see your true colors are coming out now, are they no'?"

The woman bared her teeth, snapping them like a wild animal. She began furiously bucking beneath Greer, which was unexpected. Though Greer held on to the maelstrom beneath her, the fourth or fifth violent buck tossed her off-balance. She fell to the side, and that gave the madwoman a moment to gain a little bit of footing. She rolled away from Greer and leapt to her feet. As she did, she pulled a dagger from her boot and brandished it at Greer, swiping madly at the air in front of her.

"Walk slowly from the chamber. We're going outside. Dinna argue, or I'll no' hesitate to gut ye."

Greer didn't move. She just stared at her and blinked blankly. "Will ye at least tell me who ye are? I should think if ye're willing to pull a weapon on me, ye'll share your identity. Seems only natural."

The woman straightened only slightly, still keeping her feet spread apart the way Greer knew most warriors did for hand-to-hand combat. "Dinna spout to me about natural. I'm your worst nightmare."

To this, Greer grinned. "Och, nay, not by half. I nearly died a few days ago upon the firth. Not even that was my worst night terror."

This seemed to surprise the woman, for the baring of her teeth faltered. "Dinna cause me more trouble than ye already have. Be a good lass and walk out that door."

Greer shook her head. "Ye dinna know me, so 'tis understandable ye'd think because I'm a lady I'll be compliant when a weapon is pointed at me. But ye see, I'm most assuredly not going to comply. In fact, if ye know what's good for ye, ye'll simply put the dagger away and walk with *me* down the stairs, where I might hand ye over to my men."

The madwoman laughed aloud, an eerie hawk-like screeching. Greer had to temper the urge to cover her ears with her hands.

"Ye wee stupid, wench. Ye think this is a jest?"

"Quite the contrary." Greer shrugged and rolled up her sleeves, prepared to fight if need be. She'd spent plenty of time wrestling with her brothers and trying to keep up with them. This would be nothing compared to that. "Much time has passed since I've had a scuffle. But I'm certain the movements will come back to me."

"If 'tis a fight ye want, wee lass, that is what ye'll get. But I promise ye, I'll win. I've got more experience than ye by half."

Greer rolled her neck from side to side, laced her fingers, and bent them back to crack them. "I dinna believe that experience is always what wins out. Sometimes 'tis simply having more heart."

The woman waved her hand dismissively, as though Greer were a stupid child. But she wasn't going to take offense to it. For quite frankly, Greer didn't care.

"My parents call me a hellion."

"They should call ye an idiot."

Greer laughed. "Sometimes they do." And then she lunged forward, ducking beneath the woman's stabbing dagger. Greer kicked out her foot, sweeping it toward the woman's legs, satisfied with the connecting crunch and the subsequent howl of the hag as she fell backward.

As predicted, she lost hold of her dagger, and it clattered across the floor. When she rolled to scramble for it, Greer grabbed her by the ankles and dragged her away.

"Oh, nay, Mistress of the Dark. I said no weapons in this fight, and ye dinna want to play fair." She sat on the woman's back, pinning her arms on either side of her body with her knees.

"There is no *fair* in battle."

"Well, that is a good point, I'll give ye that. Pray tell, what are we fighting for?"

"*Everything*," she sneered and spat on the ground, but given her position, it only landed an inch or so from her own face.

Greer couldn't even begin to imagine what *everything* meant. She'd never met this woman before in her life. How could they possibly have anything to war over? "Who are ye? Who do ye work for?"

"I work for myself, now and always. Ye really are a dimwitted chit."

Greer ignored the insults. Why did this feel like a game of ridiculous riddles? "And who is yourself?"

"I'm Ina Ross, ye miserable pus."

The saucy grin fell from Greer's face, and she stared at the profile of the woman pinned beneath her. The name rang instantly familiar. *This* was Ina Ross? She'd heard tales of this woman since she was a child. A cruel madwoman who'd spent her entire life in pursuit of everything that wasn't hers. Now that Greer knew who the woman was, saying they were fighting for everything made sense. Ina wanted everything. From the stories she'd heard, the woman was completely deranged.

And she'd come after Greer. What did Greer have that she wanted? Nothing truly, except her own life. Perhaps it had been Ina's intention to abduct her and issue a ransom note to Greer's father.

But wasn't Roderick somehow involved with the Ross clan, too?

The reason he'd been on his way to speak to her father was because of raids from the Ross clan. And wasn't it his cousin who'd been held hostage by Ina Ross? Emily or Emilia? She couldn't quite recall as she'd only heard the information secondhand, and that had been years before.

Whatever the case might be, she had a wanted criminal beneath her, and if the men below stairs hadn't heard the scuffling and shouting already, she would have to handle this herself.

With her knees on Ina's arms to keep her in place, Greer tore at the hem of her own chemise.

"Ye can struggle all ye want, but I'm quite sure I'm stronger than ye. It takes a lot to sail a *birlinn*, to swim, and to run my brothers into ragged heaps. 'Tis really no use—ye might as well submit to me." She tied a length of linen onto one of Ina's wrists, and then a length of linen to the opposite one. She couldn't risk letting go of her captive, so the next best thing was to tie the two strips together and slowly bring the older woman's wrists behind her back. Ina did not make it easy. Good heavens, Greer's muscles strained against the woman's struggles, but at last, she got the two ends tied together.

"Ye're going to pay for this," Ina snarled.

"Somehow, I really doubt it."

"My husband will come looking for me." Though this was likely meant as a threat, Greer could sense the woman's doubt in her tone.

"Does he know ye're here?"

"Aye." The slight hesitation before she answered gave Greer all the information she needed.

Greer tsked. "A man can only come for his wife if he knows where she is. Ye see, if I were in your shoes, I would have made certain he knew. If I wanted to be as sneaky as ye were, I would have left a missive somewhere for him to find later. But I'm guessing ye didna think to do that, either."

Greer stood and yanked up her prisoner, who tried to kick her, but Greer was able to leap out of the way in time.

"Ye're tied up, remember? Ye'll not be getting far, and I'm not opposed to tying your feet."

"I willna go anywhere with ye." Ina barreled forward, her head coming at Greer like a battering ram.

However, as proven already, Greer was a might faster, and she simply sidestepped. With all the power behind her rush, Ina fell to the ground in a heap of curses, a thin line of blood seeping from a cut on her forehead.

For a brief moment, Greer actually felt sorry for the woman. But then she remembered all the pain she'd caused people over the years. The only thing she should feel now was satisfaction in having caught her, and pity that Ina Ross had spent so many years of her life tormenting others. With a cluck of her tongue, Greer moved forward, yanking Ina up.

If she were to believe in the adage that everything happened for a reason, which she didn't typically, she would say perhaps her boat had capsized because she was meant to catch Ina, something that men had been seeking to do for years without success.

"Time to face your crimes." Greer flashed her prisoner a brilliant smile.

RODERICK, Magnus, and a few of their men rode around the perimeter of the village in different directions, but not once did they run across anyone who was *not* supposed to be there. By the middle of the night, the men decided to call it quits and return to the tavern, fully expecting everyone to have gone to bed, save for those on watch.

What they found was quite the opposite. The windows glowed from the light of the candles, and when Roderick entered the tavern, he was greeted by a woman tied to a chair, and Greer standing before her with arms crossed over her chest and a satisfied grin on her face.

Beside her, Liam and Angus stood, their shocked expressions as stunned as Roderick's. What the bloody hell had happened while they were gone?

"Good God," Magnus breathed out beside him. "'Tis Ina Ross."

Roderick's eyes widened. "With Greer."

"Tied to a chair."

"Holy hell."

"Hell has frozen over, lad."

The men approached cautiously, coming to stand beside Liam and Angus respectively.

"What is going on?" Magnus asked.

Ina shot him a look that said she very much wanted to murder him, and she murmured what sounded like a string of obscenities, but it was all muffled by the gag in her mouth. Roderick had rarely seen so much venom in his life.

"If ye're quite done with that part, I'll let ye speak." Greer reached forward and plucked the gag from Ina's mouth.

"Ye've created a devil," Ina ground out, spitting on the floor at Magnus's feet.

"A devil? Nay, Ross, but an angel, if ye're referring to my daughter." There was such pride in Magnus's voice that Roderick felt his own chest swell.

Had Greer captured this woman herself?

"Devil bitch is what she is." Ina spit on the wooden planked floor near Greer's feet next.

But surprisingly, the lass's smile didn't budge, not at the insult or the spittle sprayed on her boots.

"She came to abduct me." Greer beamed, unable to contain her pride. Then shoved the gag back in Ina's mouth. "A mistake, of course. I leave her with ye all." She gave an exaggerated yawn, tapping her palm to her lips. "I'm exhausted. I think I'll turn in."

Roderick couldn't help but smile, and he was further taken aback when she winked at him and sauntered off up the stairs.

Magnus glanced at Liam. "Were there others?"

"Nay, Da, she came alone. We didn't even hear her come in, but there was a great ruckus about back when the tavern owner's wife was found. Seems she was attacked when she went to fetch wood. We were all outside dealing with that while Ina and Greer were upstairs fighting."

"I canna believe she came alone." Roderick shook his head as he stared into the dark, beady eyes of Ina Ross. "Seems rather foolish."

She glowered at him. He was certain if she had not been gagged, she would try to spit at his feet, too.

"What happened to ye?" Magnus asked Ina with a pitying shake of his head. "Ye must have lost your sense. Ye couldna have thought to win alone."

She spouted something, but they couldn't discern her meaning, so they removed the gag.

"Ye only think I'm alone. Tell me, where were ye when I was here? Out on a fruitless hunt, no doubt."

The men grunted, but Magnus replied, "Ye've taken too much of a risk this time."

"Maybe I let her catch me."

"I doubt that, Ross." Magnus laughed. "Anyone who crosses my daughters ought to be wary, and Greer is no exception."

Roderick glanced back toward the staircase in awe, hoping to catch a glimpse of Greer's retreating figure, but she was already gone. "Well done on raising such a hellion, my laird."

Magnus chuckled. "She is certainly full of surprises."

"Aye." Roderick swallowed. Damn, would the pain of not having her in his life ever dim?

"Och, please, ye sorry horse's arse. Untie me, and I'll issue ye a swift death instead of one where I get to pull your guts out through your ballocks."

Roderick had no doubt that Ina Ross would make good on such a threat, but given she was tied to a chair and surrounded by enemies, he chose to ignore her.

"Will ye go and watch after her?" Magnus nudged him.

"Pardon?" Roderick tore his gaze from the staircase to examine Magnus. Had he gone mad, too?

"In case Ina has sent reinforcements, keep watch on my daughter."

Roderick glanced toward her brother Liam who suddenly made himself very busy. What was going on? "Will her betrothed not be disturbed by such?"

Magnus frowned. "Her betrothed?"

"Aye, the man ye said she was to marry?"

"There is no man yet. There will be soon. But who he is has yet to be determined."

Roderick let those words sink in. *Not betrothed*. The truth of it hit him like a boulder to the solar plexus. There was no one else.

Greer could still be his.

Chapter Nineteen

C limbing the stairs of the tavern seemed to take forever. Greer put one foot in front of the other, coaxing herself to hold on tightly to the rail and pull herself up. She finally made it to the landing and lurched down the hall toward her chamber. She burst into the room, slammed the door shut behind her, and leaned heavily on the wood.

The bravado she'd shown in both the tavern below and when she'd discovered Ina Ross barreling into her bedchamber had completely depleted whatever energy she might have had. She felt like an empty husk staring into a precipice.

Of course, it wasn't truly that bad. She was just in need of a good night's sleep, a good meal, and the good comforts of home.

Since Roderick had found her washed up on his shore on the brink of death, she'd put forth a brave face and tried as hard as she could to show everyone that she was fine. That a little drowning wasn't going to slow her down. That being chased by madmen and then attacked by a madwoman was no big deal.

Greer was a Sutherland, after all. She was the daughter of one of the most powerful men in Scotland and one of the strongest women she'd ever had the privilege of knowing. She'd made a name for herself as a hellion and fully lived up to that moniker.

Up until about sixty seconds ago, she'd felt very much like that was exactly who she was, but as soon as she caught sight of the bed and felt her body dropping onto it, the decision to succumb to exhaustion was made.

Greer batted away the dust clouds that floated around her face. The straw mattress sagged beneath her, and she could feel the weaving of hemp that made up the brace of the bed beneath the mattress. But she did not care. She would have gladly slept on the ground one more night if only she could close her eyes.

All she wanted to do was sleep.

And cry.

She didn't know why she wanted to cry, only that she did. She could cry over missing Jewel, over nearly dying, or maybe even over a kiss. Probably her overtiredness. Normally, such things didn't bother her so much. She was a doer. Not a philosopher.

Greer let out a sigh and rubbed at her eyes, feeling the ache of tiredness deep in their sockets. She should sleep. But for some reason, despite the exhaustion, her brain did not want to shut off.

Ina was contained below. Since the Ross warriors were without their leader and probably didn't know her whereabouts, they should be safe for the night, unless the Ross clan accidentally stumbled on this village. The chances of that were slim, though not completely out of the realm of possibility. However, if they were to cross over to Sutherland lands, there would be hell to pay, and Greer was confident they would not want to get into such hell without the approval of their leader.

Both Roderick and her father were back under the roof of the tavern, so she didn't have to worry about never seeing either one of them again, as had been her concern before. They were no doubt downstairs making a ruckus with the rest of the men. And they deserved it. They'd all cheated death, and a great enemy had been caught.

Goodness. Ina... That had been a surprise. Even more of a surprise had been the swift way she'd been able to react. Greer wasn't a fighter. Aye, she'd practiced, but it had always seemed like her older sister had more desire to leap into brawls. Bella had even met her first husband as a child when she'd punched him square in the eye and challenged him during a tournament. Her older sister was tough. Greer could be tough, too, but her idea of raising hell had always been causing trouble, not shooting arrows. Of course, after knowing she'd thrown a spear through Roderick's leg, no one would believe that. But that had been an accident, and if she could go back and do things over again, she would.

Pinning down the woman had been a test of her instincts, and so had tying her up. She supposed she should be proud that her instincts had allowed her to do as much. Well, she *was* proud. And she didn't expect any sort of praise or reward for it. Greer was simply doing her duty, and she could now bask in the glory of knowing she'd detained one of the Highlands' worst criminals.

The only thing that would make this particular moment perfect was if she were at home in her own bed. Soft linen sheets, thick down pillows, furs upon soft woolen blankets, and warmed stones at the foot of the bed to keep her toes from becoming icicles.

At Dunrobin, she'd shared a room and bed with Bella until her sister had gotten married. Now the chamber and bed were hers alone. When Bella had wed and moved away, their youngest sister, Blair, hadn't even asked to come in and share with Greer. Of course, most of the time, she was glad to have a space all to herself. When they'd been growing up, five children running about the castle had been wonderful and chaotic. But now that her older siblings were mostly gone—moved away or out on campaign—the castle was rather quiet. Blair was the calmest of all the Sutherland children, never wanting to join in any of the schemes Greer cooked up. She was usually satisfied to sit quietly. Greer had hedged bets with her siblings that one day Blair was going to break free from that calm exterior and they would all be surprised.

In any case, Greer had thought she'd be excited about the relative calm of the castle. But in the stillest quiet of her room, she often missed the chaos. Sometimes she thought about asking her youngest sister to share a room, because there was something to be said about sharing warmth, and for loneliness, too.

Maybe, she'd ask when she got home. After all, it wouldn't be long until the both of them, and Liam, too, were also married and gone away from Dunrobin. The thought of home left her with a dull ache in her chest. She didn't want to leave. Family meant everything to her, as much as she gave them a hard time. The idea of leaving made her heart physically ache.

And yet there was nothing she could do about it. She had to get married. Being married meant she would have to leave home. Go wherever her husband was. But what if whomever she married lived in the very north, or the very south—or the middle of nowhere, like the Isle of Mull? Oh, that would be a heinous torture. Even now, she could picture herself walking across the lonely gray battlements, staring out into the vast void of isle water, dreaming of climbing into a birlinn and sailing home, only to be dragged back into the endless hollow that was her new life.

Greer closed her eyes, breathing in slowly and deeply. But what if it were Roderick? Instantly, and image of his lip twitching into a smile flashed in her mind. The teasing way he grinned at her, the way he winked as though they shared a secret. His castle wasn't far from her home, either. Just across the firth. And she really liked him...more than liked him. She might even... Nay, she couldn't think it. They'd only kissed. Kissing him had been incredible. She wouldn't mind at all having to kiss him every day for the rest of her life. It wouldn't be a hardship; in fact, it was something she'd gladly volunteer to do.

Wasn't that what she wanted? To *want* her husband? Not only to desire him, but to enjoy his company? To laugh, to play?

Greer sunk further into the bed, letting her arms flop outward and take up all the space. The room was quiet, and the roar of the voices from below had melded to become a buzz of noise that faded soothingly into the background.

It was then she realized that this was the still and quiet that both Roderick and her father talked about. The time she could think about herself and what she wanted out of life.

What did she want?

Before she'd gone off on this journey, she'd thought she'd known exactly what that was. She wanted to sail, to be free to do whatever she liked. To put off marriage for as long as possible. In fact, during the first hour or two on the *currach* before the storm, she'd been coming up with a plan to thwart any of her would-be suitors. Her plans had included such things as putting herbs that induced stomach upset into their supper, letting Jewel loose in their chambers, setting their horses free, and sewing all the cuffs and neck holes closed in their shirts. She still kind of wanted to try these things on someone. It would be fun...

A realization thrummed in her mind. She'd known all about the still and quiet for a long time. She experienced it when she was out to sea in the silence, with the waves gently rocking her boat, the squalls of seagulls, her oars dipping into the water, wind rushing past. Those were soothing sounds that lulled her into moments of deep thought.

She knew exactly who she was and what she wanted. What she needed to do was stop listening to what *everyone else* wanted her to be. She needed to trust in herself, in her convictions and desires.

Sailing meant everything to her. Quitting wasn't an option, even if the idea of being in the water terrified her right now. That would fade. It had to. One little accident that almost resulted in her death shouldn't hold such power over her. It was like riding a horse. When one got tossed, they didn't simply give up, even if they broke their leg. Roderick was a perfect example of that. He still fished even though he'd gotten a spear through the leg for it.

The only thing Greer thought she would not try again was cooking. That was hazardous to her health and the health of others. Best leave that particular passion to those who actually had a talent for it.

She chuckled at the thought and curled onto her side, tugging at the threadbare blanket to keep warm, what little good that did.

When she returned to Dunrobin, she needed to implement a plan of getting back on the water. This time, she wouldn't do it alone. Well, maybe not always alone. There would still be times that she would need to be alone to think, but maybe those could be done on shore—

or at least close enough to shore that she could swim the distance if necessary.

Saints, but she prayed her parents wouldn't completely forbid her from ever sailing again. They couldn't, could they? She wouldn't let them. Roderick wouldn't... The man was always invading her thoughts. And with good reason. Because of what she wanted most. But her heart's desire would be harder to attain.

Roderick.

She wanted him body, heart, and soul. The very thought of him sent shivers racing along her limbs and caused her belly to do an excited flip. Aye, she wanted him.

A loud thump against her door pulled Greer from her thoughts, jolting her from the stillness. Her heart leapt, and she had a sudden fear that someone was going to be bursting through the door again— Ina specifically. And she had no weapon ready. After a frantic search of the room, she was able to pinpoint a fire poker, a candlestick, and her tiny eating knife.

But if someone were going to burst through her door, she'd have heard a warning of some sort. After the Ina incident, her father had tripled the men on watch. Greer sank back down onto the bed with relief. But still, whoever was out there knocked persistently.

She didn't have the energy to get up and see who it was, so instead, she called out, "Who is it?"

"'Tis Grim."

Grim. Just hearing his voice sent a smile to her face. A glance at the door showed she'd forgotten to lock it, quite an oversight given what had just happened. "Come in," she said.

She probably should have gotten up. Might have actually done so if it were any other man knocking, but Grim had seen her at her very worst—more than once. They were at a point that if she were to suddenly act as though propriety were important, she'd feel foolish, and likely he would, too. And who was she kidding? She would have turned away any other man, but she'd not the power to send her Grim off.

She wanted to spend the rest of her days with him just walking in, taking the knocking out altogether. Hadn't she just been thinking that? Was this a sign?

The door handle lifted, and he slowly pushed the door open, revealing the breadth of his massive frame as he ducked beneath the doorframe to lean against the jam. He crossed an ankle over the other, arms over his chest, stretching the linen of his shirt. His dark hair hung wet and loose around his face, and his beard was freshly trimmed. Even in the dim light, she could see the blue in his eyes. *Lord, he's striking.*

The shift in the air from him opening the door brought her the crisp, clean scent of him. A deep inhale was extremely satisfying. She could breathe him in all day. She just lay there basking in all things Roderick.

She sighed. Now she was starting to sound like her sister Bella, the way she gushed over her husband, Niall, who seemed a prince among men.

But Greer didn't want a prince, as sweet and marvelous as they might be. She wanted a hellion—someone like her. And even though Roderick tried as hard as he could to keep himself contained, she'd been able to break open his shell more than once.

Greer grinned at him, propping her head up on her elbow. "I would have stood and given ye a proper welcome, but I'm too tired to move."

The intensity of his gaze swept over her, sending chills over all of her limbs. He examined her from head to toe, and even though she lay with a light blanket and was fully clothed, she felt stripped bare and breathless.

"Are ye hurt?" he asked.

Her heart pounded at his perusal and the concern in his tone.

"No more than the aches and pains I came with." She managed a small smile, smoothing the blanket over her hip and watching the way his gaze glittered as he followed the movement. His gaze swept back up to lock on hers.

"I've a feeling ye often have aches and pains, if my own are any indication." He chuckled.

"I'm too proud to take your jest as an insult," she teased back.

"Good, for I offer it only in good fun."

He was the perfect man for her.

"Why do ye not come in? Sit." She glanced down at his leg, taking note that he was favoring his weight on the other side. "If ye've the salve, I'll be happy to rub it into your leg."

The intensity of his gaze darkened, and her throat went dry. What that gaze said... Every inch of her skin stretched taut, reaching for him, straining. Was this what it was like to be infatuated? She craved him. Craved everything about him.

"Lass..." he drawled. "I dinna think that's such a good idea."

"Why not?" She sat up a little straighter, pressing her palm into the mattress, clinging to it so she didn't get up, race across the room, toss herself into his arms, and kiss him as though her life depended on it. "It helped last time, did it nae."

"Aye." His voice had grown gruff.

A piece of hair fell across her cheek, and she puffed a breath to get it off her skin. "Go and get your salve, Grim, and stop standing there brooding."

"Nay, and I'm nay brooding." The muscles on his chest flexed as if he were bracing himself, or holding himself in place.

"What would ye call it then?"

"Practicing willpower." The dark intensity of his expression did not change, but there was a light in his eyes, a hunger that seemed to have been revealed.

Greer pursed her lips, digging her fingers harder into the mattress. "Practicing willpower? How?"

"I'm no' certain ye're ready to hear it." His eyelids were hooded now, his voice gruff, skating over her nerves like a sensual caress.

"Try me." Greer held her breath, feeling as though the air in the room crackled with whatever invisible tension was tugging them together.

Roderick gazed at her, roving the length of her body once more, and with every inch, she felt as if she were being devoured. Her body heated, little pinpricks of excitement picking their way along her limbs. Nipples hardened. Breath hitched. Goodness... She could barely think beyond wanting him to come fully into the room and firmly shut the door behind him, locking out the world.

"It's taking every ounce of willpower I possess to stay right here. Because all I want to do is..."

He stopped. She wanted to leap off the bed and demand he tell her exactly what he wanted. She let out the breath she'd been holding, and when she spoke, her voice came out a near croak. "What do ye want?"

He broke his gaze, staring toward the window on the far wall and running his hands through his thick hair. She could tell he was trying to regain control, traction. "The same thing I've always wanted."

"What's that?" She sat up and dangled her legs over the side of the bed, her bare toes brushing the floor.

His gaze slowly rolled back to hers. "Ye."

Greer sucked in a breath. That one word, that simple admission, changed her whole world in that instant. He wanted her. And she wanted him.

The truth of it weighed between them—a line drawn, and one of them needed to cross over. To do something about the fact that they both wanted each other.

Had she not just been lying there thinking the same thing?

Greer pressed her feet to the floor, let go of the mattress, and stood. She no longer felt the aches and pains of travel, or the exhaustion that had her collapsing a few moments before. She walked toward him with purpose. She wasn't going to let him back away now.

He watched her approach, his eyes dark with hunger, and she could see the war going on inside him. She could see he wasn't certain whether he should leave or meet her halfway.

It didn't matter. She wasn't going to let him walk out of her door, not before she told—*showed him*—that she wanted him too. And not just for a kiss. But for much more than that.

The closer she got, the straighter he stood, until he uncrossed his ankles, and his arms fell at his sides. When she was a foot away, he started to shake his head, but she ignored him, grabbed his hand, encircled her fingers around his and tugged him toward her. Roderick didn't argue. He stepped closer, and the heat of his body enveloped her even though they weren't yet close enough to touch. His heady scent intoxicated her, as did the powerful feeling her boldness gave her.

"Shut the door," she said.

His eyes widened, lips turning down slightly. He wanted to tell her no. "Greer..."

God, how she loved the sound of her name on his tongue. "Shut it, Grim."

He shook his head. "I shouldna."

"Ye should. If not, everyone will see us."

"See us what?" His voice was a low murmur now that had her pulse leaping.

It was too late to stop now, and she didn't want to. "See us doing this." She reached up, wrapped her arms around his neck, and tugged him down for a deep, hot kiss.

Her lashes fluttered down to her cheeks, and she put herself fully into that kiss. She tasted him, stroking her tongue over his just the way he'd showed her, the way she liked. The way that sent tingles racing all over her and made her squirm. It made sparks of pleasure and want race between her breasts and her core. It had her squirming where she stood, aching to be close to him. Flush to his body. Chest-to-chest, thigh-to-thigh, toe-to-toe.

The door slowly clicked, and she grinned against his mouth at the knowledge that he'd followed her direction and shut it. Then she felt herself being lifted, her body indeed flush to his. She gasped against his kiss, delighting in that connection. Her breasts crushed to his chest, pebbled nipples brushing with stimulating pleasure. Roderick carried her in the direction of her bed, and she wasn't going to stop him. She'd known the moment she pressed her feet to the floor and marched toward him that this was what she wanted—to have Roderick in her bed. To have his body pressing her down, claiming her for his own. To be his.

They tumbled down upon the dusty, saggy mattress, the hemp bands creaking, and the wooden legs of the bed clunking against the floorboards. But neither one of them seemed to care about the noise. Only this moment. Themselves. Their mouths slanted again and again with frenzied, primal need, each of them intoxicated with the other and the pursuit of pleasure.

"I want more than kissing," Roderick whispered against her mouth, his hand sliding over her hip, massaging the round flesh there.

Greer's eyes blinked open and stared into his. "I want so much more." Boldly, she lifted her leg and pressed her knee to the side of his body, wanting to feel more of him against her. She gasped at the way they fit, at the hardness of his arousal pressed to the sensitive parts of her. She rolled her hips and bit her lip at the frisson of pleasure that move sparked. What would it feel like without clothes?

"More than...this." His lips skimmed to her ear, tongue flicking out to tease the sensitive skin. "I want to marry ye."

Marry her... Greer had dreamed he'd whisper those words. Her entire body clenched with surprise and elation. "I love ye," she said, surprising both herself and him when the words left her lips. She'd never allowed the words to be spoken in her own mind, and the admission was a shock and a relief all at once.

"God, ye have no idea how much I've wanted to hear ye say it." His mouth crashed against hers, tongue sliding with urgent need between her lips. He kissed her until she could barely make sense of anything. "I love ye so much I'd let ye throw spears at me every day for the rest of our lives."

Greer laughed, and he chuckled, nipping at her bottom lip. "I can promise ye it will nae be every day."

"Marry me, *mo ghràidh*."

His love...

Greer could have leapt off the bed and danced around the room, flung open the curtains, and shouted to the village and hills beyond. Instead, she smiled and squeezed his shoulders. "Aye, I'll marry ye."

Roderick sucked in a breath, as though he'd feared she'd deny him, and then he let it out slowly. The heat in his gaze somehow doubled, and her body answered with a shiver. He bent low, kissing her long and hard, their bodies rocking together in a way that had her soaring higher and higher for something. The hardness of his arousal stroked with expert undulations against her middle. His hands cupped her breast, and his lips were on her mouth and her neck, his teeth tugging at the achy points of her breasts. Then she found whatever it was her body had been reaching for. She was shocked as rapture exploded, crushing her, and she cried out.

Roderick let out a low groan, swallowing the rest of her cries in his kiss. What was happening? Was this love making? They'd not undressed. No parts of him had entered parts of hers. Their bodies had just rocked together and created a friction so intense, she was certain never to move from this spot ever again.

With his forehead pressed to hers, and his breathing coming in heavy pants, he said, "We'd best save the rest of this for our wedding night."

Greer clung to him. "We've made our promises. I dinna want to wait. I canna spend another night not sleeping beside ye."

"Your da is downstairs. Your brother. A dozen Sutherland warriors. I'll nae die before we wed, love, else what would be the point?" Even as he said it, his hand explored above her hip to her ribs, edging closer to her breasts once more.

She arched her back, desiring to feel his heavy palm on her, wanting to shed her clothes and feel his skin on hers. She sought to fulfill the ache in her body that seemed to strain for his touch once more. That same shatter. Still, he hesitated with his thumb on the underside of her breast and left her nipple a hard, aching point.

"I'll no' let them kill ye," she promised.

At last, he cupped her breast, dipped his face low, and nuzzled the hardened nipple. This time, he tugged away the fabric. The heat of his tongue seared her skin. Greer groaned, feeling that slice of pleasure all the way to her core. Who would have ever thought that *doing* business was so...incredible?

"I want to make love to ye for days," he murmured, skimming his teeth over the jutting point.

"Weeks," she murmured, running her fingers through his damp hair.

He kissed her again, pressing his hips forward, rubbing the thickness of his arousal against her. Knowing what his touch could do to her, her body suddenly surged with desire all over again. Och, she needed to remove the fabric that strained between them, feel the length of his hard, naked body against hers. The pleasure that even the smallest glance from him promised.

"I dinna want to wait," he said, sliding a hand beneath her buttock to press her closer. "But we must."

"Nay," she moaned as the closer contact sent a rush of thrill through her. "No one has to know."

"Everyone will know."

She remembered how they'd all seemed to know he'd kissed her before, so that notion seemed entirely possible.

"They probably know I've got ye in bed right now."

"How?"

"The walls are thin, lass. And my boot heels are heavy."

And then she recalled how the bed had creaked and bumped against the floor as they'd fallen onto it. She'd tried hard not to make noise, but gasps and moans had slipped from his kiss.

As if to prove that point, a thunderous knock jolted both of their gazes toward the door.

"*Mo chreach*," Roderick groaned. "I didna lock it."

Chapter Twenty

Roderick leapt off the bed, traversed the length of the room in two strides, and yanked open the door, completely blocking Magnus Sutherland's view of his daughter.

"Why is the door closed?" The older warrior's eyes narrowed, his hand on the hilt of the sword at his hip.

A prickle of apprehension skated up Roderick's spine. Warning flashed in Sutherland's gaze. Though he did not pull out his sword, the threat was evident enough. If Roderick didn't give a good explanation, or get the hell out of the way, blood was going to be shed.

Roderick didn't want to lie to his future father-by-marriage, but he also didn't want to tell him he'd been moments away from despoiling his daughter. Nay, admitting that much was sure to get his head sliced clean off his neck or at the least, get him castrated on the spot.

"Da." Greer's cheerful voice sounded from behind, and then she was squeezing beside Roderick.

He dared a glance down toward her, half expecting to see her hair and clothing rumpled. For her to look as thoroughly ravished as she had moments before when her lips parted on a cry of release. Good God, he could still hear her in his head, and his blood pumped to slam the door closed and keep going.

She didn't even glance up at him, thank the saints, else Sutherland would see every thought that passed through Roderick's mind.

"There was a draft, and since I was getting ready for bed, I told him to shut it. Nothing untoward, Da." She gave a little laugh as though he'd be silly to think such.

Magnus stared at the two of them, knowing eyes traversing back and forth before finally locking on Roderick's. Despite Greer's easy lie and the smoothing of her hair and garments, one glimpse of her lips was enough of an admission. She looked thoroughly kissed, her cheeks even still held a hint of pink flush. The woman was breathtaking, and damned arousing. Roderick swallowed, glanced back toward Magnus, and prepared to take his punishment like a man.

Sutherland cleared his throat, fingers still dancing on the hilt of his sword. "I've been in this situation afore, but then I arrived minutes later than this and found my sister being debauched by her lover. I've nae doubt had I arrived less than a quarter hour later, ye'd be in the same position."

Roderick's mouth went dry. The man was not wrong.

"Da!" Greer breathed out, color coming to her face. Roderick stiffened beside her. "I've never heard this afore. Was it Aunt Lorna? Aunt Heather married her captor—"

"Ye dinna deny it." Magnus cut off her inquiry, yet he still kept his steady gaze on Roderick. Because Roderick was certain it was nay Greer he was speaking to. Sutherland was letting him know that he'd had practice dealing with despoilers of virgins in the past. "This isna the first time ye've been untoward with my daughter, is it? Only a confident man would do so right beneath my nose."

To this, Roderick had no problem speaking the truth. "Your daughter is as much a maid as she was when I found her on my beach."

Magnus's brow furrowed. "But she wouldna be by morning."

"I wish to make her my wife," Roderick said in answer to that.

"Then 'tis a good thing I called for a priest." With that, Magnus turned on his heel and started for the stairs.

Roderick stared after him. If the man knew what was happening above stairs, why had he taken the time to call for a priest before coming up? Had that been his plan all along? Is that why he'd sent Roderick to protect his daughter upstairs, when they both knew good and well nothing would happen now that Ina had been caught and the men on watch had tripled? The tricky bastard.

Greer shoved past Roderick and rushed toward her father. "Wait, Da."

Magnus stopped then, gazing down at his daughter with great affection. He cupped her cheek and gave it a slight tap. "Ye have my blessing. I could tell by the way the two of ye've been acting that this was not far off. But your mother would never forgive me if I let what was about to happen continue without the bonds of marriage being put in place."

Sutherland's words confirmed what Roderick had guessed, but that didn't mean it would be as simple as that. The older laird was going to need to save face, and to prove a point. No one could despoil one of his daughters and get away with it. Especially not be given the gift of her virtue and her hand in marriage.

"We were no'..." A pretty shade of pink, even in the dimly lit hall, covered Greer's cheeks.

"I dinna need to know more, sweet child. Prepare yourself to be wed." He nodded his head toward Roderick. "Ye can join me downstairs, lad."

"Nay, Da. Not like this." Greer tugged her father's sleeve. "Mama will want to be there. Let us wait until the feast. I beg ye."

Sutherland's lips pressed firmly together, his nostrils flaring with slight irritation, but Greer persisted, her eyes pleading.

"Ye truly wish to wait? This is nae a ruse to get out of it."

"Nay, nae a ruse, Da." She glanced back at Roderick. "I love him."

"Och, ye sound like Lorna." Magnus visibly gritted his teeth, sliding Roderick a fierce glower. "And ye can keep your hands off my daughter until then?" Magnus's gaze promised murder if his answer were anything other than the affirmative.

Roderick gave a curt nod.

Greer beamed at them both, threw herself into her father's arms, and kissed him on the cheek, thanking him. Fascinatingly, she did not seem at all embarrassed at having been caught with her skirts nearly up. And even more interesting was that Roderick was still breathing. Then again, it seemed like Magnus had guessed that there was something brewing between the two of them.

"Get some rest, lass," Magnus said and then he pointed at Roderick. "Ye, downstairs."

There was a promise of retaliation in that glower. Perhaps he wouldn't be breathing soon after all.

As Greer passed him, she squeezed his fingers and winked. Then she disappeared behind her door, leaving the two men in the hallway, her scent lingering. With her gone, all pretense of happiness left Magnus's face and was replaced by fury.

"Because I want to make my daughter happy, I'll no' be killing ye tonight, but I am going to beat your arse bloody. Dinna think that because I saw this coming that I'll go easy on ye, either. A father and laird has to protect what's his."

Roderick nodded. "Seems only fair."

"We'll get along splendidly then." Magnus walked down the stairs, and Roderick followed, their heavy boot falls echoing in the tiny stairwell.

At the foot of the stairs, the older man held out his arms, announcing for all to hear, "There's to be a wedding as soon as we arrive at Dunrobin!"

This announcement caused a few seconds of blank stares as the MacCulloch and Sutherland men regarded each other with confusion. Should they be fighting, cheering? The only two who didn't appear confused were Liam and Angus, both of whom seemed to have formed a friendship. They stood at the back of the tavern, arms crossed and equal ye're-an-arse looks on their faces.

Magnus marched outside, and Roderick followed. The older warrior began to disarm himself, and Roderick did the same. Warriors filed out of the small tavern and formed a circle around them, all of them now fully aware of exactly what was happening. His own men were about to witness him allowing his future wife's father to beat his arse.

No less than he deserved, and he well knew it.

"If ye would avoid the leg your daughter already destroyed so I may continue to see to her safety when she's mistress of Gleann Mórinnse?" Roderick noted the irony in that request, as did several others judging by their smirks.

"With pleasure," Magnus said, cracking his knuckles.

The man threw a wicked punch, knocking his meaty fist into Roderick's jaw hard enough that his head snapped back and he instantly tasted blood.

Was it right to fight back? Seemed like he should at least attempt to block after the first few blows. But to retaliate seemed dishonorable given the reason Magnus was wailing on him. Roderick stood there, allowing Magnus to get in a punch to his ribs on the left, another on his right.

That seemed a fair enough amount of free shots. Then he started to block, if only so he could actually make love to his wife when their vows were complete. Though he wasn't certain Magnus would want that anyway; it was his daughter, after all.

The men shouted, the Sutherlands calling for a more brutal beating, and the MacCullochs encouraging their laird to continue taking it like a true Highlander.

GREER KNEW it was too good to be true. How could she have been foolish enough to believe her father would simply allow them to get married after catching them in the compromising position he assumed them to be in? She'd had every intention of being in that compromising position, and he knew it.

But what she was witnessing outside of the tavern window was ridiculous. Roderick shouldn't simply stand there and let her father punch him again and again. Yet if Roderick didn't, he'd not be giving her father the due he deserved at finding his daughter in bed with a man.

She wanted to shout for them to stop. But if she did that, Roderick would lose face in front of the MacCullochs and the Sutherlands.

Biting her tongue and holding her hand over her mouth was proving hard, for she kept gasping and catching herself just as the words were rolling off her tongue.

However, she also could not just watch, for every crunch of her father's fist against the man she loved made her belly roil. So, instead, she clamped the shutters closed tightly and made use of the wine jug the tavern owner's wife had left her. Several sips into her mug later, she noticed the noise outside had finally died down and been replaced by rowdy shouts beneath her feet. Thank the saints! She'd been afraid her father would beat Roderick bloody, but in the end, it had to have been less than a dozen blows.

Now she just had to force herself to stay put when what she really wanted to do was go and tend his injuries.

Och, who was she kidding?

An hour later, when the noises had dissipated, Greer snuck down the stairs, catching the gaze of her brother, who pinned her with a dinna-dare glower. She raised her chin, prepared to fight him on this. Instead, he just shook his head and glanced the other way.

"Do ye know where he is?" she whispered.

"Aye. The stables."

"With the other men."

"Aye."

"And Da?"

"There, too."

She groaned. "There is no way I can see him?"

"Not unless ye want him to get his other eye swollen shut."

"Da left him one eye?"

"Of course, he's not a bloody monster."

Greer sighed in relief. "I wanted to help—"

"Och, sister, leave the man his pride. He doesna need ye to come and fuss over him."

To this, she also wanted to argue, but knowing there was no way she could reach Roderick anyway, she decided that perhaps it would be better to try and get to him when they were on the road.

This time when she collapsed on the bed, she was asleep before her head hit the pillow. It took her father placing a cold, wet cloth on her neck before she woke the following morning.

THE NEXT TWO days of travel were not easy on either Greer or Roderick. They were the butt of every jest, for it seemed the entire caravan knew just what had transpired, and whenever he could, her brother Liam teased her mercilessly.

Whenever they happened to get close enough to each other, the men swooped in to drag them apart. If they were intent on making her want to be near Roderick all the more, they were winning, because as it was, she was considering making them a poison pie just so she could ask him how he was doing.

Roderick, bless him, was being a good sport about all of it. One eye had been swollen shut the morning they'd left the tavern, but at least that had faded to a black eye to match the bruise on his jaw. There were certain to be more bruises beneath his shirt, which she vowed to kiss as soon as she could get him alone and naked.

The two times she'd managed to escape the view of her father and race after Roderick in the wood, she'd been caught by her brother and dragged back to camp while he berated her.

"Do ye want to marry the bastard or not?"

"I do," she huffed.

"Then quit going after him, else Da will make certain it never happens, ye foolish lass."

Greer sat heavily beside the campfire and glared up at her brother, crossing her arms over her chest. "I hope when ye find the one ye love, that everyone thwarts ye just as much."

To this, Liam averted his gaze, shifting uncomfortably before stalking away. What in blazes was that about? Did Liam have a secret he was keeping from her? But her mind was quickly averted when Roderick returned to camp, winked at her with his good eye, and then went to take watch.

Their arrival at Dunrobin the following late afternoon was met with fanfare. The men on the wall shouted their arrival for all to hear, and when the portcullis was lifted, men, women, and children from their clan lined the bailey. But the faces Greer was most excited to see leapt out of the crowd. Standing at the base of the stairs to the keep were her mother, her sister Blair, and surprisingly, her sister Bella and their brother Strath. Beside Strath was his wife, Eva, and behind Bella was her husband, Niall.

It was all Greer could do to not jump from her horse. Her father dismounted and lifted his wife in the air, greeting her as he always did upon his return in a way that warmed Greer's heart. Roderick came up beside her mare and reached for her.

"Allow me, my lady," he said with a wink.

"Are ye certain it will no' result in your death?"

"Nay, but I may die if I have to go another day without your hand in mine."

Heat rose to her face, but she didn't care. She placed her hand in his, daring anyone to come and tear her away. "I missed ye."

"And I ye, *mo ghràidh.*"

Greer sighed as he helped her from her horse, wishing she could slide right into his arms, but for propriety's sake she kept a few inches between them.

As soon as her feet hit the ground, they were surrounded by her family. She embraced her mother, squeezing her tightly, and breathing in her familiar floral and herbal scent.

"Sweet Greer, you scared me half to death." Her mother clung to her, pressing her lips to the side of her face and whispering in her melodic English accent how much she'd missed her.

"I'm sorry, Mama." Tears sprung to her eyes, and her voice croaked.

"Nay, we mustn't become all weepy. Not yet anyway." She pulled away and held Greer at arm's length. "You look different. Happier."

Greer smiled. "I am."

But before she could expound on that, the rest of her siblings grabbed her up in a tight hug.

"Ye're all here," she said with a laugh.

"We came as soon as we heard ye were missing." Bella eyed Roderick, who stood behind Greer, his fingers lightly brushing the small of her back.

"Mama, may I introduce to ye Laird MacCulloch. He saved my life." She glanced behind her. "And we're to be married." Greer reached behind her, threaded her fingers in his, and pulled him to her side.

Her family stood in silence for several breaths, and she feared her father would say something to humiliate them both. Greer flashed her father a pleading look not to ruin this moment with the news of how she'd compromised herself, and he winked.

Strath was the first to break the silence. "Thank ye for saving her, and welcome to our family."

"Married!" Lady Sutherland rushed them both, hugging Greer tightly, and then placing a kiss on Roderick's cheek.

At last, her father spoke. "Aye, the feast we'd planned will now be in celebration of their union. A great match and a strong alliance for both of our clans."

Greer could have cried. She was so happy at the easy acceptance of Roderick into their family.

But then her mother's face paled as she stared behind them all toward the gate. In all the excitement, Greer had completely forgotten about Ina Ross, who'd been traveling with them in Angus's care.

"A gift for ye, my love," Magnus said, nodding in Ina's direction.

So much of their married life had involved torment from Ina. In fact, her mother had been sent to Scotland on orders of her king to marry Ina's first husband. It was only because of a battle and because Magnus Sutherland had swept her away from the battlefield that she'd been spared that fate, and the two of them had wed. But the torment had seemed to never end. Incredible that one vile woman could continue to pester so many people for such a long time.

"Ina Ross." Her mother let out a long exhale. "I hoped you were dead."

Greer's mouth fell open in shock. She'd never heard her mother wish ill on anyone, let alone death.

"I'm not surprised," Ina hissed.

"I'm sending a missive to the king," Magnus said. "Ina will make a good prisoner of war. Perhaps she'll be used in an exchange for one of our men held by the English."

Ina railed obscenities at that, but with one nod from her father, several Sutherland warriors dragged Ina off to their dungeon, where she'd have plenty of time to contemplate her fate.

Lady Arbella watched Ina until she disappeared and then turned back to face Roderick. "How can we ever repay you for saving our Greer?"

"He's been repaid," Magnus said, a hint of sarcasm in his tone.

Greer blushed madly, a thousand ideas of what her father might mean by that rushing through her brain, only to see her mother's eyes widen with knowing.

"I see." Her mother looked to be hiding her amusement.

"See what?" Blair asked staring between the two of them, the face of innocence.

"Blair, come inside," Bella said, grabbing for her sister's arm. "Let me practice on your hair how we'll do Greer's for the wedding feast."

From the irritated set of her mouth, Blair did not want to comply. However, it was not in her nature to argue, and so she went off with their oldest sister, leaving Greer to wallow in the heat of her mortification.

Liam winked at her as he slung his arm over Strath's shoulders. "Where'd Niall run off to?"

"He's in the stables," their older brother answered. "I saw him take Da's horse."

"I've need of advice from the both of ye." Liam directed their older brother toward the stables. The rest of the bailey seemed to catch the hint of her siblings' quick disappearance and also made themselves scarce, leaving Greer, Roderick, and her parents the only remaining occupants.

Greer shifted on her feet, scuffing the toes of her boots into the hay-strewn bailey, thinking now would be a good time for the skies to open up and give her a chance to escape. But the heavens did not comply, for not a single cloud was in the blue sky.

"I'm glad to see you made a full recovery," her mother said to Roderick, obviously referring to his leg.

"Thank ye, my lady." Roderick gave a slight bow.

"And that you didna hold a grievance against my daughter for having caused the injury."

"Och, far from it," Magnus said, slapping Roderick on the back a little too hard.

"Da," Greer said through gritted teeth.

"I love her with all my heart," Roderick said, winking down at Greer with a grin that felt like a secret message.

"And I love him." Greer kept her gaze on his, wishing they were alone so she could leap into his arms and tell him just how much he made her feel whole. "I'd be lost without him."

"Och, lass," he said in a low voice. "'Tis ye who've made me whole again."

A loud bark broke them apart as Jewel came rushing from within the keep. Greer let out a shriek of excitement and crouched down to greet her hound. The massive black animal barreled into her mistress, knocking her flat on her back and filling her face with kisses.

"Oh, how I missed ye," Greer said, wrapping her arms around the dog and burying her face in her thick fur.

Jewel made yipping and yowling noises in reply as she licked Greer, wagged her tail, and wiggled her large body with excitement at being reunited.

"My wife greets me the same way after battle," Magnus teased, wrapping his arm around Arbella's shoulders. She scoffed with mock indignation, and he bent to kiss her.

Greer glanced up at Roderick to see him smiling down at her, and she knew without a doubt, their life together was going to be just as incredible as her parents'.

Chapter Twenty-One

The next few days were filled with preparations for the wedding feast, and much like during their journey, everyone did what they could to keep the two lovebirds apart—including Roderick's brother, Jon, who'd arrived on the third day.

Well, everyone but Liam, who seemed to enjoy bringing the two of them together, only to then point it out to her father. And she kept falling for it, too. Greer was going to make him pay for that. Except, she had been able to steal a few kisses from Roderick, so perhaps she ought to thank him instead.

The king's men arrived swiftly to take Ina. A message was sent to her husband in the form of a regiment of the king's army, causing Ughtred to flee back to England, though not before he'd threatened to return with a vengeance. Oh, how Greer would have liked to have seen that. It wasn't every day one got to witness a traitorous *Sassenach* tucking tail and running.

Of course, thoughts like that always made her feel a little guilty, given she was half-English herself, but her mother always waved away those guilty thoughts with the easy explanation that not all English were created equal. They fell in one of two camps—either they believed in a free Scotland or not. And she and her family believed in freedom.

However, the threat of the English king coming after them on the word of Ughtred, however small the threat was, could still be taken as one. Alas, there was nothing she could do about it now. Besides, she wanted to celebrate, for she was soon to wed.

At last, the feast was upon them, but Greer barely paid attention. The brief kiss she and Roderick had been able to share when they'd exchanged vows had only lit a torch inside her. She couldn't wait for it to burst into brighter flames. Of course, her father seemed to want to prolong the torment by continuously pulling Roderick away from her.

At last, her mother insisted they sit and eat together.

"Let's sneak away," Greer leaned over and whispered as they sipped wine and watched the dancing in the center of the great hall.

Roderick dipped his chin. "I like the way ye think. How do ye propose we do that?"

"I dinna care, but I canna take it anymore. I dinna want them to follow us up, nor do I want to be undressed by all the ladies as my sister Bella was. All I want is to be alone with ye."

"I've never heard anything better, and I've an idea that might suit." Roderick set down his cup of wine on the table and inched closer to whisper into her ear.

Of course, those who witnessed him doing such felt the need to shout out bawdy jests, which were followed by raucous laughter. But she didn't pay them any attention.

If only they knew just what he'd been whispering. Greer nodded, then leaned over to Strath's wife to seek her help, praying that her sister-by-marriage, Eva, would oblige. Eva gave her a conspiratorial wink and then crept from the great hall in a swish of skirts.

Roderick leapt up and shouted for Strath's attention, drawing him into a Highland dance to keep his attention away from Eva. Greer watched from her place on the dais, marveling at the sight of her husband's strong legs leaping and crisscrossing over swords that had been placed on the ground. One would never know there was a thick scar that oft caused him pain beneath his plaid. She was glad it didn't seem to be bothering him in the slightest today.

Greer sat back, took another small sip of wine, and waited for the scene to unfold, for certainly at any moment, their plan would come barreling into action.

And it did just as they hoped. All Eva had to do was whisper to Jewel, "Cat! Get it!" and her hound went on a tear through the great hall. One minute the men were dancing, the ladies clapping, and the next thing everyone knew, a massive blur of black fur was racing through the great hall on a mission to catch an imaginary cat. Of course, every other dog in the vicinity wanted in on the action.

Greer smiled, finding Roderick's face in the chaotic crowd, each of them with satisfied grins in place.

They met halfway. Roderick swept her up in his arms, and they disappeared into the kitchen and took the servants' stairs two at a time. At last, they reached the level her bedchamber was on, laughing at the chaos in the great hall that echoed up through the floorboards. Once they were in her chamber, he set her down, shut the door firmly behind him, and put the bar in place.

"I've a feeling ye've used that tactic more than once." He eyed her. "Did ye do that on purpose at Glenn Mórinnse?"

She laughed aloud. "I didna, I swear."

Roderick took quick strides to close the distance between them and capture her in a kiss. "I love ye." He swept her back up in his arms and marched toward the wide oak bed with four carved posts and a floral-tapestried canopy overhead.

Greer let out a squeal when he tossed her on the center, and then teased, "Alone at last, and ye can finally ravish me."

He chuckled and nodded toward the table before the hearth. "Seems we got lucky and they already prepared your chamber."

Greer pushed up on her elbows to peer over the end of the bed. Settled on the table was a platter of berries, scones, sugared almonds, and wine.

"My mother knows me well. Alas, I am only hungry for one thing— my husband." She turned her gaze back toward Roderick, letting him see in that one glance just what she wanted. "We need to finish something we started."

Roderick's regard darkened as he swept it over the length of her. "Aye. We'll eat after, for I canna wait to taste every last inch of ye, *mo ghràidh*."

Greer nodded, her belly fluttering and every part of her coming alive at the images he brought into her mind. With his gaze on her, he unpinned his plaid and slowly stripped out of every stitch of clothing, tossing his boots behind him. He stood gloriously nude in front of her, and her mouth went dry and then was suddenly very wet. He wasn't the only one who wanted to taste.

Muscles rippled from his corded shoulders and down the length of his strong arms. His chest was broad and had a sprinkling of dark hair that traveled down the sinewy bands of his abdominal muscles, and then lower still, reaching a thatch of hair from which a thick staff jutted.

Greer licked her lips, studying the member, fascinating by the length and breadth, the plush head at its tip, the drop of dew that beaded there, and the way her body yearned for that particular piece to fit with her.

As much as she wanted to linger her curious gaze there, she looked lower still, catching sight of the scar on his muscled leg. It was truly a miracle he could move and fight as though the wound had never happened at all. And that was only because he was strong as steel on the inside, pushing past the pain. She admired him for that. Loved him for it, too. Admired that he'd been able to forgive her, to love her, despite her giving him a lifetime of pain.

He stalked forward then, and her gaze was drawn back to the jutting appendage that swung gently while he walked. "Undress."

Greer flicked her gaze back up to his, and she nodded, though she didn't move. Prickles of anticipation and a little bit of fear coursed through her. Never once had she questioned what this moment would bring. Heavens, just a week ago, she'd been ready to revel in it at the tavern. She wasn't scared or filled with regret, but all the same, her nerves were firing.

Roderick reached out a hand to her, and with complete trust, she placed her palm against his. Gently, he tugged her from the bed, cupped her cheeks, and bent to kiss her. Within minutes, she forgot all about being nervous and wrapped her arms around his neck, fully absorbed in their kiss. Her body came alive as she vividly recalled the sensations he could give her.

It was only with the breath of cold air around her legs that she realized he'd removed her gown, and then a moment later, their kiss was broken. He knelt before her, pressing his lips to her belly covered only by the thin veil of her chemise. This time, he didn't have to ask. She wrenched her chemise over her head and tossed it onto the pile of his clothes, wanting to feel his breath on her skin, wanting to slide together on the soft linen sheets.

What she didn't expect was that he would put his mouth...*there*. Nor did she expect to like it so much.

Hot breath fanned over the thatch of hair, and then his tongue darted out to stroke the crease between her sex and her inner thigh. A moment later, he parted her folds with his thumbs and pressed his lips to the very center of her. Greer groaned, threading her fingers in his hair. She followed his lead as he pushed her back toward the bed and spread her legs wide to...feast. Oh, there was no other way to think of it other than her being the meal he craved.

But as soon as her arse hit the bed, he stood abruptly and wiggled his brows. Greer blinked up at him, her mind a fog of pleasure.

"I've an idea, lass." He moved toward the table and retrieved the berries.

"Roderick...I want..." How could she say she wanted him to make love to her, not to eat? Well, eat...*her*, not berries.

But his wicked wink in her direction had the words dying on her tongue. Why did she have a feeling that he was still going to do just what she wanted?

He set the bowl on the table beside the bed, picked up a berry, and pressed it between her lips before he kissed her, the taste of the tart fruit between their tongues. He feasted on her lips like he was a starving man, and she was the only thing he could survive on. Dear God, would she ever be able to eat a berry again?

His mouth skimmed from her lips to her chin and down her neck. Then he grabbed another berry, dragged the fruit along the column of her neck, and licked the juicy path he created down the length of her torso. He dripped juice on her nipples and lapped it up. Then he moved lower to her belly button, until his hot breath washed over her core once more. He pressed the berry between his teeth, gaze locking on hers as he bit through the juice, and then dipped his head between her thighs. He swept his tongue in wicked long strokes between the folds of her most private place. The scent of berries mixed with something sensual and intoxicating.

Nay, never would she be able to eat a berry again without her body bowing with pleasure, she was sure of it. With every caress of his tongue, nuzzle of his lips, her body sang with rapture, and she moaned aloud to match. His fingers stroked at her breasts, massaged her buttocks, then dipped into the very center of her, stretching her wide while his tongue circled the bud of firing sensation.

The bliss surging through her entire being was so much more than what she'd imagined. It was good she hadn't known it would feel this incredible. Because if she'd imagined it could be like this, the moment she woke up naked in his bed, she would have climbed all over him and virtue be damned.

She buried her fingers in his hair as her body spasmed and bowed with what could only be described as rapture. Pleasure even more potent than the climax she'd experienced with him before.

When the shudders had nearly died down, Roderick stood between her legs and slid his palms slowly up the length of her thighs, over the sides of her hips, and underneath her buttocks. He lifted her gently and slid her back on the bed. She gazed up at him with dilated pupils and shivered with growing anticipating at the heated look he cast her. Saints, but that gaze... It had the power to make her body weep.

Roderick climbed onto the bed like a wolf stalking his prey. The length of his hard body slid along hers, the steel of his arousal pressing hotly to the very wet center of her. Greer lifted her legs around his hips, and he tucked them up farther, bracing himself on his elbows as he stared down.

"I love ye," he murmured.

"I love ye, too."

He leaned down, kissed her languidly, and rocked his body on hers until she was trembling. "Ye're ready," he whispered, then he took hold of his shaft and positioned the head at her entrance.

"Aye," she agreed, stroking down the tightened muscles of his back. Boldly, she slid her palms over his buttocks and tugged.

Roderick groaned and surged forward in one swift thrust. The pain was shocking but gone as quickly as it had come, leaving her with a full, stretched, and slightly uncomfortable sensation. She wiggled, trying to get used to the feel, only to hear him hiss.

"Are ye all right?" she asked, suddenly concerned. Did it hurt him the way it had hurt her?

"I'm perfect, love, and I should be the one asking ye that."

Greer's lips curled along with her toes. "I'm fine. It doesna hurt."

Roderick pressed his forehead to hers. "Good... I've never...taken a maiden before."

Greer was surprised but pleased to hear that. "I'm glad to be your first."

"And only."

She sighed with pleasure, lifting her legs higher and nuzzling his face until his lips pressed to hers in a languid and delicious kiss. As their tongues stroked, their bodies began to move. Slowly at first, in long, sensual slides, until they were both barely able to breathe, their hearts pounding. Roderick buried his face in her neck, his thrusts growing faster, harder. Little moans and gasps escaped Greer's throat, growing louder as the delicious sensations inside her increased. She was very close to the same place of rapture he'd brought her before.

And then it happened. Her body shattered with a euphoria that rocked her from the tips of her toes to the top of her head. With her cry of passion, Roderick's pace quickened, until he too was letting out his own moan of release, his body shuddering. He surged forward once, twice, and a third time, then he collapsed on top of her. He rolled them both to the side and remained inside her.

Their breaths slowed, as did the pounding of their hearts, and still they remained connected. Greer stroked his face, their gazes locked in wonder.

"That was unbelievable." Roderick kissed her gently, then the kiss became more heated and she could feel him growing hard inside her again. "This has never happened. I want ye again. Right now."

Greer rolled on top of him, her eyes widening at the delicious feel of him inside her. She turned behind her, seeing his legs outstretched behind her, the scar on his thigh just beside her buttock. She stroked the puckered skin. "Are ye all right?"

"Never been better, sweet wife of mine."

Greer grinned. "I like the sound of that." She shifted, a gasp of pleasure escaping her. "Can we...make love this way?"

"If ye're not too sore."

She rocked her hips again and gasped. "Not sore at all."

"Thank God." Sweat beaded on his brow, and he gazed up at her with a primal hunger.

With his hands on her hips, he showed her how to move, and when she picked up the pace, riding toward climax once more, he leaned up and flicked his tongue over her breast, capturing the pink bud with his lips. Greer couldn't decide where to concentrate. Pleasure seemed to spark from all around her, and so she decided not to concentrate at all, but simply ride the waves as they crashed down around her.

An hour later, they found themselves in a very similar position on the floor before the hearth—and the bowl of berries completely empty, the evidence of the juice on both their skin and tongues.

Chapter Twenty-Two

A round midday the following day, Roderick and Greer finally left the chamber, pleased no one had tried to interrupt them the night before or that morning. They would have remained abed longer, but they ran out of food and drink, and with all the exercise... Well, they'd grown quite famished. They'd made love at least half a dozen times, maybe more. Who was counting? They'd been too busy learning what each of them liked, and memorizing every dip, curve, and ripple of each other's bodies.

Between lovemaking, they shared their inner most fears and dreams. He told her about Jessica, how the guilt he felt at her death had kept him a brooding mess for years, that when she'd tossed the spear at him and he'd not died, he thought it God's punishment for not saving his sister. Greer lay upon his chest, stroking a path up and down his ribs as he told stories about his sister. She listened intently, laughing, crying, growing sober as he did. She didn't try to brush off what he needed to say, nor to solve the guilty emotions he struggled with. She only whispered that time and love and remembrance would aid in healing his wounds. And he loved her all the more for it.

When they reached the last stair, the sounds of the great hall a soft murmur in the background, Roderick stopped her and pulled her into an alcove just under the circular stair and away from sight.

"I'm not yet ready to share ye," he murmured, pulling her into his embrace.

Greer snuggled against him, pressing her face to his chest. He leaned down, kissed the top of her head, and breathed in the floral scent of her hair.

"This is my new still and quiet," she whispered, pressing her lips to the place where his heart beat, her palms flat to his back. "The place where I can be free."

Her words struck a chord in him that left him speechless. When he'd confessed his guilt about his sister, he'd not told her about the note.

Ye are free, and so am I.

As if over the last weeks the notion of being himself with Greer wasn't evident enough, it had been made clear last night, again in the early morning hours, and even more so now.

"And we are safe with each other," he murmured, startling himself by saying the words. He was a warrior, a laird, and the concept of being safe never struck him before. But it wasn't being physically safe that worried him. Nay, it was the stuff upstairs, in his mind, where the dark guilt haunted.

Greer glanced up at him, a small furrow between her brows. "Always."

"There is something I kept from ye when I told ye about Jessica."

There was no judgment on her face, only curiosity.

"She left a note in which she professed to be free, and to be giving me my freedom."

Greer's lips parted in surprise, eyes watering. "I'm sorry. I didna know..."

"Ye need not apologize, sweetheart." He blinked, feeling a lightening in his chest. "I think I understand now."

She waited patiently as his mind worked in slow-turning circles.

"This void I've felt... 'Tis not that ye filled it, but that ye allowed me to fill it myself."

"She will always be a part of ye."

"Aye."

"But the guilt need not be. She didna want that."

"She would have liked ye."

"And I would have liked her."

They stayed quiet, their arms wrapped around one another for a few moments longer, until boot heels on the stairs and someone shouting their names made them realize it was time to show their faces to those they'd been avoiding since the wedding feast.

In the great hall, an eruption of cheers sounded upon them stepping off the last stair, to which Greer curtsied, and Roderick bowed. The woman was a constant and pleasant surprise. She took what she was given and ran with it, making every moment interesting.

He could not have been prouder to call her his wife.

"To Laird and Lady MacCulloch!" Jon shouted, rushing forward to thrust two cups of wine at them. "Ye disappeared afore we could toast ye last night."

The quickly growing crowd shouted their congratulations and then teased them about sneaking out during all the chaos. As if to remind them and to make them feel a bit of guilt, Jewel nudged her way forward and then between them. She leaned her head on Greer's thigh and gazed up at Roderick with what could be nothing other than a judgmental stare.

"I'll let ye have her for a moment, and then she's mine," he said to the pup, which had Greer cracking up.

The crowd parted to allow Laird and Lady Sutherland to pass. Roderick and Sutherland eyed each other for a moment or two before the older laird stuck out his arm for Roderick, who gratefully shook it.

"Welcome to our family," Magnus said.

"And welcome to mine."

Magnus gave him an appreciative nod. "If ye're ever in need of anything, ye need only ask."

"And I offer ye the same." Roderick pressed his hand to his heart. "Ye've given me a wonderful gift."

"I've given ye nothing," Magnus said. "Ye earned her."

Greer beamed at them both before she was tugged away by her sister Bella, who whispered something that made her gasp and blush.

They mingled with those in the great hall until Lady Sutherland announced the noon meal was ready, to which he and Greer eagerly found their spots on the dais to feast. When their meal was nearly over, Magnus stood and walked to the center of the dais.

"I've a gift I want to give the new couple," he announced. "Come, let me show ye."

Roderick took Greer's hand in his, and each of them eyed the other in confusion. Part of him wondered if this was going to be a final punishment. Sutherland led them all outside, down through the gardens and orchards at the back of the castle, and toward the shore where their pier was.

"I've not seen that one afore," Greer said, nodding toward a vessel with a mast that towered over the others.

When they reached the pier, Magnus turned toward them both and took his wife's hand in his, his gaze on Greer. "We had this ship commissioned, *The Hellion*. It was to be your wedding gift, and I think it no less pertinent now that ye've wed the man who saved ye. A man who ye once nearly killed on this verra firth."

"Da..." Greer groaned, but the rest of the crowd laughed.

Roderick squeezed her hand, gazing down at her, struck with the realization of how much she had changed his life—for the better. He loved her with every beat of his heart, with every breath he took. And he would spend the rest of his days trying to make her happy, protecting her from the world, and even from herself. But most of all, he would spend his days thanking her for showing him the joy in life again.

Greer could feel Roderick's gaze on her, and when she glanced up at him, there was something so much deeper in his eyes and his smile than she'd ever seen before. Love shone through, and with it was admiration and respect. *I love ye*, she mouthed, and he winked in answer.

"The two of ye have a history with the firth and with sailing," her father said. "It seems only fitting for ye to sail home to Gleann Mórinnse in a ship of your own."

Greer started to shake her head, but then she stopped herself. Roderick put his arm around her shoulder, lending her strength from his presence, his touch.

"Da." She pressed her fingers to her lips. "This means so much to me. More than ye could ever know. 'Tis more than a ship, but a blessing. An acknowledgment and support of my dreams, but also a push for me to conquer my fears." She flicked her gaze up to Roderick. "And I canna think of anyone else I'd want to share those dreams with."

Greer bit her lip, wishing she could reach up on tiptoe to kiss her husband.

Roderick shook her father's arm, pressed a kiss to Arbella's hand, and then Greer hugged both of her parents. "My sincerest gratitude for everything. 'Tis a beautiful ship, and we shall love her well."

"We will sail," Greer said, though her voice wavered.

"Aye, together." Roderick glanced down at her.

Greer nodded slowly as she gazed at the vessel. It truly was a work of art, and she could imagine it sailing through the water, cutting through the white-crested waves. She looked built not only for speed, but for defense as well. *The Hellion* was painted in large letters along the hull near the stern. A flag at the top of the mast waved proudly—a woman with her hands on her hips. Greer laughed at that. *The Hellion* indeed.

"If ye're not ready," Roderick whispered, but Greer shook her head.

It was time to face her fears in real time. Out of the two things she wanted most in life, she already had one of them right by her side.

"I'm ready."

Greer met her mother's gaze, sad to be leaving her behind after only just returning home.

"We're just across the firth," her mother said as if reading her thoughts "Only a few hours. We can visit often."

That was a comfort.

"Why dinna we all go now. Take *The Hellion* together?" Roderick offered. "Make her maiden voyage one to remember."

"Oh, aye." Greer glanced up at the sky. Never again would she simply sail on a whim. Thankfully, there was not a cloud in sight.

Two hours later, the ship full of provisions and Greer's belongings, she stood on the pier, staring hard at the gangway. Roderick held her hand, and it was only because of his hold on her that she wasn't running the other way.

"This is not the skiff, love," he murmured. "And ye've got us all here with ye."

As if to tell her she had nothing to be afraid of, Jewel was at the top of the gangway, already on the ship, letting out a loud bark.

"I know. It is more than just the ship." She met his gaze, melting. "It is leaving everything behind to start anew. I dinna want to displease ye."

"Have ye no' learned, *mo ghràidh*? There is nothing ye could do that would displease me."

She raised a skeptical brow at that.

"All right, if ye were to throw another spear at me, aye, I would not be pleased."

She giggled.

"Ye're an incredible woman. I love ye. I have nae doubt ye'll make them a brilliant mistress. And me a wonderful wife. I canna imagine my life without ye in it. Ye've taught me the meaning of conquering fear. Of taking chances."

"I have?"

"Aye, love."

A slow grin crept across her face. "Ye've taught me much the same."

With purpose, she grabbed his hand and started to march up the gangway. Her fears worked to wrap her up, to make her think of all the terrible things that could happen, but she pushed through them. There was only one way for her to get over the not-so-irrational fear—and that was to take charge on her own terms.

As they set sail across the firth, Greer took the helm, steering them out through the water. Her heart pounded, and sweat beaded on her spine, but Roderick never left her side. A short time later, she called for her da to take the helm, and she grabbed hold of Roderick's hand.

"Come to the bow with me." She led him to the back of the ship, and they peered out behind them. Dunrobin grew smaller and smaller, and with that vision, the fear of leaving lessened, and an excitement about the future took hold.

When she'd climbed onto that currach a few weeks ago, never had she thought she'd be leaving to the far shores a wedded woman, and especially not to Roderick "the Grim" MacCulloch.

"Thank ye," she said.

"For what?"

"For taking a chance on me. Well, more than one chance." She wrapped her arms around his middle and stared up at him, grinning.

"Och, lass, I'd take a thousand." He dipped down to brush his lips over hers in a gentle, loving kiss. "Thank ye for showing me that life is about taking risks to find happiness."

"A task I plan to show ye every day for the rest of our lives."

"I look forward to it with pleasure."

And then, despite the witnesses, he swept her up for a deep kiss that promised just that.

IF YOU ENJOYED **THE HIGHLANDER'S HELLION***, please spread the word by leaving a review on the site where you purchased your copy, or a reader site such as Goodreads or Shelfari! I love to hear from readers too, so drop me a line at* authorelizaknight@gmail.com *OR visit me on Facebook:* https://www.facebook.com/elizaknightauthor*. I'm also on Twitter: @ElizaKnight. If you'd like to receive my occasional newsletter, please sign up at* www.elizaknight.com*. Many thanks!*

More Sutherlands!

Are you ready for more Sutherlands? Coming Spring 2019!

The Highlander's Secret Vow

When Liam Sutherland was a lad of fifteen summers, he saved a *Sassenach* lassie's life, and secretly vowed to always keep her safe. As the prized warrior for his clan, and youngest son of the laird, his responsibilities at the castle continue to mount, and just when he's about to forge a name for himself, he receives a mysterious missive that has the power to make him leave everything behind.

Cora Segrave, daughter of an English baron, owes her life to the Scot who saved her years ago during a border raid. When her family home is destroyed, and they are taken prisoner, there is only one man she knows can save her—the one man she's never been able to forget.

Answering Cora's plea for aid will jeopardize Liam's reputation, and maybe even cause a rift with his family, but a vow is a vow, and he cannot turn his back on her—or his heart. The only choice he has is to save her before it's too late, and pray his family and king will understand. In saving her, just maybe he'll be able to save himself.

SIGN up for my newsletter to be the first to know when the pre-order link is up!

Excerpt from The Highlander's Temptation

Prologue

Spring, 1282
Highlands, Scotland

THEY GALLOPED THROUGH THE EERIE moonlit night. Warriors cloaked by darkness. Blending in with the forest, only the occasional glint of the moon off their weapons made their presence seem out of place.

'Twas chilly for spring, and yet, they rode hard enough the horses were lathered with sweat and foaming at the mouth. But the Montgomery clan wasn't going to be pushed out of yet another meeting of the clans, not when their future depended on it. This meeting would put their clan on the map, make them an asset to their king and country. As it was, years before King Alexander III had lost one son and his wife. He'd not remarried and the fate of the country now relied on one son who didn't feel the need to marry. The prince toyed with his life as though he had a death wish, fighting, drinking, and carrying on without a care in the world. The king's only other chance at a succession was his daughter who'd married but had not yet shown any signs of a bairn filling her womb. If something were to happen to the king, the country would erupt into chaos. Every precaution needed to be taken.

Young Jamie sat tall and proud upon his horse. Even prouder was he, that his da, the fearsome Montgomery laird, had allowed him to accompany the group of a half dozen seasoned warriors—the men who sat on his own clan council—to the meeting. The fact that his father had involved him in matters of state truly made his chest puff five times its size.

After being fostered out the last seven years, Jamie had just returned to his father's home. At age fourteen, he was ready to take on the duties of eldest son, for one day he would be laird. This was the perfect opportunity to show his da all he'd learned. To prove he was worthy.

Laird Montgomery held up his hand and all the riders stopped short. Puffs of steam blew out in miniature clouds from the horses' noses. Jamie's heart slammed against his chest and he looked from side to side to make sure no one could hear it. He was a man after all, and men shouldn't be scared of the dark. No matter how frightening the sounds were.

Carried on the wind were the deep tones of men shouting and the shrill of a woman's screams. Prickles rose on Jamie's arms and legs. They must have happened upon a robbery or an ambush. When he'd set out to attend his father, he'd not counted on a fight. Nay, Jamie merely thought to stand beside his father and demand a place within the Bruce's High Council.

Swallowing hard, he glanced at his father, trying to assess his thoughts, but as usual, the man sat stoic, not a hint of emotion on his face.

The laird glanced at his second in command and jutted his chin in silent communication. The second returned the nod. Jamie's father made a circling motion with his fingers, and several of the men fanned out.

Jamie observed the exchange, his throat near to bursting with questions. What was happening?

Finally, his father motioned Jamie forward. Keeping his emotions at bay, Jamie urged his mount closer. His father bent toward him, indicating for Jamie to do the same, then spoke in a hushed tone.

"We're nearly to Sutherland lands. Just on the outskirts, son. 'Tis an attack, I'm certain. We mean to help."

Jamie swallowed past the lump in his throat and nodded. The meeting was to take place at Dunrobin Castle. Why that particular castle was chosen, Jamie had not been privy to. Though he speculated 'twas because of how far north it was. Well away from Stirling where the king resided.

"Are ye up to it?" his father asked.

Tightening his grip on the reins, Jamie nodded. Fear cascaded along his spine, but he'd never show any weakness in front of his father, especially now that he'd been invited on this very important journey.

"Good. 'Twill give ye a chance to show me what ye've learned."

Again, Jamie nodded, though he disagreed. Saving people wasn't a chance to show off what he'd learned. He could never look at protecting another as an opportunity to prove his skill, only as a chance to make a difference. But he kept that to himself. His da would never understand. If making a difference proved something to his father, then so be it.

An owl screeched from somewhere in the distance as it caught onto its prey, almost in unison with the blood curdling scream of a woman.

His father made a few more hand motions and the rest of their party followed him as they crept forward at a quickened pace on their mounts, avoiding making any noise.

The road ended on a clearing, and some thirty horse-lengths away a band of outlaws circled a trio—a lady, one warrior, and a lad close to his own age.

The outlaws caught sight of their approach, shouting and pointing. His father's men couldn't seem to move quickly enough and Jamie watched in horror as the man, woman and child were hacked down. All three of them on the ground, the outlaws turned on the Montgomery warriors and rushed forward as though they'd not a care in the world.

Jamie shook. He'd never been so scared in his life. His throat had long since closed up and yet his stomach was threatening to purge everything he'd consumed that day. Even though he felt like vomiting, a sense of urgency, and power flooded his veins. Battle-rush, he'd heard it called by the seasoned warriors. And it was surging through his body, making him tingle all over.

The laird and his men raised their swords in the air, roaring out their battle cries. Jamie raised his sword to do the same, but a flash of gold behind a large lichen-covered boulder caught his attention. He eased his knees on his mount's middle.

What was that?

Another flash of gold — was that blonde hair? He'd never seen hair like that before.

Jamie turned to his father, intent to point it out, but his sire was several horse-lengths ahead and ready to engage the outlaws, leaving it up to Jamie to investigate.

After all, if there was another threat lying in wait, was it not up to someone in the group to seek them out? The rest of the warriors were intent on the outlaws which left Jamie to discover the identity of the thief.

He veered his horse to the right, galloping toward the boulder. A wee lass darted out, lifting her skirts and running full force in the opposite direction. Jamie loosened his knees on his horse and slowed. That was not what he'd expected. At all. Jamie anticipated a warrior, not a tiny little girl whose legs were no match for his mount. As he neared, despite his slowed pace, he feared he'd trample the little imp.

He leapt from his horse and chased after her on foot. The lass kept turning around, seeing him chasing her. The look of horror on her face nearly broke his heart. Och, he was no one to fear. But how would she know that? She probably thought he was after her like the outlaws had been after the man, woman and lad.

"'Tis all right!" he called. "I will nay harm ye!"

But she kept on running, and then was suddenly flying through the air, landing flat on her face.

Jamie ran toward her, dropping to his knees as he reached her side and she pushed herself up.

Her back shook with cries he was sure she tried hard to keep silent. He gathered her up onto his knees and she pressed her face to his *leine* shirt, wiping away tears, dirt and snot as she sobbed.

"Momma," she said. "Da!"

"Hush, now," Jamie crooned, unsure of what else he could say. She must have just watched her parents and brother get cut to the ground. Och, what an awful sight for any child to witness. Jamie shivered, at a loss for words.

"Blaney!" she wailed, gripping onto his shirt and yanking. "They hurt!"

Jamie dried her tears with the cuff of his sleeve. "Your family?" he asked.

She nodded, her lower lip trembling, green-blue eyes wide with fear and glistening with tears. His chest swelled with emotion for the little imp and he gripped her tighter.

"Do ye know who the men were?"

"Bad people," she mumbled.

Jamie nodded. "What's your name?"

She chewed her lip as if trying to figure out if she should tell him. "Lorna. What are ye called?"

"Jamie." He flashed her what he hoped wasn't a strained smile. "How old are ye, Lorna?"

"Four." She held up three of her fingers, then second guessed herself and held up four. "I'm four. How old are ye?"

"Fourteen."

"Ye're four, too?" she asked, her mouth dropping wide as she forgot the horror of the last few minutes of her life for a moment.

"Fourteen. 'Tis four plus ten."

"I want to be fourteen, too." She swiped at the mangled mop of blonde hair around her face, making more of a mess than anything else.

"Then we'd best get ye home. Have ye any other family?"

"A whole big one."

"Where?"

"Dunrobin," she said. "My da is laird."

"Laird Sutherland?" Jamie asked, trying to keep the surprise from his face. Did his father understand just how deep and unsettling this attack had been? A laird had been murdered. Was it an ambush? Was there more to it than just a band of outlaws? Were they men trying to stop the secret meeting from being held?

There would be no meeting, if the laird who'd called the meeting was dead.

"I'll take ye home," Jamie said, putting the girl on her feet and standing.

"Will ye carry me?" she said, her lip trembling again. She'd lost a shoe and her yellow gown was stained and torn. "I'm scared."

"Aye. I'll carry ye."

"Are ye my hero?" she asked, batting tear moistened lashes at him.

Jamie rolled his eyes and picked her up. "I'm no hero, lass."

"Hmm... Ye seem like a hero to me."

Jamie didn't answer. He tossed her on his horse and climbed up behind her. A glance behind showed that his father and his men had dispatched of most of the men, and a few others gave chase into the forest. They'd likely meet him at the castle as that had been their destination all along.

Squeezing his mount's sides, Jamie urged the horse into a gallop, intent on getting the girl to the safety of Dunrobin's walls, and then returning to his father.

Spotting Jamie with the lass, the guards threw open the gate. A nursemaid rushed over and grabbed Lorna from him, chiding her for sneaking away.

"What's happened?" A lad his own age approached. "Why did ye have my sister?"

Jamie swallowed, dismounted and held out his arm to the other young man. "I found her behind a boulder." Jamie took a deep breath, then looked the boy in the eye, hating the words he would have to say. "There was an ambush."

"My family?"

Jamie shook his head. He opened his mouth to tell the dreadful news, but the way the boy's face hardened, and eyes glistened, it didn't seem necessary. As it happened, he was given a reprieve from saying more when his father and men came barreling through the gate a moment later.

"Where's the laird?" Jamie's father bellowed.

"If what this lad said is true, then I may be right here," the boy said, straightening his shoulders.

Laird Montgomery's eyes narrowed, jaw tightened with understanding. "Aye, lad, ye are."

He leapt from his horse, his eyes lighting on Jamie "Where've ye been, lad? Ye scared the shite out of us." His father looked pale, shaken. Had he truly scared him so much?

"There was a lass," Jamie said, "at the ambush. I brought her home."

His father snorted. "Always a lass. Mark my words, lad. Think here." His father tapped Jamie's forehead hard with the tip of his finger. "The mind always knows better than the sword."

Jamie frowned and his father walked back toward the young laird. It was the second time that day that he'd not agreed with his father. For if a lass was in need of rescuing, by God, he was going to be her rescuer.

Chapter One

Dunrobin Castle, Scottish Highlands
Early Spring, 1297

"I've arranged a meeting between Chief MacOwen and myself."

Lorna Sutherland lifted her eyes from her noon meal, the stew heavy as a bag of rocks in her belly as she met her older brother, Magnus', gaze.

"Why are ye telling me this?" she asked.

He raised dark brows as though he was surprised at her asking. What was he up to?

"I thought it important for ye to know."

She raised a brow and struggled to swallow the bit of pulverized carrot in her mouth. Her jaw hurt from clenching it, and she thought she might choke. There could only be one reason he felt the need to tell her this and she was certain she didn't want to know the answer. Gingerly, she set down her knife on her trencher and took a rather large gulp of watered wine, hoping it would help open her suddenly seized throat.

A moment later, she cocked her head innocently, and said, "Does not a laird and chief of his clan keep such talk to himself and his trusted council?" The haughty tone that took over could not be helped.

After nineteen summers, this conversation had been a long time coming. It was Aunt Fiona's fault. She'd arrived the week before, returning Heather, the youngest and wildest of the Sutherland siblings, and happened to see Lorna riding like the wind. Disgusted, her aunt marched straight to Magnus and demanded that he marry her off. Tame her, she'd said.

Lorna didn't see the problem with riding and why that meant she had to marry. So what if she liked to ride her horse standing on the saddle? She was good at it. Wasn't it important for a lass to excel in areas that she had skill?

Now granted, Lorna did admit that having her arms up in the air and eyes closed was borderline dangerous, but she'd done it a thousand times without mishap.

Even still, picturing her aunt's look of horror and how it had made Lorna laugh, didn't soften the blow of Magnus listening to their aunt's advice.

Magnus set down the leg of fowl he'd been eating and leaned forward on the table, his elbows pressing into the wood. Lorna found it hard to look him in the eye when he got like that. All serious and laird-like. He was her brother first, and chief second. Or at least, that's how she saw it. Judging from the anger simmering just beneath the surface of his clenched jaw and narrowed eyes, she was about to catch wind.

The room suddenly grew still, as if they were all wondering what he'd say—even the dogs.

He bared his teeth in something that was probably supposed to resemble a smile. A few of the inhabitants picked up superficial conversations again, trying as best they could to pretend they weren't paying attention. Others blatantly stared in curiosity.

"That is the case, save for when it involves deciding *your* future."

Oh, she was going to bait the bear. Lorna drew in a deep breath, crossed her arms over her chest and leaned away from the table. She could hardly look at him as she spoke. "Seems ye've already done just that."

Magnus' lips thinned into a grimace. "I see ye'll fight me on it."

"I dinna wish to marry." Emotion carried on every word. Didn't he realize what he was doing to her? The thought of marrying made her physically ill.

"Ye dinna wish to marry or ye dinna wish to marry MacOwen?"

By now the entire trestle table had quieted once more, and all eyes were riveted on the two of them. However she answered was going to determine the mood set in the room.

Och, she hated it when the lot of nosy bodies couldn't get enough of the family drama. Granted at least fifty percent of the time she was involved in said drama.

Lorna studied her brother, who, despite his grimace, waited patiently for her to answer.

The truth was, she did wish to marry—at some point. Having lost her mother when she was only four years old, she longed to have a child of her own, someone she could nurture and love. But that didn't mean she expected to marry *now*. And especially not the burly MacOwen who was easily twice her age, and had already married once or twice before. When she was a child she'd determined he had a nest of birds residing in his beard—and her thoughts hadn't changed much since.

She cocked her head trying to read Magnus' mind. Was it possible he was joking? He could not possibly believe she would ever agree to marry MacOwen.

Nay, Lorna wished to marry a man she could relate to. A man she could love, who might love her in return.

"I dinna wish to marry a man whose not seen a bath this side of a decade." Lorna spoke with a reasonable tone, not condescending, nor shrill, but just as she would have said the flowers looked lovely that morning. It was her way. Her subtlety often left people second guessing what they'd heard her say.

Magnus' lip twitched and she could tell he was trying to hold in his laughter. She dared not look down the table to see what the rest of her family and clan thought. In the past when she'd checked, gloated really, over their responses it had only made Magnus angrier.

Taming a bear meant not baiting him. And already she was doing just that. She flicked her gaze toward her plate, hoping the glance would appear meek, but in reality she was counting how many legumes were left on her trencher.

"Och, lass, I'm sure MacOwen has bathed at least once in the last year." Magnus' voice rumbled, filled with humor.

Lorna gritted her teeth. Of course Magnus would try and bait her in return. She should have seen that coming.

"And I'm sure there's another willing lass who'll scrape the filth from his back, but ye willna find her here. Not where I'm sitting."

Magnus squinted a moment as if trying to read into her mind. "But ye will agree to marry?"

Lorna crossed her arms over her chest. Lord, was her brother ever stubborn. "Not him."

"Shall we parade the eligible bachelors of the Highlands through the great hall and let ye take your pick?"

Lorna rolled her eyes, imagining just such a scene. It was horrifying, embarrassing. How many would there be in various states of dress and countenance? Some unkempt and others impeccable. Men who were pompous and arrogant or shy or annoying. Nay, thank you. She was about to spit a retort that was likely to burn her Aunt Fiona's ears when the matron broke in.

"My laird, 'haps after the meal I could speak with Lorna about marriage...in a somewhat more private arena?" Aunt Fiona was using that tone she oft used when trying to reason with one of them, that of a matron who knew better. It annoyed the peas out of Lorna and she was about to say just that, when her brother gave a slight wave of his hand, drawing her attention.

Perhaps his way of ceasing whatever words were on her tongue.

Magnus flicked his gaze from Lorna to Fiona. Why did the old bat always have to stick her nose into everything? Speaking to her in private only meant the woman would try to convince Lorna to take the marriage proposition her brother suggested. And that, she absolutely wouldn't do.

"'Tis not necessary, Aunt Fiona," Lorna said, at the exact same time Magnus stated, "Verra well."

Lorna jerked her gaze back to her brother, glaring daggers at him, but he only raised his brows in such an irritating way, a slight curve on his lips, that she was certain if she didn't excuse herself that moment she'd end up dumping her stew on his head. He had agreed on purpose —to annoy her. A horrible grinding sound came from her mouth as she gritted her teeth. Like she'd thought—brother first, chief second.

"Excuse me," she said, standing abruptly, the bench hitting hard on the back of her knees as so many people held it steady in place.

"Sit down," Magnus drawled out. "And finish your supper."

Lorna glared down at him. "I've lost my appetite."

Magnus grunted and smiled. "Och, we all know that's not true."

That only made her madder. So what if she ate just as much as the warriors? The food never seemed to go anywhere. She could eat all day long and still harbor the same lad's body she'd always had. Thick thighs, no hips, flat chest and arms to rival a squire's. If only she'd had the height of a man, then she could well and truly pummel her brother like he deserved.

She sat back down slowly and stared up at Magnus, eyes wide. Was that the reason he'd suggested MacOwen? Would no other man have her?

Nestling her hands in her lap she wrung them until her knuckles turned white.

Magnus clunked down his wooden spoon. "What is it, now?"

"Why did ye choose MacOwen?" she whispered, not wishing the rest of the table to be involved in this particular conversation. Not when she felt so vulnerable.

He shrugged, avoiding her gaze. "The man asked."

"Oh." She chewed her lip, appetite truly gone. 'Twas as she thought. No one would have her.

"Lorna..."

She flicked her gaze back up to her brother. "I but wonder if any other man would have me?"

Magnus' eyes popped and he gazed on her like she'd grown a second head and then that head grew a head. "Why would ye ask that?"

She shrugged.

By now everyone had gone back to talking and eating, knowing there'd be no more juicy gossip and Lorna was grateful for that.

"Lorna, lass, ye're beautiful, talented, spirited. Ye've taken the clan by storm. I've had to challenge more than one of my warriors for staring too long."

"More than one?" She couldn't help but glance down the table wondering which men it had been. They all slobbered like dogs over their chicken.

"None of the bastards deserve ye."

She turned back to Magnus. "And yet, ye picked the MacOwen?" She raised a skeptical brow. Ugh, of all men, he was by far the worst choice for her.

Magnus winked and picked up another scoop full of stew, shoveling into his grinning mouth.

Lorna groaned, shoulders sinking. "Ye told him nay, didna ye? Ye were baiting me."

Magnus laughed around a mouth full of stew. "Ye're too easy. I'd see

ye married, but not to a man older than Uncle Artair," he said, referring to their uncle who had to be nearing seventy.

"Ugh." Lorna growled and punched her brother in the arm. "How
could ye do that? Ye made every bit of my hunger go away and ye know
how much I love Cook's stew."

Magnus laughed. The sound boomed off the rafters and even pulled
a smile from Lorna. She loved to hear him laugh, and he didn't do it
often enough. When their parents died, he'd only been fourteen, and
he'd been forced to take over the whole of the clan—including raising
her, and her siblings. Raising her two brothers, Ronan and Blane, and
then the youngest of their brood, Heather was a feat in itself, one only
Magnus could have accomplished so well. In fact, the clan had pros-
pered. She couldn't be more proud. If anyone deserved a good match,
it was Magnus.

Her heart swelled with pride. "Ye're a good man, Magnus. And an
amazing brother."

He reached toward her and gave her a reassuring squeeze on her
shoulder. "I'll remember that the next time ye wail at me about
nonsense."

Lorna jutted her chin forward. "I do not wail—and nothing I say is
nonsense."

"A true Sutherland ye are. I see your appetite has returned."

Lorna hadn't even realized she'd begun eating again. She smiled and
wrapped her lips around her spoon. Resisting Cook's stew was futile.
The succulent bits of venison and stewed vegetables with hints of
thyme and rosemary played blissfully over her tongue.

"My laird." Aunt Fiona's voice pierced the noise of the great hall.

Magnus stiffened slightly, and glanced up. Their aunt was a gem, a
tremendous help, but Lorna had heard her brother comment on more
than one occasion that the woman was also a grand pain in the arse.
Lorna dipped her head to keep from laughing.

"Aye?" he said, focusing his attention on their aunt.

"I'd be happy to have Lorna return home with me upon my depar-
ture. Visits with me have helped Heather so much."

Lorna's head shot up, mouth falling open as she glanced from her brother to her aunt. Good God, no! Beside her on the bench, Heather kicked Lorna in the shin and made a slight gesture with her knife as though she were slitting her wrist. Lorna pressed her lips together to keep from laughing.

"I'm sure that's not necessary, Aunt," Lorna said, giving the woman her sweetest smile. At least she'd not told her there was no way in hell she'd step foot outside of this castle for a journey unless it was on some adventure she chose for herself. She'd heard enough horror stories about the etiquette lessons Heather had to endure.

"Magnus?" Fiona urged.

There was a flash of irritation in his eyes. Magnus didn't mind his siblings calling him by his name, but all others were to address him formally. Lorna agreed that should be the case with the clan, but with family, Lorna thought he ought to be more lenient, especially where their aunt was concerned.

Aye, she was a thorn in his arse, but she was also very helpful.

Before her brother could say something he'd regret, Lorna pressed her hand to his forearm and chimed in. "'Haps we can plan on me accompanying Heather on her next visit."

That seemed to pacify their aunt. She nodded and returned to her dinner.

Ronan, who sat beside Magnus on the opposite side of the table, leaned close to their brother and smirked as he said something. Probably crude. Lorna rolled her eyes. If Blane was here, he'd have joined in their bawdy drivel. Or maybe even saved her from having to invite herself to stay at their aunt's house.

As it was, Blane was gallivanting about the countryside and the borders dressed as an Englishman selling wool. Sutherland wool. Their prized product. Superior to all others in texture, softness, thickness, and ability to hold dye.

She stirred her stew, frowning. Blane always came home safe and sound, but she still worried. There was a lot of unrest throughout the country, and the blasted English king, Longshanks, was determined to be rid of them all. It would only take one wrong move and her beloved brother would be forever taken away.

Lorna glanced up. She gazed from one sibling to the next. She loved them. All of them. They loved each other more than most, maybe because they'd lost their parents so young and only had each other to rely on. Whatever the case was, they'd a bond not even steel could cut through.

Magnus raised his mug of ale. "A toast!" he boomed.

Every mug lifted into the air, ale sloshing over the sides and cheers filled the room.

"Clan Sutherland!" he bellowed.

And the room erupted in uproarious calls and clinks of mugs. A smile split her face and she was overcome with joy.

She'd be perfectly happy never to leave here. And perfectly ecstatic to never marry MacOwen.

Even still, as she clinked her mug and took a mighty gulp, she couldn't help but wonder if there was a man out there she could love, and one who just might love her in return.

❦

*Want to read more? Check out **The Highlander's Temptation** and the rest of the **Stolen Bride** series wherever ebooks are sold...*

About the Author

Eliza Knight is an award-winning and *USA Today* bestselling author of over fifty sizzling historical romance and erotic romance. Under the name E. Knight, she pens rip-your-heart-out historical fiction. While not reading, writing or researching for her latest book, she chases after her three children. In her spare time (if there is such a thing...) she likes daydreaming, wine-tasting, traveling, hiking, staring at the stars, watching movies, shopping and visiting with family and friends. She lives atop a small mountain with her own knight in shining armor, three princesses and two very naughty puppies. Visit Eliza at http://www.elizaknight.com or her historical blog History Undressed: www.historyundressed.com. Sign up for her newsletter to get news about books, events, contests and sneak peaks! http://eepurl.com/CSFFD

facebook.com/elizaknightfiction

twitter.com/elizaknight

instagram.com/elizaknightfiction

bookbub.com/authors/eliza-knight

goodreads.com/elizaknight

Manufactured by Amazon.ca
Bolton, ON

41492004R00146